SHADOWS ON GLASS AND OTHER STORIES

SHADOWS ON GLASS AND OTHER STORIES

JAMIE LACKEY

ISBN: 979-8-9850216-2-2

CONTENTS

DEDICATION

To my grandfather.

I wouldn't be who I am today without your influence.

I've collected some of the weirdest of the "weird stuff" I write, and I am dedicating it to you. I hope something in here touches your heart.

SHADOWS ON GLASS

Originally appeared in *Metaphorosis Magazine*

Theodora Rhodes stood in the doorway and stared out at the field. The corn was chest-high and green, growing in neat rows.

It seemed impossible that this place remained, that the war could leave a single thing untouched. And yet, here she was, familiar boards creaking under her bare feet, familiar smell of hotcakes and burnt coffee wafting from the kitchen. And in front of her, corn swayed in the summer morning breeze, just like it always had. If she closed her eyes, she could almost hear her brothers shouting at each other.

But she could also almost hear injured soldiers moaning and horses screaming, and see the purple haze of magic staining the western sky. She shuddered and opened her eyes.

She leaned against the doorframe and winced as the stump of her left arm caught against the rough wood. She scowled down at the thick bandages wrapped around her elbow joint, and the empty space beyond it. The constant pain had faded to a dull ache, but the ghosts of sensation remained.

Last night, she had reached with her missing hand to take her dinner plate. Her father had been unable to meet her eyes ever since.

"Teddy, come on in here. The food's ready."

Her father had set two places at the too-large table, and Teddy sat in what had been her brother Toby's chair, next to their father's place at the head of the table.

None of the boys had come home from the war. Teddy imagined their bones bleaching in a field, and wondered if corn grew around their scattered remains.

"I hear there's a man in town selling prosthetics," her father said.

Teddy had to put her fork down to pick up her coffee. "Doc says I'm not ready for a prosthetic yet."

"You ought to go take a look anyway. It'd be good for you to get out of the house. He's set up at the old Methodist church."

Teddy stacked plates and carried them to the sink, but her father waved any further help away. "Get on with you."

So, she struggled out of the clothes that she'd managed to get herself into—a pair of Danny's old trousers and her mother's old sleeping shirt—and tried to make herself presentable.

All of her old things had too many buttons. She managed to fasten a skirt, but it slid right off of her hips.

Resigned, she pulled on her uniform. The hems on the pant legs were worn through, and the bloodstains refused to wash out, but the left sleeve was already tied up, and it was the only thing that fit. The nurses had replaced all of the buttons with snaps, so she could get into and out of it herself. Even now, the uniform felt right. Even now, when all that it stood for was defeat and ashes.

There was nothing she could do about her hair—it was growing out around her face, uneven and split at the ends, too short to braid even if she'd had the use of both hands.

She had a bit of money—the Western government had offered to handle all the back pay that was owed to the defeated Eastern soldiers. Maybe it was time to invest in a new wardrobe—she could head to the store after she stopped in at the church. It felt good to be dressed, to get out of the house. The sun was warm on her face, the path familiar under her feet.

She pushed the church door open and froze.

The prosthetic vendor was a Western dandy, pale-haired and wire thin. His wares glowed with an eerie purple light. Teddy's stomach turned. This dark magic was what they'd been fighting against—what her brothers had died in vain trying to destroy.

The dandy hit her with a charming smile that looked out of place on his narrow face. "Good morning, miss. You must be the Rhodes girl."

He, and his wares, made her skin crawl. She chastised herself for being irrational and reminded herself that the war was over, but took a step back anyway. "Look now, I don't know who told you what, but I'm not interested."

She stepped back again, but he grabbed her shoulder before she could escape. His hand was cold and soft. "Now, now," he said in a hearty, earnest tone. "Let's not be hasty. My prices are very reasonable, and you can't really want to be a cripple for the rest of your life. I know that's not what your father wants for you."

Anger and shame and pride mixed uneasily in Teddy's belly. He'd spoken with her father?

She shrugged his hand away. "I'd be happy to explain just what I'd like you to do with yourself, but that's not a discussion for polite company."

He stepped close—too close, and Teddy almost choked on the the lightning-strike scent of magic that clung to his skin—and lowered his voice. "Do you really intend to let fear and ignorance destroy what is left of your life? What are you going to do with yourself, Miss Rhodes? The back pay that my government is so generously providing won't last forever. How will you support yourself? With one hand, you're a burden on your poor father. With two, you'd be able to help him, to support him in his twilight years. Maybe even get yourself a husband to help with the farm. I know it's hard to believe, but I'm here as a friend."

"You don't know anything about me," Teddy snapped. "Don't pretend like you do." She turned away and let the church door fall closed behind her, then headed back home. She didn't have it in her to try to do any shopping today.

How could her father have sent her here? What had he said to the dandy that made him so determined to strap one of his abominations to her arm?

Her father tried to hide his disappointment when he saw her still-empty sleeve. Teddy tried to hide everything she was feeling, too.

•

Her father invited the dandy for dinner that night. "Teddy, I believe you met Mr. Duncan."

"In passing," she said. Her fingers itched for her repeater, but it was gone, surrendered on the battlefield along with her pride in exchange for her life.

Her father served bland stew and hard biscuits, and had the dandy sit in her mother's chair.

Her father looked tired. And old.

Teddy dunked a biscuit in the stew and watched it closely. It was hard to look at either man's face.

Her father leaned forward. "Mr. Duncan was telling me about a new model of prosthetic—"

"No," Teddy said.

"But Teddy—"

She slammed her single fist against the table. "I said no, Dad. Absolutely not. I will not attach myself to one of his monstrosities."

"I am offering a significant discount to all veterans, on either side," Mr. Duncan said.

"So the cost would be something other than my soul?"

"As I said, my prices are reasonable. You can have a state-of-the-art prosthetic for the cost of a single memory. You won't get that deal from anyone else."

"I'm not interested," Teddy said.

But Mr. Duncan reached across the table and grabbed her jaw in a grip like iron. His eyes burned into hers.

The smell of blood and cordite, the sound of ragged screams and hopeless moans. The doctor's face looming over her, exhausted and pale. The taste of harsh whisky, the cold, ragged edge of the saw pressing into ruined flesh. The endless rasping against bone before the darkness came.

Teddy jerked away, and she was in her father's kitchen again. Her biscuit had dissolved in her stew.

"It's not one you'll miss," Mr. Duncan said.

"Please, at least think about it, Teddy." Her father took her one hand between his. "I just want to know that you can take care of yourself."

Teddy stood up, shaking with her bottled rage. "I already know that I can take care of myself, Dad. I learned it over and over again, these past five years. And I'd rather have no hands at all than make the very thing I fought against a part of myself."

She'd never bothered to unpack her kit, so there was no need to take time to toss necessities into a bag. She grabbed her cash and slung her rucksack onto her shoulder.

Her father stood in the doorway. "What are you doing?"

"Leaving. Don't worry about me. I'll be fine. But I can't stay here, not after this."

"I don't understand."

"That's because you haven't seen what their magic can do, and what it costs. Their factories will keep churning out products—there's nothing I can do to stop that now—but I will never, ever use one."

More memories flooded her mind, of purple-tinged mist, creeping over a hillside, of fallen men getting back up, their eyes and fingernails and gaping wounds glowing that same purple, turning and shambling back toward their own line. Of rain that ate through tents and blankets and flesh, of cannons that fired severed heads that exploded when they impacted or shot jagged purple lighting that cut men down like a scythe through wheat

"Some of our methods have been regrettable, but that doesn't make everything we touch evil," Mr. Duncan said. His earnest tone grated on her nerves. "This technology proves that we can harness our magic for the good of mankind."

"I hope you're right," Teddy said. "I really do. But I'm going."

Her father didn't move. "Please don't. You're all I have left."

"I thought I was a burden," Teddy snapped.

"I never said that. I just want what's best for you."

"But you can't trust me to know it for myself?"

Her father sagged. "I'm sorry. Please, just—just stay, Theodora."

Mr. Duncan held out his hand. "My offer stands, Miss Rhodes. If you ever change your mind—"

"I don't think that's likely, son," her father said. "And I know myself that my cooking isn't anything to stick around for, so you'd best be going."

Mr. Duncan tipped his hat to them. "As you wish. Goodbye, Mr. Rhodes. Miss Rhodes. I do wish you well."

They stood on the porch and watched him go. "I do believe that he meant every word," Teddy said. "And it might even be true. But I can't use their magic. Can't make it a part of myself. I—I just can't."

"I don't understand, but it's your life, your arm. Your choice. I'm sorry I pushed you. Will you stay?"

Teddy closed her eyes at the pain in his voice. "Yeah. I'll stay."

•

Teddy stared out at the corn. It was taller than her, now. She wondered if the fields her unit had watered with blood had higher or lower crop yields than normal, this year.

Or if blood didn't change a thing.

"I was thinking of trying to plant a rose garden," her father said, handing her a cup of coffee. "Your mother always wanted one."

"Would they be able to survive the winter?"

He shrugged. "I dunno, we never tried it. Come on in, food's ready."

Teddy followed him, then poked at what she could only assume was meant to be oatmeal. "Dad, let me cook. Even one-handed, I think I can manage better than this."

"Are you sure?"

"Yes."

He grinned at her. "Thank the Lord, I was starting to worry that we'd starve."

Teddy's arm healed, and she got a simple prosthetic with a hook. In her first week with it, she shredded four shirts, one skirt, and dropped two plates. She kept practicing.

One of the town boys who'd lost a leg got a fancy Western prosthetic, and could walk—even run, Teddy heard—like he was whole. Teddy told herself that it wasn't her place to judge. He didn't meet her eyes when they crossed paths, but he muttered, "I figured that we couldn't beat them, so...." He trailed off and shrugged.

"Having that thing attached to me would give me nightmares," Teddy said. "I was at Tikamat."

"Our unit never saw any purple action."

"Count yourself lucky."

"I do, Miss Rhodes. Believe me, I do."

"What memory did you give them?"

"A week in hospital, after I lost the leg. I was feverish, almost died."

"Do you miss it?"

"The memory?"

Teddy nodded.

"You know, I do. You wouldn't think so—I know it was a bad week, even not recalling it. But the empty space—well, it feels a bit like my leg did, before."

•

The next Westerner to come into town was different from the first. His fine brown suit was worn through at the knees and elbows, and he didn't smile. He drove his cart to the farm and stopped. He hopped down, hat in hand. "I hear you were in the war, miss."

"That's right. I'm Theodora Rhodes." She held out her hand, and he shook it. He had a nice, firm grip.

"Name's Tim Brady. I'm a photographer. I was on the front lines, and I'm looking to sell some pictures. I've got them on glass plate." He patted the wagon.

"Do you still have your camera?"

He shook his head. "It was government property. I couldn't have kept it fueled on my own, anyway. I've got no gift for memory-taking."

"Did they turn you out after the war was done?" Teddy asked as she glanced through a stack of glass plates. Nightmare images stared back. Ghostly outlines of dead men, charred fields, smoking houses. Piles of corpses frozen to the ground, a horse melted by the deadly rain, a nurse tossing an amputated arm into a pile of discarded body parts.

"Not exactly." Mr. Brady's tone hinted at a longer story, but didn't invite more questions.

The last one in the stack was a blurry shot of a horde of purple shamblers. Teddy shuddered. "I can see why you're having trouble selling these."

He pointed at another section. "These tend to be my better sellers. They're more scenic shots of places before the battles started. I'd be happy to trade a few for a place to stay and something to eat."

Teddy couldn't imagine wanting any of the pictures—her memory already held enough horrifying images. "Did you take portraits?"

"I did."

"Ever join up with the 17th regiment?"

He shook his head. "No, sorry."

Teddy shrugged. "That's the unit my brothers were with. Anyway, come on in, we've got extra beds, and I should be able to scrounge up an unbroken plate for you."

"Thanks, Miss Rhodes. I'll see to my mule first, if you don't mind."

"That's fine, Mr. Brady. Come on in whenever you're done."

Dinner wasn't fancy, but it was hot and filling and a far sight better than anything on the lines. Mr. Brady tucked in with enthusiasm.

"You've arrived at an opportune time, if you're looking for a bit of work," Teddy's father said. "I could use some help bringing in the harvest. Can't pay, but you'd be welcome to stay here till we're done."

"That's mighty kind of you, Mr. Rhodes. I'm much obliged."

He had a nice smile. Small and tired, but nice.

Days slipped by. "That Brady's a hard worker," her father said one morning, while Mr. Brady was out seeing to his mule. "We'll have the harvest in pretty soon, now."

"That's good news. Do you think the weather will hold?"

"I think so."

"Good."

"Teddy, I know you never gave much thought to marriage, but with the boys gone, we're gonna need help around here, and we can't afford a hired hand."

"I understand, Dad."

"I think he's a good man."

"I think so, too."

Teddy sat on the porch after dinner, trying to mend one of her torn skirts. Mr. Brady wandered out and stared up at the sky. "Do you have nightmares, Miss Rhodes?" he asked.

"Of course I do."

"Yeah. Me too."

"Why are you here? Why aren't you back West, selling your pictures to the government? I'm sure they'd take them."

"I'm sure they would, too. And they'd print the ones that serve them and dispose of the rest. And maybe that's a good thing. We all have to move forward together, now. Western magic is the way of the future. The past is done, and should be buried along with the dead. But I'm not ready to let it go. The things in those pictures—they're real. They happened, and no number of cheap prosthetic limbs will change that."

"So, what do you plan to do? Travel around, selling off plates one at a time?"

He shrugged. "No one wants them, Miss Rhodes. No one but the one group that I don't want to sell them to."

Teddy set her mending aside. "So don't sell them."

"I can't cart them around forever—they're not exactly sturdy."

"Don't do that either."

"What are you suggesting, Miss Rhodes?"

"Stay. Stay here, with us. Call me Teddy. Help me build a greenhouse so that we can grow roses."

"You want to use the glass plates to build a greenhouse?"

"Yes."

"The sun will bleach them to nothing, eventually."

"That's the way it is, with time."

"Your father calls you Teddy."

"My brothers did, too."

"Can I call you Theodora, instead?"

"If you'd like."

"I've always liked roses."

"So did my mother. But I worry that the winters would be too harsh."

"Okay."

"Okay?"

"I'll stay with you, Theodora. And I'll build your greenhouse, and let the sun bleach my photographs."

Teddy took his hand. "And maybe someday, our nightmares will fade, too."

"Maybe they will." His hand was warm, and chapped from working in the fields. "Maybe I'll get a new camera, one that doesn't run on memories, and take pictures of our roses."

"I'd like that," Teddy said. She laced her fingers through his, and they watched the stars come out together.

ANOTHER WILL OPEN

Originally appeared in *What Fates Impose*

Bahiti ripped her napkin into tiny pieces and kept her eyes away from the clock. Her water glass was empty, and the menu was no distraction. She always ordered D5. She loved teriyaki chicken.

Her blind date should have been here twenty minutes ago. She hated waiting. The waiter refilled her water. Another ten minutes passed. A man entered. He wasn't bad looking, and Bahiti smiled at him. He blinked at her, and a woman entered behind him and took his arm.

"You want a fortune cookie?" the waiter asked, filling her water glass again.

Bahiti forced a smile. "Sure."

Her fortune said *He's not coming.*

Rage curdled in her belly. "Really?" she snapped at the waiter, waving the tiny slip of paper. "Is this a joke?"

He glanced at it. "When one door closes another will open?"

Bahiti looked at her fortune again. *Hurry home if you don't want to get soaked.*

The hair on the back of her neck stood up. "I—I'm sorry, I must have misread it." She left a few dollars on the table for the water and the cookie, and fled.

She stopped in the middle of the street in front of her house. "This is stupid," she muttered. She turned on her heel. "I'm going for a walk."

Brakes squealed, and a car missed her by inches.

It started raining.

•

Take a sweater.

Bahiti stared at the slip of paper, walked halfway down the stairs, then ran back and grabbed a sweater. It was a beautiful spring morning. "Hmph," she muttered. She wasn't sure if she was relieved or disappointed. She waited at the bus stop, hugging her sweater and feeling like an idiot. The air inside the bus was stuffy and still.

She fought off her disappointment and reminded herself that it'd been what she expected. Then she walked into the office, and cold air hit her like a slap.

"The AC won't stop blowing," the secretary said. She rubbed her arms. "The facilities guys don't think they'll be able to get it fixed today."

Bahiti pulled on her sweater.

●

Fortune favors the bold. Bahiti glared at it. "Nice platitude," she muttered. She folded it, and noticed the lucky numbers on the back.

The lottery was up to 327 million. She bought a ticket. The paper was thin and smooth. It reminded her of the pages in her father's bible. It didn't feel real.

She'd never watched a lottery drawing before. She sat on the edge of her couch while butterflies ate each other in her belly. "Don't get your hopes up," she told herself, remembering that every time things seemed too good to be true, they were. Evan had seemed perfect, till he hit her.

At least if this didn't work out, she'd only be out a few bucks.

The numbers popped up, one by one. Her numbers. She fell off the couch.

●

She put in her two weeks notice and shared her exciting news with a few friends. After her last day at work, sat in her small apartment alone and stared down at the worn fortune. She weighed her options. What did she want to do with her life? She wondered what good she could do with her money. Did she have enough to save the whales? And she'd always wanted to travel, but where should she go first?

She didn't want to go alone.

"What do I do now?" she whispered. But the fortune didn't answer her questions. It still said the same thing it'd said yesterday.

Good things come to those who wait.

Bahiti flopped back on her bed. "I hate waiting."

●

Bahiti checked her email. Some old friends who hadn't contacted her in years wanted money to start a project. It didn't sound very promising.

Her eye caught on a daily horoscope message. Would that work, if her fortune cookie did? She opened the message and scrolled down to her sign.

Expect an unwelcome call from an old flame. Ignoring him won't work. Do not offer him money. Threaten to call the police, and he will leave.

Her doorbell chimed.

She left the chain on the door and cracked it open. Evan stood on her doorstep, wearing a shirt she'd bought for him. She could smell his cologne wafting from the hallway.

"Hey, beautiful," he said. "How're you?"

"Fine," Bahiti said.

"Can I come in?"

"Go away, Evan. You're not getting any money from me, and if you don't go, I'll call the police."

"You can't still be mad at me. I know I made a mistake, but I swear, I'd never do it again. I've missed you, sweetie. Come on, can't we just sit and talk for old time's sake?"

He'd been drunk and angry, and she'd left the next day. She was so lonely. She remembered the smell of his shampoo, the feel of him asleep next to her—the way he'd made her feel stupid and small.

"Go away. I will call the cops, Evan." She slammed the door.

The doorbell didn't ring again.

•

Bahiti checked her horoscope again. *Now is the time to wait, to catch up on unfinished tasks, and rest.*

She glared at the screen, then she waited. She ate chocolate ice cream and watched old television shows and slept till noon. She read all the books that she'd promised herself she'd get around to. She cleaned. She wrote a very large check to the wildlife federation. She baked 26 different kinds of bread and taught herself macramé.

By the end of her first month as a millionaire, she'd gained ten pounds, and she was tired of waiting. Her fortune and her horoscope didn't change.

She went for a walk.

•

Birds sang, the sun shone, and people bustled around on their lunch breaks. Bahiti checked her fortune every few blocks. She sat down on a park bench and shook it. "Are you broken?" she asked. Terror licked at her heart at the thought. How was she going to decide where to go if it was broken? How would she decide what she wanted to be, or find someone to share her life with?

"Why are you shaking that slip of paper?"

Bahiti jumped, and a gust of wind ripped the fortune from her fingers. She swore and chased it. The wind taunted her, keeping the fortune just out of her grasp.

An arm reached past her, and the fortune vanished in the stranger's hand. He was tall, with warm brown skin, gold-rimmed glasses, and short, messy hair. He looked down at the fortune. "When one door closes another will open?"

"Give it back!"

He put his hand behind his back. "Why's it so important to you?"

Panic welled up in Bahiti's throat. "Please," she managed. "Please give it back."

The man blinked, then handed it to her. "I'm sorry," he said. "It must have a lot of sentimental value."

Bahiti clutched it to her chest. "It tells me the future."

She wished she could take the words back the instant they were out of her mouth.

"Well, what does it say about having lunch with me?"

Bahiti gaped at him. Was he flirting with her? Was that what that playground display had been? She glanced down at her fortune. *Say yes.*

"It says that it's a good idea."

"Really?"

She nodded. "Where do you want to go?"

•

Shivers ran down her spine as he led her into the Chinese restaurant where it had all started. She glanced down. *It's okay.* She took a deep breath.

She ordered D5 without looking at the menu.

"I'm Senet," he said.

"Bahiti."

"A nice, Egyptian name," Senet said, smiling.

"Yours, too."

He opened his menu. "Have you ever been?" he asked.

Bahiti shook her head.

"Me neither. I've been obsessed with the history and culture my whole life, but I can't afford to go."

"Why are we here?" Bahiti asked.

He blinked at her. "Like in a deeper, philosophical sense?"

"Why did you ask me to lunch?"

"You're cute. You were sitting on a park bench, shaking a fortune from a fortune cookie that says 'When one door closes another will open.' It just seemed like the thing to do. Isn't this how people meet?"

"I—I don't know. I'm not good at meeting people."

"Me neither."

She glanced at her fortune. "Do you want to go to Egypt?"

"Of course I do. Who doesn't?"

"Then let's go."

Senet laughed. He had a nice laugh. "Okay. How are we going to get there? Do you have a reed raft?"

Bahiti shook her head. "I'm thinking we'll fly first class."

•

Senet stared at the ticket and the itinerary. They'd spent over an hour sitting with a travel agent, figuring out the schedule. "Are we missing anything that we really need to see?" she asked.

Senet shook his head. "It's my dream trip." He sighed. "I hate to ask this, but are you serious?"

"About what?"

"Did you really win the lottery by playing the numbers on your fortune cookie fortune?"

Bahiti nodded.

"And you're going to take me to Egypt with you."

Bahiti nodded again.

"Because the fortune told you to."

"Yes."

"We're not surrounded by hidden cameras, are we?"

"No."

"Okay." He took a deep breath and looked around. "Okay."

"I'll see you at the airport tomorrow," Bahiti said.

"I'll be there."

•

They stood in line at airport security. Bahiti clutched her passport. She'd never used it before.

"I brought you a present," Senet said.

"Really?" Bahiti loved presents.

"I—it's probably dumb." He handed her a Magic 8-Ball. "But I figured this would be harder to lose than a fortune."

She shook the ball and whispered, "Do you work?"

The white triangle bobbed in its blue ocean. *Yes.*

She shook it again. "What should I eat for breakfast?"

Get a breakfast burrito.

Bahiti grinned. "It works!" Her mind raced with questions. She could ask it anything.

She shook it. Plastic rattled, and the water inside sloshed. "Should I put you in my checked bags?"

Go through the second security booth.

She stuffed the 8-Ball in the bottom of her purse and did as it told her. Her breakfast burrito was delicious.

•

She sat in her hotel room in the glow of the alarm clock. The door to Senet's adjoining room was locked. The numbers read 4:07. She didn't know what time it was at home. She shook the 8-Ball. "Why did Evan hit me?"

She took a deep breath before she flipped the ball over.

Because he was broken.

Bahiti hugged the ball. "Why am I alone?"

You're not alone anymore.

"Because I have Senet?"

He is a step along your path.

"My path to what?"

Your destiny.

•

She asked her 8-Ball what to eat for every meal. She asked it when she should set her alarm clock and how much to tip and what outfit to wear.

It was hot in the car, even with the AC blasting, and their driver's music blared. Senet tried to look in every direction at once.

"Bahiti," Senet said, "I can see the pyramids."

Bahiti glanced up from her 8-Ball. "Those are pyramids, all right." She shook her 8-Ball. "How old are the pyramids?"

"Put your answers away and look up," Senet said. "You're missing it."

Bahiti slipped the plastic toy into her purse and watched the pyramids grow. The sun blazed, and the sky was a new shade of blue. Senet's fingers curled around hers. His eyes shone. "Those are the pyramids. We're really here."

"They're beautiful," She thought of a thousand questions to ask about them, but she could always ask later.

•

"I've got a challenge for you," Senet said over breakfast. "I bet you can't go a whole day without your 8-Ball."

"Why would I want to?" Bahiti asked.

"You can't spend your life asking a toy questions. Even if the toy does have all the answers. Life is for living."

"Do you really believe that it has all the answers, or are you just humoring me?"

Senet shrugged. "I never expected to actually be here, and I wouldn't be if not for you. You believe that it's real, and that's enough for me."

"Okay. You're on." She stuffed the 8-Ball in the bottom of her suitcase. "What do I get when I win?"

•

She lasted about two hours before panic started edging across her sternum. She smiled at Senet and snuck to the ladies room. She pulled the fortune out of her wallet.

Your paths separate here.

She stared at the paper. "But I like him," she whispered.

Leave him and go west.

"Can't I go west and take him with me?"

No.

Bahiti stuffed the fortune back in her wallet.

"How're you doing?" Senet asked, grinning. "How does it feel to be free from your 8-Ball?"

Bahiti forced a smile. "It's great."

"Come on, I found a place to have lunch. It looks great."

The food was bland and overpriced, but there was a view out over the Nile. Bahiti stared out the window and poked at her food.

Senet sighed over his koshari. "You pick better places."

"I don't pick them," Bahiti said. She hadn't made a single decision since he'd handed the 8-Ball to her.

She'd been so busy asking her 8-Ball questions, but she couldn't remember asking Senet a single one. "What did you do before I swept you off to Egypt?" she asked.

"I worked in a shoe store."

"Worked?"

He shrugged. "I couldn't get the time off, so I quit. I can get another job when I get home. I wasn't going to get another chance at this trip."

Bahiti tried to imagine wanting something so much that she'd turn life upside down for it. She couldn't. "Do you have any family?" she asked.

"My parents, and I'm the oldest of three boys."

Bahiti grinned. "Your poor outnumbered mother."

"Oh, she held her own, believe me. How about you?"

Bahiti shook her head. "Just me. I'm all alone."

Senet took her hand. "Not anymore."

She twined her fingers through his. "So, you sold shoes. That can't be what you really want to do."

Senet rubbed his neck. "I play classical guitar. This is the longest I've gone without playing for years."

"Are you any good?"

He laughed. "I'm not bad. What about you? What do you want to do?"

Bahiti shivered in the hot, dry air. "I don't know."

•

They wandered through kiosks and bought trinkets. Bahiti helped Senet pick gifts for his parents and brothers. They ate dinner at the hotel. He walked her to her room. "So, you won," he said.

"I guess I did," Bahiti said. She wondered if checking the fortune counted as cheating. She didn't ask.

"What prize do you claim?" he asked.

Bahiti kissed him. His lips were warm, and his cheek rough with stubble. He smelled like Old Spice and hot sand. Her chest ached. "We're even. Good night."

•

She pulled out the 8-Ball with shaking hands. "Can I trust him?" she asked.

Leave him.

"Yes or no," she hissed, shaking it again.

You must follow the path.

"Or what?"

Concentrate and ask again.

Bahiti dropped the 8-Ball. The message in the generic answer was clear. If she didn't do what it told her, it would stop working. She'd be adrift. "You—you can't threaten me," she said. She picked it back up, and sat down on the bed. She rested her forehead against the cool plastic. "So, it's him or you, huh?" She shook the ball. "What do I get if I follow your path?"

Your destiny.

"And what's that?"

You will be a force in the world.

Bahiti stared at the small white letters. Did she want to be a force in the world? Would she be happy? Or would Senet make her happy? Did he even want that? Did he see her as a person, or as his crazy benefactor? She imagined meeting his mother, his brothers, his father. She wanted to hear him play guitar.

She wondered how he'd feel if she left him.

She knew how she'd feel if he left her.

She had to make a decision. She rolled the 8-Ball back and forth between her hands. "I've never been any good at decisions."

She let it fall. It bounced, the rolled under the bed. "Maybe I just need practice."

She picked up the phone and called the front desk. "I'd like to buy a guitar."

•

"I got you a present," Bahiti said. "It's no magic 8-Ball, but I hope you like it.

The hotel had sent her to the best music store in Cairo. She held the guitar out, and Senet took it from her like it was made of glass. "It's amazing, Bahiti." He cradled the guitar and ran his fingers across the strings. He tuned it one string at a time, and Bahiti watched. "Play something for me," she said.

He played a song she'd never heard before. It was light and simple, but the melody was beautiful. "I wrote it," he said. "For you."

"You can't play the guitar," she said to her 8-Ball. "I bet Senet would teach me, if I asked."

She pulled up her horoscope.

Decisions that you make today will affect the rest of your life. Weigh your options wisely, and you could save the whales and go down in history as the century's greatest humanitarian.

She picked up her 8-Ball. "Can I save the whales without you?"

Cannot predict now.

"I'd like to know that things would work out with him," Bahiti said. "And I wish I had a better idea of what I want to do with my life, but I know I don't want to be your puppet, no matter what the rewards are."

•

"So, we fly home tomorrow," Senet said. "I was wondering if—if when we get home, if you—well, if you'd want to keep seeing me."

Bahiti took his hand and kissed his knuckles. She noticed the calluses on his fingers for the first time. She wondered how many other little things she'd missed. "I'd like that," she said.

•

Senet snored, and hogged the covers. Bahiti stuffed things into her suitcase while he slept. A strange, tiny smile tugged at her lips every time she looked at him. She picked up the 8-Ball. "Am I doing the right thing?" she asked.

Reply hazy, try again.

She shook it again. *Very doubtful.* She shook it again. *Without a doubt.*

She wondered about the destiny she'd turned away from and if she'd ever stop feeling lost. She pulled the fortune out of her wallet.

When one door closes another will open.

She put the fortune back in her wallet, and left the 8-Ball on the bedside table. Then she stuffed it in her suitcase. It was a fun toy. Maybe one of Senet's brothers would like it.

THE SPIDER'S GARDEN

Originally appeared in *Daily Science Fiction*

The spider grows invasive plants in her garden. Morning glory crawls up the walls, its leaves green and glossy, its tendrils curling into brick and crumbling it slowly to dust. Mint and lily of the valley choke each other in shady corners. Forsythia hedges stand under the weight of creeping kudzu vines.

The spider spins her webs and catches insects that venture into her domain. She wraps them in sticky thread and bites them. Her venom flows into their bodies, altering them. Shaping them to her will. Then she lets them go. Once, she would have devoured them, pulled them into her body to use them as a part of herself.

But that is no longer necessary.

•

One day, a young buck finds her garden. It ventures inside, each step carefully placed, its brown eyes wide and watching for any dangers. The spider admires the smooth brown of his coat, the feathery velvet of his new antlers. She's unsure of her venom's ability to change him—he is so much larger than she is. Still, she drops down behind one twitching ear and bites. Her fangs sink through his fur and skin, barely pricking the flesh beyond. The deer's ear flicks at her, and he takes two jittery steps. She injects all the venom that she has, then lets go, lets her silken thread carry her back to the safety of the wall.

Days pass before the deer returns. More than long enough for her body to produce all the venom she can store. He is calmer now, more confident within the garden's walls. She bites him again. Soon, he is coming every morning in the gray dawn, and standing perfectly still when she bites him.

•

The next creature to venture into her garden is a cat. It is large and long-furred, with alert green eyes and dangerous claws and teeth.

The spider considers just letting it leave. Staying out of its reach, up in a delicate web stretched between closed morning glory blossoms.

But it is so much smaller than the deer. And the spider enjoys a challenge.

The cat strolls along below her, stopping to dig at the soft soil around the mint, batting at a brown-edged fallen leaf. It flops onto its side in a pool of sunlight, and its eyes fall into the spider, perched at the edge of her web.

She shudders under its regard. But eventually its eyes slip closed and it twists onto its back.

The spider considers its exposed belly. Its vulnerability is almost certainly a trap. She was once a predator, too. She knows all about luring prey to its doom.

Still.

Still.

She drops down from her web, suspended on a silken thread.

She pauses, just outside of easy reach. The cat remains still, its position relaxed and boneless. Its eyes closed, its ears motionless.

The moment stretches, as thin and fragile as her thread.

She drops and burrows into its long fur and bites. Its back legs rake toward her, take one hard swipe. One of her legs rips away. But it is done. She lets go and climbs.

The cat jumps after her, swiping now with reaching front claws. But she is fast and small and it is already changing.

She settles back into her web as it licks its extended leg, between each clawed toe, and casually scrubs at its ears. Then it flops down again in its pool of sunshine.

The spider is pleased. The cat is a good addition to the garden, and her leg will grow back.

•

Her reach spreads one creature at a time. The cat brings mice and moles and shrews and birds into the garden, stunned and terrified, but still alive. The deer, his antlers rubbed smooth and shiny, leads his herd to her. A swarm of wasps build a papery nest in one corner. When new wasps are born, they are already hers.

She surveys her domain, and is pleased.

•

The daylight hours grow shorter, and the nights grow cold. Her creatures crowd into the garden, sharing the heat of their bodies and breath. The spider connects each of them with strands of sticky webbing, spins a thick cocoon in the very heart of her garden. As the gray clouds spit the first snowflakes, she climbs inside.

She dreams of long summer days, and wakes as a thousand daughters, who will claim a thousand gardens.

SEEKING THE GREAT RAYMUNDO

Originally appeared in *Beneath Ceaseless Skies*

I squeezed into my snug, bright red dress, pasted a big smile on my face, and followed Freddy on stage. We were playing for a crowd of kids in a dilapidated theater, but it was quickly apparent that they were too busy throwing popped corn at each other to care about the act. Which was fortunate for us, since he was intoxicated again and there's only so much covering I can do.

I paraded around the stage, handing Freddy trick hats, rainbow scarves, and silk flowers. I tried not to think too much.

Then one of the brats threw a handful of popped corn at me.

It was the last straw.

I stepped away from the box I was supposed to be disappearing in, squeezed my hands into fists, then snapped them open. Balls of flame burst to life in each of my palms. I'd been watching Freddy for years—I was better at his tricks than he was, and I'd even managed to pick up a bit of the deep magic.

I pointed at the brat who'd thrown the popcorn. His face had gone slack and white in terror. "You spoiled little worm!" I shouted. "I can destroy you with my mind, and I deserve some respect!"

The rest of the kids screamed and ran for the exit. The brat just whimpered. I was tired of tight, sequined dresses. Tired of contorting into boxes while plastering a happy, surprised expression on my face. Tired of bleaching my hair.

Freddy put his hand on my shoulder. "Felicity," he slurred. "Let the boy go."

I gritted my teeth and clenched my fists closed. The fire sputtered out around my fingers, then died. The brat darted after his friends.

I wanted the tux, the hat, and the wand.

I wanted to cry. I was tired of being a joke.

"You mustn't do magic," Freddy slurred, his hand still heavy on my shoulder. "Women are assistants. It's the way things are. You know that."

31

I shrugged him off. The Brotherhood of Magicians wouldn't like it, but I was going to be a magician. If I managed to get The Great Raymundo on my side, they wouldn't be able to stop me.

"Freddy, I'm sorry. I can't do this anymore. I quit."

•

They say that as he lay dying, The Great Raymundo discovered a way to force his soul into his battered copy of *The Magician's Manual*. Any magician who gets his hands on that book would have the key to becoming the greatest magician of our time—maybe of all time. But any magician who's claimed the book has quickly lost it.

However, no woman had ever tried to claim the book, and they say that The Great Raymundo was quite the womanizer. Maybe, he'd be willing to stay with me. I had to try. I couldn't go on the way things were.

I stared deep into my dressing mirror, letting my focus drift till the glass went dark. "I seek thee, Great Raymundo," I whispered. Then I twisted my voice around the words of deep magic that would seal me to the task. I imagined the Great Raymundo peering out at me from within the darkness. Magic shivered across my skin, and my reflection reappeared.

I left without saying goodbye to Freddy. I couldn't think of anything to say. I packed my things into a sturdy carpetbag and marched to the train station.

The ticket to San Francisco cleaned out most of my savings. Working for Freddy hadn't been the most lucrative job.

I climbed into an empty car and found a seat next to the window. I leaned my forehead against the cool glass.

"Is this seat taken?" A well-dressed, handsome gentleman tipped his hat to me. I shook my head. "Where are you heading?" he asked as he settled in beside me.

"San Francisco. You?"

"The same. My brother went out last year looking for gold, and I'm to fetch him back. Our mother tires of his foolishness."

"Seems to me like it's your brother's life. If he wants to spend it in the west digging for gold, that's his business."

"That's a very enlightened attitude." The gentleman arched an eyebrow at me. "And what takes you west?"

I shrugged. "I've got nothing holding me here." I snapped my bag open, intending to pull out one of the penny dreadfuls I'd bought for the ride.

Instead, I found a dark gray leather-bound journal perched on top of my things. I glanced over at the gentleman. He'd pulled out some correspondence and had devoted himself to perusing it. I opened the journal, and a note slipped into my lap.

Felicia, I know you don't think much of me, but I've grown to see you as a daughter over the years. I should have told you how much I appreciated you taking care of me. And I should have taught you, Brotherhood be damned. Maybe this'll make up for things a little.

He'd signed it "The Fabulous Frederick." He hadn't called himself that in years. I smiled and stroked the soft leather of the cover. In spite of everything, Freddy wasn't a bad guy. I tucked the note into the journal and noticed a hastily scribbled p. s. on the back of the note.

Trust nothing! Raymundo can make liars of your very senses!

I glanced at the gentleman from the corner of my eye. He seemed enthralled with his letters. Possibly from his poor wayward brother. Or worse, his overbearing mother. I fought to keep from rolling my eyes.

Freddy's journal was fascinating reading. He explained his familiar tricks with complicated diagrams that defined and explained things that I'd always just felt were right without really understanding.

Freddy really had been fabulous once. I wondered what happened. Why had I never bothered to ask?

"So, what are you reading that's so engaging?" the gentleman asked.

I jumped a bit. I'd forgotten he was there. "A gift from a friend."

He arched his eyebrow again. I wondered if he'd practiced the expression. "A male friend?"

I wished I could kick him and make it look like an accident. Or light him on fire without getting into serious trouble. Instead I just closed Freddy's journal and shot the gentleman a quelling frown. "I don't see how that's any of your concern."

He shrugged. "I hate to see a lovely lady traveling alone. I was just wondering what has become of your chaperone."

"As far as I'm aware, I've never had a chaperone."

"Well, then it's high time you did."

I glared at him, since my frown garnered no result. "That's very... neighborly. But unnecessary. I can take care of myself."

"We're both traveling to California. I insist on seeing to you till then."

I hoped he wasn't a junior member of the Brotherhood sent to spy on me. I couldn't think of any other reason for his concern, but I also didn't see any polite way to put him off. "Well, if you're to be my protector, I should at least know your name."

"Jeffry. Jeffry Hawk."

"I'm Felicity Banks."

"Lovely to make your acquaintance, Miss Banks."

The train stuttered, and I barely kept myself in my seat. I grabbed Freddy's book, clutched it to my chest, and whispered a quick protection spell. Mr. Hawk slid to the floor. Brakes squealed, and the train slammed to a stop. This time, I failed to keep my seat. I tumbled directly into Mr. Hawk's lap. He wrapped his arms around me and absorbed the worst of the blows.

"What happened?" I asked.

Mr. Hawk shook his head. "It seems we've hit something." He was bleeding from his temple, but seemed otherwise unharmed.

"What kind of obstruction could stop a train?" I asked.

He shrugged, and I realized that his arms were still wrapped around me. I pulled away. For an instant, he seemed unwilling to release me. I tucked Freddy's book into my skirt and helped him to his feet.

"We should go see what's going on." I said.

"Why in the world would we do that?" he asked.

"Someone might be hurt out there." I moved toward the door.

Mr. Hawk grabbed my hand. "It might be dangerous."

"Then you'd best come along, in case I need your protection."

He frowned, but came with me. He didn't release my hand. The train had gone eerily silent. Where were all the other passengers? Shouldn't there be shouts? Groans? Something? I looked into another car and found it deserted. There was luggage, scattered about by the crash, but no people.

Fear edged through my belly.

"What is going on here?" Mr. Hawk asked. His voice was too loud in the eerie silence.

I led him toward the engine. Maybe it would hold some answers. His hand gripping mine had become a comfort instead of an annoyance.

The engine was gone. The front car had been ripped open, and the bright midday sunlight streamed in. There were claw marks in the metal, and a trail of huge three-toed footprints deep in the sand.

A familiar tingle passed along my skin. Someone had worked deep magic here.

"It can't be safe for us to stay," Mr. Hawk whispered back.

I looked outside. Desert stretched out in every direction. "Should we have reached the desert yet?"

Mr. Hawk shook his head. "Not unless my geography classes were seriously misleading. Or the train was moving much faster than it seemed."

I stared down the tracks that led out into the vast desert. "We're in serious trouble."

·

We gathered what supplies we could from the abandoned luggage and headed down the train tracks. Mr. Hawk only let go of my hand when absolutely necessary.

I no longer minded. In fact, my fingers found his at least once. We set out across the desert, following the train tracks. I studiously avoided looking at strange footprints. They were perpendicular to the tracks—hopefully whatever monster left them would see no reason to return. Eventually, they fell behind us.

Of course, that meant the train did, too. There were no other landmarks.

The sun beat down on us mercilessly, and the sand was unstable and made walking difficult. Grit coated my skin and found its way into my socks. Our ragged breathing and muffled footfalls were the only sounds. Mr. Hawk's palm grew sweaty against mine, but neither of us moved to let go.

"I wasn't really going to bring my brother back," Mr. Hawk said.

I was too winded to answer, but I managed a small, curious noise to encourage him to continue. The sound of his voice was a welcome break from the oppressive silence.

"I was going to join him. I just needed a bit of capital from Mother, so I pretended to go along with her wishes."

I kept encouraging him to talk, and he kept talking, mostly about his plans for finding riches in the mines. We struggled across the sand until every step was torture.

Then, the earth trembled beneath us. "What was that?" he asked.

It happened again. "I don't know." I glanced back over my shoulder and bit back a horrified cry.

A great, reptilian monster charged toward us. It was well back along the tracks, but closing fast. Wooden railroad ties splintered beneath its feet. Its gray-green body was larger than a house and balanced on its two massive hind legs. Great black horns curved up from its forehead, and a line of delicate yellow sails lined its spine. It roared, and its foot-long teeth gleamed in the desert sun.

It ran incredibly fast. The ground rumbled beneath our feet as if it were a train approaching.

"What the hell is that?" Mr. Hawk shouted.

I shrugged and hoped it was flammable. I squeezed his hand, then pulled away. "We're not going to be able to outrun it."

Mr. Hawk drew a pistol from his boot. "You go. I'll see if I can slow it down."

"Let's see if we can stop it, together." I clenched my fists and summoned fire.

Mr. Hawk didn't have time to be shocked. The monster was bearing down on us. He took careful aim and fired six times. I threw both balls of flame.

The monster roared in pain, but it didn't slow its charge. It lunged toward us. Its breath smelled of death. Mr. Hawk shoved me away and the monster swallowed him whole.

Rage unlike anything I'd ever known surged through me. I screamed, and bolts of fire shot down from the heavens. The monster's scaly flesh charred off of its huge skull, and it slumped to the ground.

I clawed at its mouth, frantic to pry the teeth apart. "Mr. Hawk! Jeffry!" I prayed for him not to be dead. I couldn't face this strange wasteland alone.

A muffled moan reached my ears, and I managed to shift the monster's jaw. Jeffry tumbled into my arms. He was covered in foul-smelling slime.

I wiped off his face as best I could, and his eyes fluttered open. "Felicity?" he croaked.

"Yes, Jeffry?"

"I've figured it out."

"Figured what out?"

"This has to be some kind of vision."

I ran my fingers through his hair. It was stiff with drying slime. "I hope you're right."

•

Night fell, and Jeffry managed to build us a fire using the trail of broken railroad ties. The smell was acrid and foul, but the desert night was too cold to do without.

I cut off hunks of monster flesh and roasted them. The smoke imparted an oily, chemical flavor. But I'd had worse dinners.

"We need to figure out how to escape," Jeffry said. He poked at the fire with one of the monster's claws.

"Why are you so certain that this is a vision?" I asked.

"Because this," he paused to shake the claw, "is impossible."

"It's magic," I said.

"Wouldn't it be easier for a magician to trap us in a vision than summon some huge carnivorous lizard?"

I considered his point. "I suppose it would be. But I did feel the presence of magic back on the train, where the monster clawed its way out of the car. I haven't felt it anywhere else."

"What happened to all the other people, then? And the engine? Why are we in the desert?"

"I—I don't know."

"Do you feel tired? Or thirsty? Is it hunger that drove you to roast us dinner, or habit?"

Our thirst should be crippling by this point. But he was right. While the thought of water was appealing, it wasn't a necessity.

"You must concede that my idea does make sense."

"Yes," I said. I tapped my finger against my lips. "But how do we escape it?"

"That was my original question," Jeffry said. "You seem to know some things about magic."

"Yes," I said. "Does that bother you?"

He shrugged. "Why should it? I'm not a member of the Brotherhood. And we're in this together—I'm glad one of us knows about magic."

No one had been glad about my interest in magic before.

I kissed him. He tasted like sweat, and the monster's stink still clung to him, but it was an enjoyable kiss, in spite of that.

His expression, when I pulled away, was a mix of shock and delight. It was the look of a child who'd just been informed that Christmas was going to come early this year.

I kissed him again.

He pulled me close, and we stayed like that for some time. The fire burnt down, and the temperature dropped.

"Look at that," Jeffry whispered, pointing at the sky.

I rolled over and stared up. The stars were unlike any I'd ever seen. They glimmered every color of the rainbow in unrecognizable patterns strewn across the sky. "If we're not in a vision, we're in serious trouble," Jeffry said.

I nodded. "We must be in a vision."

"Any ideas on how to extricate ourselves?"

I shook my head. I could look through Freddy's book in the morning, but it was too dark now. "Let's go to sleep and see what the morning brings."

●

I dreamed that The Great Raymundo, resplendent in his tux and top hat, handed me a wand. "It's only proper that wands belong to men," he said. "But I never understood why The Brotherhood didn't want women to play with them." He leered and winked at me.

I kicked him in the knee.

●

Waking in Jeffry's arms was perfectly pleasant, but the day went quickly downhill. My dream had left me restless and edgy, and the fact that I'd dreamed at all was worrisome. Did one dream if trapped inside a vision?

Freddy's book held no insights to our predicament. There was a fascinating diagram about teleportation, but I didn't think it would be applicable to our current crisis.

Jeffry smoked strips of monster, rubbed my shoulders, and offered encouragement. Eventually, though, I gave up. "I don't have any ideas."

Jeffry squeezed my hand. "Well, then, we should keep walking. These tracks have to lead somewhere, don't they?"

●

We walked for days. We never grew thirsty, or hungry, or tired, but we stopped when the sun went down. Jeffry rambled on about his brother's gold claim, his mother's fortune, and his schooling.

I told him about life with Freddy—bratty kids, annoying parents, and life on the road.

"Why in the world do you want to be a magician, if that's the life they lead?" he asked me after one particularly bloodcurdling story about an angry mother.

"I don't want to do stage magic. I want to learn the deep magic."

"But what do you want to do with it?" he asked.

I shrugged. I'd never really thought of it. "I guess I'm hoping that the right path will reveal itself. When I'm ready."

●

Eventually, we reached the station at the end of the tracks. A man in a tux and top hat stepped into the sun and waved at us.

"Who's that?" Jeffry asked.

"The Great Raymundo," I said, suddenly understanding Freddy's warning.

"The dead guy? The one in the book?"

"The very same!" The Great Raymundo strode toward us, grinning. The lines of his tux were razor sharp, and his white shirt glistened in the sunlight.

I felt very grimy. "And we're in the book with you, aren't we?" I asked.

He grinned at me and winked at Jeffry. "Quite a clever one, isn't she?"

"So it's not a vision?" Jeffry asked.

The Great Raymundo shrugged. "Where is the line between what is real and what isn't, really?"

"Why have you brought us here?" I asked.

The Great Raymundo leaned toward Jeffry and stage whispered, "Impatient, too."

Jeffry looked ready to strike him, and for that I was certain to always love him. "Just answer the lady's question."

The Great Raymundo laughed. "Well, I brought you here to test you, girl. You are the only interesting candidate I've seen in half a century. You're the one who dragged him along."

"Did I pass your test?" I asked.

The Great Raymundo beamed at me. His teeth were even whiter than his shirt. "What makes you think it's over?"

"The fact that you're here," Jeffry snapped.

"I just wanted a closer look at you," The Great Raymundo said. "It's been a long time since I've had the chance to look at a—what did you call her—oh, yes. A lady."

I grabbed Jeffry's arm before he could swing. "Well, you've had a look at me."

The Great Raymundo leered. "Indeed."

"So, now what?" I asked.

"I will consent to teach you. But only if you carry my book with you always, over your heart."

"You mean in my bodice."

The Great Raymundo nodded. "Indeed."

"And we'll wake from this vision?"

The Great Raymundo nodded.

"And if I refuse you?"

The Great Raymundo shrugged. "Who knows? Perhaps I'll keep you here forever, to amuse me. Perhaps not. You'll definitely never become the magician you so long to be. You need me, girlie."

Jeffry squeezed my hand and leaned in close to my ear. "We managed to slay his monster. Maybe we can rid ourselves of him, too,"

I remembered Jeffry vanishing into the monster's mouth, and shook my head. "It's too dangerous."

"There must be another way," Jeffry said. "You can't bind yourself to this... lecherous cad."

I thought of Freddy's book, already tucked into my belt. I turned to The Great Raymundo. "I want your word that you'll release us and never try to harm either of us again, and that if I carry you in my bodice, you'll teach me."

"I swear it upon my very soul," The Great Raymundo said.

"Very well."

The Great Raymundo waved his hands with impressive flourish. There was a flash of light, and I found myself back on the train, click-clacking along just as it should. My head was resting on Jeffry's shoulder.

He opened his eyes and looked around. Then he looked down at me. Worry shadowed his eyes. "Miss Banks?"

I kissed him. For the first time, we were clean and comfortable. We didn't rush.

Eventually, though, I grew aware of an uncomfortable pressure against my breastbone. I pulled away, and pulled the book from my bodice. It was bound in red leather and The Magician's Manual was embossed on the cover in gold leaf.

"The cheek," Jeffry grumbled.

It was a beautiful book. And it was my key to becoming the greatest magician who ever lived—to The Brotherhood of Magicians accepting me—to whatever it was that my dreams would hold.

I tossed the book through the open window.

Jeffry gaped at me. "But—"

"I don't want to keep him in my bosom, so he is under no obligation to teach me." I pulled out Freddy's journal. "I already have a book that I can learn from. And this one doesn't ogle or give orders. I will write to Freddy when we arrive, and see if we can arrange some sort of correspondence course."

Jeffry took the book from my hand, carefully tucked it back into my bag, and kissed me. "Maybe you can help me look for gold."

The happiness that shivered along my skin felt almost like magic. "Maybe I can."

REFLECTIONS OF DUST

Originally appeared in *Lakeside Circus*

A thin stream of gray brown dust slipped through the roof over Heddie's bed every time the wind shifted. It pooled next to her face, and puffs danced like smoke every time she exhaled. It looked like a living thing, asleep on her pillow. She rolled away, scrunched her eyes, and tried to sleep. "It's just dirt," she whispered. The wind screamed across the wasted cornfields, and dust hissed against the walls.

Pa had done his best to seal it out, but it kept finding new ways in.

Matilda coughed from her tiny bed in the far corner—a familiar, dry, wrenching cough.

Their mother had coughed just like that just before the dust pneumonia took her. Heddie's throat ached, and she blinked back her tears. Their mother was gone. It was her job to take care of Matilda now. She took a deep breath and pushed her covers back.

The pool of dust puffed into the air and floated, hovering in front of her face. It shifted in the still air, formed into a rough oval, with a bulge in the middle, with two hollows above it and a horizontal gash below.

The dust face smiled at her.

Heddie hit it with her pillow, and it flew apart and drifted to the already gritty sheets.

She scrambled out of bed, still clutching her pillow in her shaking hands, and ran to Matilda's bed. Two forms curled on it, one above the sheets, one below. One flesh, and one formed of dust. Both stirred and looked up at Heddie. "Five more minutes," Matilda muttered sleepily and buried her face in her pillow. The dust copy coughed.

Heddie attacked it with her pillow. Matilda sat up and screamed. The dust-Matilda held its form through three blows, then disintegrated.

Matilda kept screaming, but so did the wind. It swallowed Matilda's voice.

Heddie pulled Matilda into her arms and pulled the sheets over them. "Shh. It's okay. It's gone."

Matilda sagged against her chest. Tears left muddy tracks in the thin layer of dust on her cheeks. "It looked just like me."

"I know."

It was dark under the sheet, and their breath thinned the warm air. "Do you think one of those things took Ma?" Matilda whispered.

"I dunno." She imagined their mother, consumed by dust and trying to cough it up till her heart stopped.

"Pa won't believe us, will he?"

Heddie shook her head. Their mother had begged him to leave the farm for months. She'd told stories about California and oranges and ocean breezes. Then she'd started coughing.

"What are we going to do?" Matilda asked.

Heddie pushed the sheet away. Two dust figures peered at them from the foot of the bed, their faces like dark mirrors. "Give us our mother back," Heddie said.

Her dust reflection coughed. It held its hand out, palm up. "Don't," Matilda hissed. "We should run. Maybe if we show Pa—"

It didn't look threatening, sitting with its hand outstretched. Maybe it just wanted to talk. Maybe it really could give their mother back. Heddie reached out and laid her palm against the dust. It was soft and fine and powdery, like flour. Heddie's fingers sank into it, and thin streams of dust crept up her arm. She coughed. She tried to pull her hand away, but the dust curled around her. Its surface swirled, and her hand burned as the grit scoured skin away.

Matilda swung her pillow with a feral scream, and both figures dissipated. She hit the scattered dust again and again. "You can't have her! She's my sister!" She stopped, panting, her pillow black with dust. She clung to Heddie. "I—I won't let you leave me."

Heddie stared at the raw skin on her hand. "I—I thought maybe we could get mom back, somehow."

"She's gone, Heddie."

They sat together and listened to the dust hiss. "Even if they hadn't eaten her—just taken her someplace, would you really want to go get her?" Matilda asked.

Heddie imagined a whole world made of dust. The image was too familiar. She shuddered. "No."

"Let's go check on Pa." Matilda twined her fingers through Heddie's. They were warm and solid.

"I'm supposed to take care of you," Heddie said. "Not the other way around."

"Let's just take care of each other." Matilda pulled her out of their room.

They found Pa sitting in the kitchen, still in his working clothes, staring at a sputtering fire and sipping burnt coffee. "This is the fourth dust storm this month," he said.

"We know, Pa," Heddie said.

"My father came out here with nothing. He built this house with his own hands before he sent for us." He stared into his coffee. "It used to be easier."

Heddie lifted Matilda into his lap, then wriggled in beside her. They hardly fit.

"You girls should be in bed," Pa said, but he wrapped his arms around them.

"Let's go to California," Heddie said.

Pa sighed. "There's no guarantee that things will be any better out there."

"Can things get much worse?" Heddie asked. She thought about her mother's grave and wondered what exactly they'd put in the ground. She shivered, and snuggled closer to Matilda and Pa.

"We—we'd be leaving our whole life behind."

"Just like grandpa did?" Matilda asked.

Pa chuckled. "Yeah. I guess so. When did you get so smart?"

"Please, Pa," Heddie whispered. She didn't want to sleep in their house for another night. She wondered if the neighbors would even notice when they left, or if their dust reflections would carry on for them.

She hoped not. She wanted them to crumble and blow away. She remembered the dust copy's hand in hers. She shuddered and coughed.

Her father looked at her in alarm. "Heddie—"

Matilda coughed, too. Her whole body shook with it. "Please, Pa. California has to be better."

He brushed muddy tears off of Matilda's face, then nodded once. "All right, girls. All right."

⚫

Heddie shook out her sheets, then folded them. No matter how much she shook, she couldn't get all the dust off. It coated everything. Her skin, her hair, her teeth.

Maybe she was already a dust copy of herself. She took a deep breath and let it out. Maybe it didn't matter.

They loaded the truck then piled into the cab. Pa's knuckles were white on the steering wheel. He jerked the truck into gear, and they rolled forward. Heddie craned around and watched as her home fell away.

A dust figure stepped out of the doorway and waved. Dust streamed from its fingertips. She thought about oranges and ocean breezes, and waved back.

LETTING GO

Originally appeared in *Weird Tales*

The sun pounded down on the graveyard, blasting the grass to brittle brownness and casting harsh shadows on the dry earth. Marigolds and roses shriveled next to faded plastic bouquets.

Alissa perched on a headstone, her thighs resting on griddle-hot marble. She twisted her engagement ring around her finger and stared at the sparkling diamond. Her fiancé had wanted to spend today together. Instead, private tradition had driven her here. She let go of the ring and fidgeted with the chain of her silver locket. It felt far more familiar to her fingertips.

The locket itself was frozen in place against her breastbone. She'd stolen it from her father's desk when she was six, and hadn't been able to remove it since.

She'd never seen what was inside.

It was the twenty-fifth anniversary of Alissa's mother's death—Alissa's twenty-fifth birthday. She always spent her birthdays here.

Her friends called her morbid.

Cicadas buzzed. Alissa knelt on her mother's grave and planted mums and lilies, rosemary and lavender. She poured a gallon of water over them, and they didn't wilt immediately. Drops of sweat rolled down her chest and froze against her locket.

The shadows grew, and the dying sunlight painted her locket blood red. It looked like a window to her heart. A hot breeze lifted the scent of rosemary and lavender, and a ghostly hand reached out of the muddy earth.

Alissa laced her fingers through the hand's cold, shimmering ones. Her skin burned.

This time, she pulled.

Her mother's ghost emerged from the grave as the sun slipped below the horizon. The ghost wore a stained hospital gown, and her hair fell in ragged tangles around her face. She reached forward and pulled the locket away from Alissa's heart. She unclasped the latch with gentle fingers and looped the chain around her own insubstantial neck.

She pressed an icy kiss to Alissa's forehead, then started to sink back into the ground.

"Wait," Alissa said, grabbing her mother's arm. "I don't know what's in it."

Her mother just smiled and shook her head. "It's not for you." Her voice was like the winter wind, and suddenly Alissa was cold. The hand against her mother's arm started to ache.

"Please. I wore it for so long," Alissa begged. "I need to know. I have a right to know."

The ghost shook her head.

The moment stretched. Alissa started to shiver. A blue tinge spread across her fingernails. Ice formed on her engagement ring. Her mother tried to pull away. If Alissa held on, she might have her answers. But were they worth the cost?

She let go.

The ghost sank into her grave. Alissa stood and listened to the crickets. Her chest felt strange—light and warm. Her engagement ring glinted in the moonlight.

She could spend her next birthday somewhere else.

GROWING UP

Originally appeared in *Daily Science Fiction*

I didn't realize I was property till my progenitor sold me. The last time I saw zir, ze looked deep into my eyes and said, "All children are assets, little one. Someday, if you are able to earn a place among the adults, you'll understand."

Ze patted me on the head with a heavy, soft, short-fingered hand, so unlike my own childish hands with their long, nimble fingers. Then ze lumbered away, leaving me with my new owner.

My new owner was kinder than my progenitor had been—ze thanked me for the cooking and cleaning that I did, and ze never needed me to drag zir from one room to another when ze was too drained to move.

But I could never forget that I was property, an owned thing. An asset. Resentment grew in me like a deep-buried seed, sending thin roots into every crack in my soul.

One night, after my owner dragged zir's bulky body to zir's sleeping chamber, I crept from my resting alcove and down to the library. The tapping of my feet seemed to echo like drumbeats, but there was no response from my owner's chamber.

The books were designed for adult hands, but I was strong from dragging my progenitor, and I managed to pull one book from the shelves, then another. The words were meant for adult eyes, and looking at them too long gave me a headache. But after that first night, I spent all of the time I could in the library. The hours of practice strengthened my eyes, and eventually I unlocked the puzzle of written language.

I discovered the adults' secrets, and my resentment bloomed into hate.

But there was nothing I could do. Without my owner's protection, I'd be claimed by another adult. There was no way I could survive on my own. I worked and I read and I tried to ignore the anger that simmered in me like a sickness.

Eventually, my owner reached zir's reproductive cycle, and produced another child. The child hatched and grew quickly, and my owner didn't bother to differentiate between us.

I trained the child, as was my duty. And I taught the child, knowing it could be my doom. But it was nice to not be alone, to voice my anger and see another face mirror my own rage. To listen when the child had questions and find any answers I didn't know together.

The child and I both knew what to expect when my owner, the child's progenitor, called us down into the depths of the house. We had read the stories that were not meant for our childish eyes.

"You must fight," my owner said. "The victor will consume the body of the fallen, and only then will you ascend to adulthood."

Ze opened a heavy-lidded box. Inside, sharp knives with chitinous handles glistened against dark velvet. I wondered if an adult had made them, somehow, or if children created them.

My owner put a heavy hand on each of our heads. "It is time to grow up," ze said.

The child and I exchanged a look as we each took a knife. We had not discussed what we would do when the time came. I thought about lunging forward, burying the blade deep in the child's side. I was the stronger of us. I could win, take my place among the adults.

Instead, I lowered the blade to my side. The child did the same. Then, as one, we turned on my owner. Flesh parted easily under our blades, and we shared zir's huge body equally between us.

The change is upon us now. I don't know what we will become. But I am at peace, knowing that I will never earn a place among the adults, never understand the choice that every adult made.

We will not be like them.

TRYING TO BE HAPPY

Originally appeared in *The Colored Lens*

The veranda steps groaned as the movers dragged our things into our newly-purchased, sprawling, dilapidated house. I stood in the shade by the car, drained by the heat. My head throbbed, my feet ached, and I felt fat, sweaty, and resentful. The baby kicked, and I glared down at my distended stomach. I wished I was back home, with air conditioning and a cold cocktail.

John rushed back and forth, giving instructions and grinning like an idiot.

I took a long drink from my water bottle. It was blood-warm.

Motion fluttered in an upstairs window. A teenage girl with dark, elaborately curled hair frowned down at me. She was wearing a filmy, white dress that seemed to flow into the thin curtains. Her eyes met mine. She mouthed something—I've never been much of a lip reader—then she vanished.

Chills cut down my sweaty back, and I dropped my water bottle.

John was at my side in an instant. "What's wrong, Donna?" he asked.

A moment ago, I would have given him a list. "N—Nothing," I stammered. "Just my imagination playing tricks on me."

He kissed my forehead and laid a hand over my belly. "Maybe you should sit down. I had them put your rocking chair on the porch. I'll get you some more water."

He filled my bottle from the tap. It was only a little cooler, and it tasted like iron.

•

I stood in what was to be my office, staring at the mess of boxes. I walked over to the window and looked out at where I'd been standing when I saw the girl. I trailed a finger down the limp curtains. She'd been standing right here.

A cold, transparent hand appeared over mine.

I screamed, and the hand vanished.

John thundered up the stairs. "What happened? Are you okay?"

"This house is haunted," I said.

John blinked at me. "What?"

"There's a ghost. She just touched my hand."

John frowned. "Are you sure it wasn't just a draft?"

"Yes, I'm sure it wasn't a damn draft! It's a ghost! I saw her yesterday, and today she touched me!" I hugged my arms tight around my belly. "I want to go home."

John sighed. "You promised that you wouldn't do this."

"That was before there was a ghost."

"You're just feeling unsettled because this is such a huge change. Unpack. You'll feel better once you have some familiar things around. You just need to recontextualize. This is your home now. This is where we're going to raise our baby." He took my hand, covered the skin that the ghost had touched with his warmth.

I wanted to tell him to stop talking down to me. I wanted to insist that the ghost was real, that I'd seen her, but it seemed so absurd, standing next to him in the sunshine.

"You can be happy here," he said. "You just have to try."

I nodded, forced a sickly smile. "I did promise."

"There's my good girl. Want me to stick around, help you deal with these boxes?"

I nodded. Part of me wanted to tell him off for his condescending tone, but I wasn't ready to be alone again. "I'd like that."

•

John started his new job at the hospital the next day. I was alone in the house. I spent the morning organizing the kitchen, getting the flowerbeds ready for planting, hanging clothes in the huge closets. Avoiding my office.

But if I avoided it all day, I knew John would notice. And he'd say something. And I couldn't think of anything to respond with.

So, after my lunch—peanut butter and pickles on a toasted English muffin—I took a deep breath and faced the haunted room. I opened a box full of books and started arranging them on the shelves.

The ghost knelt next to me and scanned the titles.

She was pretty, with a dusting of gold freckles on her white cheeks. Her eyes were the deep, clear blue of a cold mountain lake. Her white dress billowed and flowed when she moved, and faded to nothing at the edges. She trailed a finger down the spine of one of my college textbooks—a book about the formation of stars.

I took a deep breath. She wasn't threatening me. Maybe she was a friendly ghost. "Hello," I said. The word sounded silly, out loud.

Her eyes flicked to my face, then down to my wedding ring, and past, to my pregnant belly. Her gaze returned to my face, cold and angry. "You should know better," she said. "You're an educated woman."

"What are you talking about?" I asked.

"You don't want to be here," the ghost said. "You don't want that baby. You've let him trick you into giving up all of yourself for his happiness." She stared down at her almost-transparent hands. "You shouldn't have done that."

I cupped my hand over my belly and felt the baby move, another life incased in my body. Fear shivered through me. "You're wrong," I said. To her. To myself.

She shrugged, pulled one of my books off the shelf, and paged it open. "We'll see."

•

I sat on the porch till John came home. He looked tired. I hesitated to bother him with this. I was afraid he'd brush me off again.

"There is a ghost," I said.

John sighed.

I walked to the edge of the porch and looked down at him. The top of his head was sunburned. "You asked me to have your baby. You asked me to come here with you. Now I'm asking you to believe me."

He opened his mouth, then closed it. He took a deep breath. "Okay." He took my hand and brought it to his lips, then held it to his cheek.

"I'm not making her up. I'm not backing out of my promise. I want to be happy here, but I can't if you're going to treat me like this."

John nodded. "You're right. I'm sorry. I should have listened and not just dismissed you."

We went inside, and he put a frozen pizza in the oven. "Why can't I see her?" he asked.

"I don't think she likes you much."

•

John stood, still fully clothed, next to our bed. He scanned the room. "Is she here?"

I shook my head. "I can't see her."

"Good." John started undressing.

"Of course, that doesn't necessarily mean that she's not here."

He glared at me. I'd never seen him get dressed so fast. I started laughing. It felt good.

"Stop that!" he said. "There was a weird cold spot in the shower this morning. What if she was in there with me?"

"The house is haunted, and your big fear is that the ghost might see you naked?" I asked, falling back on the bed, giggling.

He crawled in bed beside me and put his head on my chest. "Well, so far she hasn't been violent. But she might have been in the shower."

"How was your day?" I asked.

He shrugged. "First days are always hard. But everyone was nice."

I kissed him and fell asleep believing that everything was going to be okay.

•

The ghost stood at the foot of the bed when the alarm went off. John groaned and rolled to his feet. He looked right through her, then he shuffled into the bathroom.

"So, he believed you," the ghost said. She watched him for a long moment, then narrowed her eyes. "That changes nothing."

"It changes everything," I said. "He didn't force me to come here. He asked me to give it a chance. I said that I would."

The ghost sat on the foot of the bed. "So?"

"So I asked him to believe me, and he did. He didn't just pretend to. He did. So I can't just pretend to give this life a chance. I have to try to be happy."

"That's idiotic. You shouldn't have to try to be happy. You should just be happy."

I laughed. She sounded so young. "It's never that easy."

John poked his head out of the bathroom. "Did you say something?"

I shook my head. The ghost was gone.

•

After John left, I made myself put on one of the cute pregnancy outfits my mother-in-law gave me. I stuffed my laptop and a couple old copies of Popular Science in my purse and drove to the local coffee shop. I ordered an iced decaf and an egg white frittata, then I stood by the counter and scanned the room. Two couples, one old man reading the newspaper, an assortment of people typing away on their laptops. And one woman about my age, sitting in the corner flipping through a National Geographic. I took a deep breath and approached her. "Hello."

She glanced up at me. "Hi?" Her southern drawl was thick, even in the single syllable.

"I'm Donna. I'm new in town, and I was wondering if you'd mind some company?"

She smiled at me and closed her magazine. "Sure, honey. Have a seat. I'm Lacey."

•

By lunchtime, Lacey and I were fast friends. She had two kids, her husband was a doctor, too, and she worked as a substitute teacher. She asked me to join her book club and invited us over to a picnic on Sunday.

I picked up some groceries on my way home, and went inside humming.

The ghost cornered me in the kitchen. "He'll hurt you eventually. I know he will. They always do. Always."

I slid eggs and carrots into the fridge. "You're wrong."

"I—I wish I could believe that," she whispered.

I bent to pick up the milk, and pain stabbed through my middle. Something warm and wet spread down my legs, and my knees crumbled beneath me.

Was the baby coming? It was too soon. Months too soon. Panic and pain tugged at my thoughts. I tried to stand up, but my body wasn't working.

We hadn't activated the landline, and my cell phone was in the car.

Another pain spiked through me. "Something's wrong," I said. "It hurts."

The ghost knelt next to me, her eyes wide. "I want to help."

"Get John," I said. Blackness edged my vision, and blood spread across the clean linoleum. "He'll know what to do."

The ghost vanished.

I passed out.

•

Hands clutched each of mine. One was warm, the other cold. I recognized the soft beeping and empty smell of hospital air.

The ghost and John were both staring at me. "Is the baby okay?" I asked. My lips were dry and my whole body felt heavy.

The ghost looked away. John squeezed my hand. His eyes were red. "She's not. She just—just wasn't ready."

I slumped back. Emotions crashed around inside me, but they cancelled each other out. I just felt numb. "Am—am I okay?"

John smiled and wiped away a stray tear. "I think so."

I closed my eyes. "Good." Long moments passed. Tears leaked out from under my eyelids. "Can I see her?"

.

John and I stood over the tiny grave. "I want to try again," I said. "Not right now. But later."

John nodded. "I'd like that."

I leaned my head against his shoulder. "I hated being pregnant."

He barked a startled laugh. "I know."

The ghost walked up the hill toward us. She was almost invisible in the sunlight. She carried a tiny bundle.

My heart caught in my throat.

"You said you wanted to see her," the ghost whispered. She pulled back the blankets, and I saw my daughter's face. She blinked and scrunched her face. A tiny hand wormed its way out of the blanket and reached toward me. I extended a finger, and her tiny, cold hand wrapped around it.

John held me. I was afraid that if he let go I'd shatter into a million pieces.

The ghost tucked the blanket back into place. "I'm going to go with her," she said. "You two—you don't need me. Just—keep trying to be happy."

"Thank you," John said. "If you hadn't been there—"

But she was gone.

.

Days slid by. Lacey came over on her days off and we'd work on the house or sit around and watch TV or just talk for hours on end. I set up my telescope, and managed to get a little work done.

Life moved on.

I tried to be happy.

Most days, I managed it.

THE SHARP EDGES OF ANGER

Originally appeared in *Apex Magazine*

Rose is ten when the blacksmith's son pushes her into the river. She lands badly, rocks scraping her knees, tearing her palms. Her dress is cold and wet against her skin as she drags herself out of the water.

Her anger forms a hard lump in her throat. The blacksmith's son smirks at her, waiting for her to swallow it down like she knows a good girl should.

She screams and rakes her nails across his face.

Later, her mother pulls the anger out of Rose's chest and stares at it. It is smooth and gray, like the river rocks. After a long moment, her mother presses it into Rose's hand. For an instant, Rose can see her mother's anger, pressing out above the collar of her dress. Then it vanishes. "You must be a good girl," her mother whispers. "You know what you have to do."

Her mother locks her in the storage shed. Rose stares down at the rock in her hand, at the blood drying beneath her fingernails.

She does not swallow her anger, or smash it and scatter the pieces. Instead, she hides it in the corner, under a bag of wrinkled potatoes.

Things are hard for her family that winter, since the blacksmith demands reparations. Rose's new anger grows inside her, but she is careful not to let it show.

•

Rose is sixteen when she catches the eye of the local lord. He likes her face and the shape of her, so he makes quiet arrangements with her father. Rose listens from the other room, and the anger in her chest grows jagged spikes. She will kill him if he touches her.

Before the appointed time, her mother sends her into the city to find work, even though there is plenty to do at home.

Her mother gives her a shawl to wrap around her neck and chest. "You must hide it better if you are going to keep it," she says, her voice still like a winter pond. "Keep your head down. Sometimes it shows in your eyes."

Before she leaves, Rose takes her old anger out of the shed. She's amazed by how small and smooth it is.

•

Rose is eighteen when she sees a girl being beaten in an alley. The girl's skin and clothes color her an outsider. Her eyes are huge and wet, and when they meet Rose's they both beg for help and scream for her to run.

One of the men looks up at her. "Move along," he says. "This is none of your concern." There is kindness in his voice. Concern that she might do something foolish.

It is hard to breathe around her anger. There are too many of them. She cannot stop this, and if she goes to the guard they will not care.

"Let her go," Rose says. The words catch on the sharp edges of her anger and choke her. She steps into the alley. "Let her go."

The man who spoke detaches himself from the group. He grabs Rose's shoulders and pushes her back. His grip is gentle. He leans down and speaks in her ear. "You can't help her. Let me help you. Just go."

Rose looks past him, at the girl. Tears roll down her cheeks, and the men's boots are wet with her blood. Rose pushes forward, slipping out of the man's grip and lunging toward the girl. Rose's hand touches a wet cheek as a boot hits her in the chest.

Her anger shatters into a thousand razor fragments.

•

Rose is still eighteen when she wakes on the dirt floor of a tiny cell. Her chest aches and her vision blurs as she sits up. Her mother sits on the other side of the iron bars.

"What happened to the girl?" Rose asks.

Rose's mother does not look at her. She closes her eyes and takes a deep breath. "She died."

Rose buries her face in her hands.

"The blacksmith has paid for your treatment," Rose's mother says. "You will be treated for your injuries, then you will be married to his son."

"No," Rose says.

Her mother says nothing, just sits with her eyes closed.

"I won't." Rose hears the fear in her voice, and shame curls through her belly.

"You don't have a choice." Her mother's voice is barely a whisper. Rose watches her mother's anger swell and vanish, swell and vanish. She stands up and brushes dust from her skirt. "I'm sorry, Rose. I wish things were different."

Her mother leaves, and two men slip into her cell. "What were you thinking, letting your anger grow like that?" one asks. "It's dangerous. Your fragile constitution isn't made for it."

The other holds her down while the first draws a long, thin knife out of his bag. "We have to remove the shards. You'll hurt yourself if we don't."

Rose screams as he cuts and pulls and cuts and pulls and cuts and pulls. He drops the shards of her anger into a bucket. They chime like crystal when they fall.

When they are done, Rose feels scraped out and empty.

She curls up in a ball on the floor of the cell and cries herself to sleep.

•

Rose is just nineteen on her wedding day. She stands silently in her white dress. "Make your mark here," the priest says, pointing to his book. Rose is too tired to argue, too weak to run. Still, she shakes her head.

The priest shrugs, and the blacksmith makes a mark for her.

Her husband takes her hand, and she wishes she had the energy to hate him.

When her anger begins to grow again, her husband pulls it from her chest and takes it to his father to destroy. "You can't be trusted with this," he says, holding the shards between careful fingers. "You could hurt yourself, and we don't want that."

Tears slip down her cheeks and she has just enough energy to hate herself.

•

Rose is twenty when she misses her menses and realizes that there is a child growing inside of her. She imagines it in her womb like a worm, eating her from the inside out.

Any kind of food turns her stomach. Her whole body aches. She dreams of cutting it out and throwing its tiny bloody body into the river.

She screams the first time she feels it move inside her.

Her husband is more attentive than ever, bringing her any food she seems to favor, taking extra care to remove any anger that grows in her chest, babbling softly with his cheek pressed against the hideous bulge of her belly.

Her ankles swell, and she cannot abide the feel of socks against her feet. She is always cold.

The texture of her hair changes. Her reflection is a soft-edged, empty-eyed stranger. Her body is not her own, and constant panic whispers under her skin.

Her labor is hard and long and she begs for death. No one listens.

When the child is finally born, it is wiped off and handed to her husband. He brings it to her, beaming.

Rose refuses to touch it.

"It's a girl," her husband says, his voice thick with joy.

Rose weeps.

Later, after the baby has been pressed against Rose's breast, it's suckling mouth hot and stinging, she does sit and hold it. She watches it breathe on its own, no longer a part of her, consuming her from the inside.

It is helpless, and its wet eyes remind her of the girl in the alley. She cannot hate it. But she can't love it, either.

Its dimpled face crumples, and it begins to wail. Rose sees a tiny bump on its chest and pulls it free.

The baby's anger is as small as a pea and as soft as a new cheese.

Rose hides it under her pillow.

●

Rose is twenty-four when her husband stops checking her chest for anger every night. It grows slower now, but is sharper than ever.

Her husband has taken over his father's forge, and comes home exhausted to find a smiling daughter, a passive wife, and a meal on the table. He is happy, and he has decided that she is, as well.

Rose pulls out splinters of her own anger, leaving enough for him to assuage any suspicion. She buries them in the garden, between the parsley and the carrots, in the same spot that she keeps the child's stolen anger.

The child takes after her father, and Rose makes herself be glad of that. She isn't angry often, and she usually swallows it before Rose can take it and hide it away.

She's a good child, and everyone else loves her. Sometimes, Rose finds herself wishing that she could just settle into this life—that she could love her daughter and her husband, that she could find happiness in keeping their home tidy and their stomachs full.

She knows that in many ways she is lucky. Blessed with fortune far beyond her deserving. If she was a different person, she could be satisfied with this life.

She is not a different person. She has no real desire to change.

So she hoards her own anger, and she steals whatever she can from the child.

•

Rose is twenty-six when the child accidentally tells her husband about the anger in the garden. They sit together over dinner, silent except for the sound of chewing. "I went to visit the forge today!" the child says, her voice bright. "Daddy showed me how to destroy my anger by throwing it into the fire. It was so pretty! It went woosh! Maybe we could go together sometime and throw some anger in together."

"Your Mommy isn't supposed to touch her anger," her husband says. "It's dangerous for her."

"Oh," the child says. Rose can see her doom working its way across that small, open face.

Rose is closest to the door, and she is moving before the child opens her mouth again.

"But what about all of the anger in the garden?" the child asks. "Is that dangerous for Mommy?"

She slams the door behind her and frantically blocks it with the shovel. It won't hold, but it might slow him. She scrambles in the dirt, slicing her fingers on tiny sharp pieces of her own anger, gathering soft lumps of the child's, all of them caked with dirt. She shoves each into her chest.

She feels alive for the first time in years.

She hears her husband coming, his steps slow. She whirls to face him.

He's holding out his hands, speaking softly, like she is a wild animal. "Calm down. I'm not angry. Calm down."

"But you won't let me keep it," Rose says.

"You know I can't. It's poison. It'll consume you from the inside."

Rose knows how it feels to be consumed from the inside. That isn't how she feels now. "Then why do you get to keep yours?" she asks.

"Men are stronger. We can contain it." He takes a slow step toward her. "I love you. Come back inside, and let me help you."

"I don't need your help," Rose says. And she runs. She hasn't run in years, and her body knows it. She is short of breath in a matter of moments. She pushes her legs faster, each step a painful impact that jars her whole body.

The anger helps, giving her energy to push through the building pain.

Her husband shouts behind her. She doesn't have to look back to know that he's chasing her. That he will catch her. That in the end, there is no escape.

She doesn't even know where she is running to.

The river is high, swollen with spring rain. She doesn't stop running. The water sweeps her off her feet, surges into her mouth, her nose, her eyes. She tumbles, rocks scraping her knees, tearing her palms. She thinks of the girl in the alley, wonders how things would be different if she had lived and Rose had died. Would she have been able to let herself be happy?

Her husband grabs her wrist and pulls her from the water. Her dress is cold and wet against her skin. For the first time, she notices a faint scar on her husband's cheek, from her fingernails when she was ten.

"If I let you keep it, will you stay?" he asks. There are tears in his eyes.

Rose sags against him. She nods. Maybe she can try.

•

Rose is twenty-eight when the child realizes that her mother doesn't love her. Rose watches her cry and wonders if she's capable of loving anything.

Even with the bits of anger that her husband allows her, she still feels empty.

"Why?" the child sobs, curled in on herself in a corner. "I've always tried to be so good."

Rose kneels beside her, puts a hand on her shoulder. "I'm sorry. I wish things were different."

"I wish you were different," the child whispers. Rose watches her anger swell, then vanish.

There's still a part of Rose that wishes for that, too. But most of her is just too tired to care.

•

Rose is twenty-nine when she chooses the river.

CHANGE ALWAYS MEANS AN ENDING

Originally appeared in *Mad Scientist's Journal*

Mother clutches my hand. "Change always means an ending," she says. The whites of her eyes are sunshine-yellow around blue irises. She doesn't have much time left. "It's like butterflies. One life ends, another begins. But the caterpillar can't look up to where the butterflies flutter, can't understand the coming change. They only see the end."

I don't bother to remind her that she has no idea what caterpillars think. She's dying—she doesn't need any lip from me.

"I love you, Dallas," she says. "I wish I could stay."

But she can't, and a moment later she is gone. Empty flesh, missing its spark. I hope she was right about the butterflies.

But the disease changed me, and I am still here.

I try not to cry, but she was my mother.

Tears slip down my cheeks, and wherever they fall, flowers bloom. New flowers, unlike any I've seen before, in every color I can imagine. They smell like springtime and beginnings.

My mother would have loved them. But what good are flowers, when I can't save anyone?

•

No one knows where the disease came from. It popped up everywhere at once, but that's because it has a long incubation period and people travelled a lot, before.

We did hear news of some other survivors before communication went down. Not many, though. And no one ever mentioned magic.

I use it to bury my mother. I ask the flowers to dig with their roots, and the ground opens up beneath her. I throw a handful of dirt on her— it's a tradition, so I do it. Then the plants cover her up. I stretch out on the grave, and the plants weave a bed for me, with soft petals pillowing my head.

I feel used up, empty. Alone. "What do I do now?"

Of course, no one answers.

I sleep, and the plants twine around me. It should be weird, but it's nice. Like a hug.

I walk through the city, looking for other survivors. Plants grow out of cracks in the sidewalk as I pass. Cats and dogs eye me warily but don't approach.

The smell of rotting bodies fills the air. Flies buzz in the distance, but the plants keep them away from me.

The old world is over. But what new world can I build by myself? I stand in the middle of the city and scream.

No one answers.

•

I wander to the park, away from the empty buildings with their windows like vacant eyes. Plants bring water up from the earth when I am thirsty, produce fruit when I am hungry, build me shelter from rain and sun. All of my needs are met without conscious thought. Am I controlling them, or do they serve me? I have no idea, no way to tell.

I think of the new flowers on my mother's grave, sprouting up from my tears. That is clearly something I did—life I created. Maybe that is my way forward now.

I cry, and flowers spread around me. I imagine new shapes for them, and the next teardrop shapes that image into reality. But my tears can't make trees or grass or vines. Only flowers.

It is hot the next day, and I run through the streets, till sweat drips down my brow. I watch it fall, and grass spreads at my feet.

It isn't hard to find a shard of broken glass.

It is hard to cut myself with it, even after I wash it four times. I choose a spot on my arm, press the glass to it. Take a deep breath. "If change always means an ending, an ending always means change."

Blood falls onto the dirt. I hold an image in my mind, and two columns of vines grow up, then twine together. Two arms and a head sprout from the torso, feet form along the bottom of the legs.

Its eyes are daisies, and they spiral open to look at me.

It reaches out and takes my hand.

And finally, something new begins in the old world's ashes.

JOINING THE FLOCK

Originally appeared in *The Cryptonaturalist*

I dashed into the woods. The trees swayed overhead—thin leaves and sturdy branches and Spanish moss moving as one. I couldn't see the birds—couldn't hear them, either. But I knew better than hope that I'd escaped them.

I stumbled and fell into thick loam. The scent of rich dirt and rot filled the air. I scrambled back to my feet and kept moving, deeper into the forest—away from the open sky. There was a cave ahead—surely they wouldn't follow me there.

Danny and I had explored the cave years ago, holding hands and urging each other around each dark turn.

I couldn't think about Danny. He was one of them, now.

A harsh caw broke the silence. I urged my exhausted body forward, my breath as harsh as the bird's cry. I spotted the cave, a black smudge in the green and brown.

The sound of wingbeats came from everywhere. Gusts buffeted at me. I threw myself forward, scrambled along the ground on all fours— maybe if I stayed low—maybe I could still escape.

My fingers brushed damp rock.

Then my fingers changed.

My body contracted, and feathers sprouted from my skin. I opened my mouth to scream, but a rough caw emerged from my beak.

We flew away together, weaving through the trees to explode up through the canopy as one.

We spread out to look for the next member of our flock.

ASHES TO DIAMONDS

Originally appeared in *Stupefying Stories*

"You have more than enough carbon material," the salesman assured Toby, pushing glossy pamphlets across the café table. Neither of them had touched their sweating glasses of ice water or the platter of dates.

Toby wrapped his lock of Janet's honey-colored hair around his finger. She'd given it to him when he shipped out so that he'd always have a piece of her with him. It shone in the desert sunlight. He wondered if it would still smell like her. She always smelled like the ocean. He carefully tucked the hair back in its envelope, then he ran his fingertips over the Ziploc bag that her parents had sent him.

Her vibrant smile, the way her skin smelled, the inviting curve of her hips, the odd little sounds she made when she was happy, all his dreams for their future—all gone forever, replaced by a baggie of gray-brown ash that her parents had mailed him, along with a few photos, his class ring, and a tear-stained sympathy card.

"We'll purify her carbon essence, then, using extreme pressure and heat, we'll form her into a diamond. An eternal tribute to your love. We have a variety of color, carat, and cut options."

Toby slid the bag and the envelope across the table. "Janet's eyes were blue. Dark blue, like the ocean." Toby wrote a blank check, and slid that across the table, too.

The salesman reached across the table and patted Toby's shoulder. "We can do dark blue." He gathered up the check, ashes, hair, and his pamphlets. "You'll receive your diamond in approximately twenty-four weeks."

•

Janet floated over her parents' house. It was a beautiful day. She wished she could feel the sunshine. She missed feeling things.

But there was freedom in not having a body. She could go wherever she wanted and look at whatever she wanted. And no one could see her.

That was the best thing about being dead.

Her funeral had been nice enough. Toby hadn't been able to make it back, but he'd sent a dozen blue roses. People had said nice things. Janet would have blushed, if she could have.

She floated up the street. She peeked into houses and businesses, listened to a woman reading to her baby, discovered the secret ingredient on old Mrs. Florsham's chocolate chip cookies, and watched a teenage couple make out on the beach.

The teenagers made her miss Toby, so she started floating east, out over the water.

She got distracted halfway across the ocean. Thousands of fish moved together in a flashing silver cloud. She chased them through the water, marveling again that she didn't need air. She could hear whales singing. She followed one song, then another, until she floated into a coral-filled cove. She felt life all around, pulsing through her.

She floated in a warm world, filled with light and color. It was a nice place to stop, to sleep, to rest.

Janet drifted. She could sense bits of herself fading away, but she couldn't remember why that mattered. A better sense of the world around her replaced them, until she was aware of the currents a hundred miles away. Weeks passed, and she thought less and less, but understood more and more.

It was really rather wonderful, being dead.

Then, something jerked her out of the ocean. It shoved her into a hot, bright, tiny space, and started to squeeze.

Janet tried to scream, to fight, to run, but she couldn't. The pressure built and built, until it was pain.

Janet had almost forgotten pain. She wondered if this was hell.

•

Toby sat in his hometown bar and slid an empty bottle back and forth in front of him.

He'd planned to spend this leave in Niagara Falls with Janet. She was going to skip a week of classes, and they'd get a hotel and do some sightseeing.

Toby had wanted to propose to her there.

Instead, she'd been dead for almost six months and he was spending his leave at his dad's house, having lunch alone in a bar.

He ordered another beer.

The girl behind the bar replaced his bottle and said, "This one's on me. I was sorry to hear about Janet, Toby."

He blinked at her. He should probably know who she was. He shrugged, then took a long pull. He was tired of sympathy. It didn't mean anything.

She'd given him a better beer than the one he'd ordered. "Thanks for the drink."

"I hear you're in town for the whole week," the girl said.

"Yeah?"

The girl rubbed her neck. "Your dad's in here a lot. He likes to talk."

Toby grunted.

The girl laughed. "But I guess you don't. I'm Alice, by the way. I was a year behind you in school. You were in my French class."

Toby remembered her now. "You got contacts."

"And cut my hair, yeah." Alice smiled at him. "You know, if you don't have anything better to do tonight, a few of my friends and I are going to go see a movie. You're welcome to come along, if you want."

"I don't need your pity," Toby said.

Alice arched an eyebrow. "You could have fooled me." She turned away. "Let me know if you need another drink."

Toby finished his beer and thought about spending the evening with his dad, watching fishing on the outdoorsman channel. "What time's the movie?"

•

Janet's prison was changing. The pressure had forced her into its physical form, so that it was like a new, immobile body. She could feel where she ended, where the rest of the world stretched away, outside of her cage. The separation wrenched.

The pressure had finally ceased, only to be replaced by the pain of some outside force carving parts off of her new self. At first, she'd been almost perfectly round, but soon she was the shape of a princess-cut gemstone—pointed on one end and round and faceted on another.

She was aware of light—of rainbows trapped inside of her—but she could sense nothing else.

She missed the ocean.

Toby's dad had signed for Janet's diamond while Toby was out on a date with Alice. It was her day off, so they'd spent it together, picnicking on the beach.

Janet had hated picnics, even though she'd loved the ocean.

Alice made him laugh. He hadn't really laughed for six months. Her hair smelled like springtime, and her lips tasted like strawberry lip gloss.

The diamond had been a stupid decision. He'd been grief-stricken and had wasted most of his life savings. It seemed unnecessarily morbid, now. He was glad that he hadn't mentioned it to Janet's folks.

Toby opened the box. The diamond glittered against a background of black velvet. The shade of blue was exactly right. He touched one of its smooth, sparking facets.

"Toby?" Janet's broken whisper echoed inside his mind.

He snatched his finger back and threw the box across the room.

●

Janet felt a touch, and somehow knew it was Toby. She called to him, but then he was gone again. She was still alone. Still trapped.

She wished she could weep.

●

Toby put the diamond back in its box, careful not to touch it.

The next day, he ignored Alice's calls. He spent the day with his dad, trying not to think. Then he got up in the middle of the night and dumped the diamond into his palm.

"Toby?" Janet's voice asked. "Is that you?"

"Yeah, sweetie. It's me."

"I—I missed you." She sounded uncertain and lost.

"I missed you, too."

●

Janet watched the world through Toby's eyes as he wandered around his dad's house. His touch extended her prison, and she flowed freely into his body. She could sense his memories, and she knew that if she wanted, she could look through them. He'd never know.

But she didn't. She stayed with him, in the present, and they sat in the morning sun and drank bitter coffee. Janet would have preferred tea.

"I could put you into a ring, and we could live like this," Toby said. "You and me. Together. Just like we always wanted."

"It would be nice to not be lonely," Janet said. But she still felt alone. And she wasn't sure if this is what she wanted. She thought about whale songs and the pull of the tide through coral stems.

"I love you, Janet. I'll always love you."

"I love you, too, Toby."

•

Toby put Janet back in her box and paced. He missed Alice. He'd carried Janet with him for three days, and he was tired of her melancholy detachment. She wasn't the same. Nothing seemed to make her happy, and she was making him miserable. Alice had made him happy.

He was supposed to leave to go back on duty in eight hours. He hadn't talked to Alice since he'd started carrying Janet, and she'd stopped calling. Sometimes, when Janet was under his pillow for the night, he'd play back Alice's voicemails just to hear her voice.

He didn't know what Janet would do if she knew that he'd been seeing someone else. He wondered if she'd even care.

He called Alice. The phone rang seven times before she answered. "I think guilt about our relationship is driving me crazy," he said.

Alice sighed. "I miss you, too."

"I need you to come over here."

"Now? Three days of nothing, and now you need me right now? It's the middle of the night. I don't think what you're feeling is guilt, Toby."

"Not funny. Seriously, Alice. I need you."

"Okay, okay. I'm on my way."

Toby paced until Alice arrived, then he thrust the box into her hand. "What is this, Toby?"

"I had Janet made into a diamond."

"That's... creepy." Alice opened the box. "Toby, it's beautiful." She turned the box, and the diamond sparkled in the light. "I've changed my mind. It's not creepy. It's wonderful. I want to be a diamond, too. Can I touch it?"

Toby wondered if he should warn her. But what if he really was just going insane? "Yeah, go ahead."

Alice tipped the diamond into her palm. She blinked, then her face went pale. "Is she—is she trapped in there?"

Toby sagged with relief. "You hear her, too?" His throat tightened. "I think I've made a big mistake, Alice, and I don't know how to fix it." He choked back a sob.

"I understand if you need time. Or even if you don't want to see me any more." She sounded like she was fighting back tears of her own.

"No, no, that's not it." Toby wrapped his arms around her. "I—I just can't be with her. Not like this. But she's trapped, and I don't know what to do. Her soul might be able to move on if we destroy the gem, but how do you destroy a diamond?"

•

Janet flashed through the woman's mind, examining memories. She learned her name, her favorite color, her best memory, her worst fear. It was wonderful to do something. For an instant, Janet was livid that Toby had moved on. But then she realized that she had, too. It wasn't him she missed, after all.

She listened to Toby through Alice's ears, felt him wrap his arms around her waist and slide his rough cheek against hers. She flowed between them and spoke into both of their minds.

"Throw me in the ocean."

•

Toby drove to the beach alone. Alice had kissed him and said, "I understand. You need to say goodbye."

He stood on the sand and stared out over the ocean. The moonlight sparkled on the waves. The diamond in his palm looked like a bit of the ocean made solid.

He could feel Janet in his thoughts, familiar, but somehow strange. "Our life would have been good," he said.

"Maybe," Janet whispered in his mind. "Maybe not. It's not for us to know, now. Goodbye, Toby."

"Goodbye, Janet."

Toby threw the diamond. It flashed once in the moonlight, then vanished without a ripple.

•

Janet sank down through the cold water, into the slippery silt. It enveloped her, and the ocean sang to her.

She drifted, and faded, and understood.

NO MORE THAN WE CAN BEAR

Originally appeared in *Theme of Absence*

The steady rain had long since soaked through Callie's layered clothing. The stone steps in front of the cathedral were dark with water, and the surfaces of the puddles were dull in the gray light. Cold water trickled down her neck from the ragged ends of her short-cropped hair.

She pressed the dented aluminum of her violin against her cheek, and her numb fingers fumbled on the strings. She urged her battered instrument and drained body through the opening "Amazing Grace." It wouldn't do to finish early.

After all, God was watching.

Finally, she heard bells tolling, and Callie lowered her violin. She felt God's gaze leave her, and she slumped with relief. She gathered the change that people had scattered at her feet and dragged herself to a nearby diner. The waitress, pert and blonde with crooked teeth and an illegible nametag, brought her a cup of coffee, a hot dog, and a blanket.

"It's awful out there today," she said, sliding the plate and steaming mug onto the table. "And He kept you late. Again."

"It doesn't matter, Darla," Callie said. She reached for the blanket and her eyes misted with gratitude. She pulled it tight around her shoulders and wrapped her fingers around her mug. The heat stung. She forced a smile. "It's an honor to play for Him."

Darla sniffed. "Better you than me. I don't see why He can't just have you play somewhere inside. You're like to catch your death."

Fear clutched at Callie's belly. "Don't talk like that!" she said. Just because she could no longer feel His eye didn't mean He wasn't listening.

Darla just sighed. "He's not going to smite me for worrying about you."

"Your worry sometimes sounds a little too close to criticism for my taste." Callie sipped her coffee. The heat spread across her tongue like a prayer.

"I'd better quit jawing and get back to work," Darla said. "You call if you need a refill. Or another dog. Or anything."

"I will," Callie said. Shivers wracked her frame, and her clammy, wet clothes clung to her. But the coffee helped.

She wished she could go home. But He didn't want her to.

She ate her hot dog and waited for Him to call again.

•

He called at midnight. Callie had drifted to sleep with her forehead pressed against the diner's window. Her clothes had stiffened as they'd dried, and her neck ached. Darla had left hours ago, after paying Callie's tab, and the overnight waitresses ignored her.

She pulled herself to her feet and walked out into the night.

It was still raining.

For a moment, it was almost too much. Callie's knees trembled, and she nearly collapsed onto the wet pavement.

His gaze sharpened. Callie wasn't sure if He wanted her to succeed or fail—to endure or give up. She wasn't sure if He even cared.

All she knew was that He was watching. And that He wanted her to play for Him on the cathedral steps.

Her family had been so proud when she'd been singled out. They hadn't hesitated to cut off contact when He'd demanded her solitude. She wondered if they missed her.

A gust of wind swept cold pellets of rain into her face. She was already freezing. She straightened her shoulders and made herself walk, one step at a time. She was soaked before she was halfway there.

It was dark on the steps. The streetlamps had burned out, and the night sky was black as sin. Callie tripped and landed badly. The step bit into her shin, hard enough to draw blood.

She felt His impatience.

She beat back her own rage. Her resentment. Her pain. She stood up and brought the violin to her chin. She closed her eyes and played.

She played the same songs she always played. There had been a time when each tune had filled her with joy. Her faith had overflowed into her music. Every note had been a celebration.

Now, they were hardly more than sounds.

And still He watched. And listened. And demanded more.

Callie's tears felt just like the rain on her cheeks.

"Hey, you!" A rough voice, from below her somewhere. The speaker was invisible in the darkness. "It's the middle of the night! Stop that damn noise!"

Callie slipped into her rendition of "The Battle Hymn of the Republic."

Pain exploded in her head as a rock the size of her fist slammed into her left temple. "I told you to stop!"

The church bells tolled. God's eyes withdrew.

Callie lost consciousness.

•

She knew something was wrong the instant she woke up.

She was in a bed. Why was she in a bed? He didn't want her to sleep in a bed.

Her head hurt, and the world around her spun when she tried to move.

She felt His eyes. His call pulled at her. She tried to pull herself up.

"Hey, what are you doing?"

A familiar voice. "Darla?" Callie asked. Moving her jaw sent waves of pain up through her temple.

"That's right. I found you a few days ago, outside that damned cathedral of yours."

Callie winced at her blasphemy. "He's watching, Darla."

"Good. I'd like to give Him a piece of my mind." Darla pulled the blankets back up and tucked them around Callie's neck.

"I have to go. I have to play."

"No. You don't. He left you on those steps, Callie. He made you go out there in the middle of the night, in the rain, and for all I know he made someone throw rocks at you. You've been unconscious for days. If I hadn't seen you, you probably would have died."

"Maybe that's what he wants," Callie whispered. "Maybe he wants me with him in heaven."

"I don't give a damn about what he wants, and I don't think you should, either."

Callie squeezed her eyes shut, sure that something terrible would happen. He did take direct action, sometimes.

He just watched.

"You've done enough for Him. You gave up your home, your job, your family. You've been living on the street or sleeping in the diner ever since His eye fell on you, all because you want to make Him happy." Darla laid a gentle hand against Callie's injured temple. "I don't think anything can make Him happy."

"He never asks for more than we can do. He never gives us more than we can bear," Callie whispered. "If he still wants me to go and play, that means that I must still be able to. Please, Darla."

Darla stepped back. "If you can stand on your own, then I'll help you."

"Okay." Callie gathered her strength. She felt His gaze upon her. His call thrummed through her like music too deep to hear. She sat up.

She passed out.

•

When she woke again, He was gone. But Darla was still there.

Callie cried until she ran out of tears. "Was it all for nothing?" she asked Darla. "I gave up so much, all for Him. Why did I fail?"

Darla shrugged. "I'm sure you'll ask a preacher that, sooner or later, and he'll have some smooth answer about lessons or intentions or some such nonsense. But I think He just wanted to see how far He could push before you snapped. He wanted to test your faith. And it wasn't the sort of test a person passes—it's the sort that just keeps getting harder till you fail."

"God doesn't work like that."

Darla arched an eyebrow. "Doesn't he?"

Callie sighed. "Have you ever felt his gaze?"

Darla looked away, out the window. "Yes."

Callie wasn't surprised. She'd always figured that was why Darla was so nice to her—she understood what his gaze was like. "Did you follow his commands?"

"Almost. He wanted me to marry my geometry teacher. I was walking up the aisle when I realized that I just didn't want to. I left him at the altar."

"What did your family say?" Callie asked. She couldn't imagine running away from God's plan. But then, she couldn't imagine marrying her geometry teacher, either. "How old were you?"

"I was seventeen. And I haven't talked to my family since. I didn't tell them where I was going."

"Do you think your life would be better? If you'd followed his plan?"

Darla shook her head. "I used to worry about it. I'd picture myself as a happy housewife, packing lunches and watching soaps. But then I saw you, saw how unhappy He was making you, and I realized that I made the right choice."

·

After a few days, Callie was strong enough to sit up. She hadn't felt His gaze upon her since she'd failed to answer his call. She hadn't touched her violin, either. She stared out the window all morning while Darla worked.

She was pretty sure that Darla had put her in the only bed.

Darla, who had always been so amazingly kind. Who had disobeyed Him and saw Callie as justification for her choice.

Callie missed the feel of His gaze.

Darla brought her a piece of pumpkin pie. Callie ate it slowly, savoring every bite. There were some things that her misery couldn't dull.

The thought carried just a touch of hope. Maybe things were getting better, after all.

They sat in silence for a while. Callie ate every crumb of pie, then licked the plate clean. Darla worked on her cross stitch.

"I wish I could be more like you," Callie said. "I wish I could give up on God."

"Why don't you?" Darla asked. "He almost got you killed."

Callie shrugged and stared at her plate. "I love Him."

·

It took a long time for Callie to heal. She hadn't realized just how exhausted she was, how far His demands had pushed her. She'd been killing herself, even before the rock.

She thought about going back to her old life, now that she'd failed God, but she couldn't face it. Her family would never understand.

She hadn't been happy before, anyway.

Darla helped her get a job at the diner. She served coffee and pie and flirted with the old men who came in at 5am every morning. The clink of silver against ceramic, the burble of the percolator, and the chatter of strangers became the new music of her life.

She and Darla walked home together after the lunch rush. They both smelled like stale coffee and bacon grease. Callie felt peaceful. Not content—the gaping emptiness was still inside her, but the sting of it had faded. Birds sang overhead, hidden in the riot of fall-painted leaves. Darla stopped in a pool of sunshine. "Do you know any songs that aren't about God?" she asked.

Callie waited for the pain to stab through her from that empty place, reminding her of her failure, of the death of her dreams. It didn't.

"I know a lot of songs that aren't about Him," she said. And suddenly her fingers itched to play some of them.

"Would you play for me?" Callie had never heard Darla sound so hesitant.

"Of course," Callie said. The hollow in her chest suddenly felt full—even overflowing. "I'd love to play something for you."

•

Nerves jittered in her belly as she tuned her violin. She was as aware of Darla's eyes as she'd ever been of God's. She took a deep breath, and started to play a sad, sweet Beethoven concerto.

Darla's eyes shone like stars.

A deep joy spread through Callie as she watched Darla listen to her. It wasn't the same as God's gaze—nothing was—but it was good.

What if Darla was her temptation? What if the exhaustion and the injury were just a set up for this moment? What if her choice wasn't to play or not, but to play for God or Darla?

Her fingers faltered on the strings.

"Are you okay? Don't push yourself too hard. Do you need to lie down?" Darla jumped up and took Callie's hand.

She squeezed Darla's fingers. "No. I'm okay."

•

The sun was just up, and the crisp air held the promise of another beautiful, sunny day. Callie was clean and dry, clad in Darla's old Easter dress. It smelled like mothballs and laundry soap. They stood together on the cathedral steps for a moment, looking up at the stained glass window. "It looks so dim from this side," Darla said.

Callie raised her violin and started to play.

But this time, instead of playing for Him, or for Darla, she played for herself.

She stood in the sunlight, and joy bubbled up in her heart. For a moment, she felt His gaze upon her again.

Then it passed.

She played till her fingers grew tired, then she and Darla went for coffee and pie.

THE PATH TO BUTTERFLY

Originally appeared in *Lakeside Circus*

Cheri stretched her tongue deep into a bright pink lily. Bitter, dusty pollen coated her tongue, but she couldn't reach the sweet nectar.

She sipped her Kool-Aid and moved on to the next flower.

She imagined her tongue stretching, narrowing, forming into a slender tube. Like a butterfly tongue.

Cheri tried all the blooming flowers in the overgrown garden, even the ones her mom had called weeds. Her eyes got itchy, her nose starting running, and she ran out of Kool-Aid.

She'd have to raid the neighbor's cupboards for sugar again.

She studied her reflection in her empty glass. She felt her tongue with dirty fingers. She turned her head as far as it would go, rounded her shoulders forward, and searched for a hint of colored, papery wings.

She looked just like she had before.

She sat on the ground and tried not to cry.

A monarch landed on her bare knee. Its tiny feet tickled. Maybe she would turn into a butterfly if she ate it. She imagined catching it—stuffing it into her mouth. Its filmy wings would beat frantically at the insides of her cheeks, its slim body would crunch between her teeth.

It would be bitter, like the pollen.

It fluttered away and Cheri watched its orange wings flash in the sun with burning envy. She wanted to fly away on orange wings. She was so tired of being alone here.

Fat tears rolled down her cheeks and plopped into the rich brown dirt.

She spotted a caterpillar inching along the ground, and she watched as it climbed up one of the flower stalks.

She wiped her tears away.

Of course she couldn't change into a butterfly.

She had to change into a caterpillar, first.

·

She examined the caterpillar carefully. Black, white, and yellow stripes covered its soft body. She took note of what leaves it ate, and what leaves it didn't.

She nibbled on one of the leaves that it had munched on. It tasted horrible. But she made herself eat a handful them. She scooped the caterpillar into her Kool-Aid glass, gave him plenty of leafy food, and went into her hollow, dusty house.

·

She practiced crawling on her stomach in bed, where it was soft and didn't hurt her knees and belly. She colored stripes on her skin with washable markers. She learned to take tiny, tiny bites of leaf, so that her nibbled leaves looked just like the caterpillar's.

She watched him spin a green cocoon hung from a leaf propped up in his glass. She made sure to open the window, while she still had hands. Then she wrapped herself in blankets. She didn't have anywhere to hang her cocoon, but she covered her face last, just like he had.

·

She woke up and pushed her way out of her cocoon. It was huge now, far too big for her caterpillar body. It took a lot of crawling to get out of the blankets.

The world looked strange to her new eyes. She crawled over to her supply of leaves and ate her fill. They tasted much better, now.

The other cocoon had grown transparent, and she could see that he'd finished his change, too. She watched her caterpillar push out of his cocoon. His orange wings were dark and wet. He tried to scramble up the inside of the glass, but his butterfly feet slipped. He dried on top of his empty cocoon.

When he flew away, Cheri watched happily.

It would be her turn, soon.

THE IRON TANG OF BLOOD

Originally appeared in *Penumbra*

The streetlights hissed and sputtered as Lady Bianca Schmidt picked her way along the muddy cobblestones. She tugged her hood down and hugged her long cloak close, thankful, for once, for the thick, acrid smog that further hid her features—it was not an acceptable time for a lady to be out alone.

Coughs racked her body, and the iron tang of blood coated her tongue. She spat into the mud.

A man-sized green dragon approached from the other direction. A layer of gray dust obscured his thick spectacles and dulled his scales. He carried his lunch in a tin box belted at the base of his long neck. His nostrils flared at Bianca's approach. "I didn't expect you to come yourself," he said.

Bianca's lungs burned. "Did you bring it?"

The dragon's jaws parted into a jagged grin. "Of course I did." He sat back and pulled his lunch from his neck. His claws clicked on the box.

"This is the last of my hoard." He sighed. "How times have changed." The latch creaked as he opened the lid. Bianca craned over him. He reached under his thermos and pulled out a small velvet bag.

Bianca snatched it and peaked inside. She could just make out the diamond's glinting edges in the flickering streetlights. She tucked the pouch into her bodice. "Your payment will be delivered by sunrise."

"Excellent. My rent's due."

"Thank you, Mr. Sherman."

"I wish you luck, Lady Schmidt. Now, I must get to work. The train engines don't stoke themselves."

The dragon vanished into the smog, and Bianca continued on her way, conscious of the diamond's hard edges pressing into her breast.

She ran up the marble steps of her family's estate. The clockwork servants were just starting to move about. She hurried past them, up the stairs to her tower apartments and finally into her laboratory. Coughs ripped their way out of her throat as she threw the heavy drapes back and shook the diamond out of its bag. Her fingers trembled as she dropped it into position. There wasn't time to run through a final test of her equipment, so she stepped back.

She twisted her hands together and tried to take deep breaths. The sun would rise again tomorrow.

The first rays of light pierced her window and fell straight into the heart of the diamond. Rainbows painted the room and a unicorn appeared in the elaborate gilded cage that she'd built against the western wall.

Bianca sagged in relief. "It worked."

The unicorn was smaller than a horse, with delicate cloven hooves, a lion's tail, and a long, spiral horn that shone like mother-of-pearl in the morning sunlight. The scent of green apples filled the room.

It screamed defiance and slammed its hooves against the bars. Silver-blue sparks flew and the room shook, but the cage held.

"You will not force your way out, unicorn."

"Release me," it said in a voice like spring rain.

"I need you to heal me."

The unicorn gazed at her. "I could repair some of the damage to your lungs, but it would not be enough to save you."

Bianca clutched at the bars. "I don't understand."

"Your lungs are flawed—they are not fit for our times, and I cannot strengthen them."

"But—but you're magic."

The unicorn stepped toward her. "There was a time when that mattered."

Her parents had already paid for the best doctors. The unicorn was her last chance.

"A little more time is better than nothing. Please."

"And you will free me if I heal you?"

Bianca nodded.

"And then, when you need me again, you will call."

Slowly, Bianca nodded again. "I suppose I would."

The unicorn folded its legs beneath it and turned its face away.

"So you would rather starve now than face me calling you at some distant point in the future?"

"I am not your slave."

Bianca coughed, and her blood splattered on the unicorn's white coat. "Fine," she snapped. "I'll summon another unicorn."

"That diamond is tied to me. It will not call another."

Bianca didn't have the time or means to acquire another diamond. "Then I will have to find a way to make you help me."

•

Bianca tossed and turned in her canopied bed. Her lungs ached and her breaths rasped. She lit a candle and slipped into to her laboratory. The unicorn still curled in the corner of its cage.

"Do unicorns sleep?" Bianca asked.

"No."

"Are you hungry?"

"No."

"Can you die?"

"No."

"So you'll wait there until I die, then hope for someone to free you?"

"Yes."

"I am begging for your help. I don't understand how you can be so cruel. It would cost you nothing."

"You hold me here against my will, and I owe you nothing."

"I'm dying. I'm afraid," Bianca whispered.

"All mortals die. You must face that truth. Have courage."

"If you do not help me, I will wall up your cage, and you will be trapped in the dark forever."

The unicorn did not respond to her threat. She blinked back tears and swallowed her guilt.

•

Bianca slipped a long dagger between the bars. "I've heard that unicorn blood has healing properties."

The unicorn did not even open its eyes.

"I know you're not asleep," Bianca said.

She cut deep into its flank, and it flinched. Red blood coated her dagger.

It looked just like her own.

The unicorn's wound closed.

Bianca smeared the blood on a glass slide and examined it with her microscope. She ran test after test, each experiment wilder than the last, but every one was a dead end. It was just blood.

But maybe it was a magic that eluded scientific explanation. She cut the unicorn again, and caught the blood in a silver cup. She swallowed it in one long quaff.

The pain did not fade.

•

Every breath burned, and the taste of blood never left her mouth. It was slippery on her teeth, and red spots stained everything she owned. Her hands trembled constantly, and she was unable to keep even simple foods down.

Even her vomit tasted like blood.

Her parents put her in bed, and her doctors pressed cool towels to her forehead. The rough grating of her breath filled the room.

"I think she will live through the night," one of the doctors whispered. "It might be best if you slept, my lord and lady. You mustn't exhaust yourselves."

They nodded and pressed teary kisses to Bianca's hair.

The doctors drew back, clustered around a low table together to talk of their research and other wealthy patients.

Bianca reached for the cord to call a servant. It took her three tries to grasp it.

A clockwork maid entered and bowed. "Bring me a pitcher of warm spiced wine," Bianca rasped.

The servant did as it was bid, then left again. Bianca emptied a tiny vial of white powder into it and watched it dissolve.

"Doctors," she called, then coughed. Hot wine slopped on her nightgown.

They hurried over and took the pitcher. "I—I had that brought for you."

The doctors clucked their thanks and drank deep. They fell asleep clustered back at their table.

Bianca rolled out of bed. Her legs would no longer hold her, so she dragged herself to her laboratory, stopping only when the coughing twisted her whole body like a ragdoll.

The unicorn stood in its cage when she pushed the door open. It shimmered in the moonlight. Bianca gazed at the curve of its arched neck, the purple depths of its eyes, the lithe muscles of its flanks that bore no evidence of her abuse.

"I think it is too late for you to wall me in," it said.

"I know."

"I will not save you."

"I know." She was past resentment, past anger, almost past fear. It was time to face her death with courage, if she had any. She gripped the edge of her workbench and pulled herself upright.

The golden key was heavy and cold, and her fingers did not want to curl around it. She held it between both hands and stumbled to the cage.

Frustrated tears blurred her vision. She found the keyhole and forced the shaking key into it, then turned it.

The door swung open. "Go," she whispered.

"I will escort you back to your bed."

She leaned on the unicorn, and they shuffled back to her bedroom. She slipped into her covers, and the unicorn vanished. A light breeze curled around her, and the green apple smell filled her lungs.

The pain eased, and Bianca let go of her fear.

HOW LOVE WORKS

Originally appeared in *Stupefying Stories*

Carl clutched the cool seed to his chest. He'd lost everything else, but at least he still had what he'd come for. It was as big as his fist, and heavy. He'd almost dropped it when the shaman handed it to him.

His bright yellow life-raft drifted aimlessly. The crash—if there had even been a crash—was an empty space in Carl's mind. He didn't know what that meant, but as far as his memory was concerned, he had gone straight from the cramped airplane to this sun-baked, half-provisioned raft. There'd been no sign of his luggage, wreckage, or other survivors.

His stomach rumbled. He wondered what would happen if he ate the seed.

The shaman had promised that it would grow into his deepest desire, once he planted it. He'd planned on going straight home and burying it in his neglected back garden. He'd imagined a huge, golden flower bursting from between the stunted weeds, and a beautiful, kind-faced woman stepping out of its petals to take his hands between hers.

If he closed his eyes, he could still see her. He knew he'd never be able to eat the seed. He'd never be able to do anything to hurt her. Even if she wasn't real.

He took a slow swig of blood-warm water. He only had half of a bottle left. He'd eaten his last protein bar for dinner last night. He pawed through the crinkly, slippery wrappers, searching for a stray crumb or smudge of melted chocolate.

Hunger gnawed at him. The slow, steady slap of water against the raft, the constant rocking motion, and the glaring sun made him queasy and dizzy. He'd never done well on the water.

He longed for land.

He wanted to live.

He wondered if he was dead already.

He held the seed to his forehead. Its cool, smooth skin soothed him. He imagined his dream-woman curled inside it.

Did she dream of him? Or of rescue? Or was there nothing inside but wood?

He drank the last of the water. His empty belly ached.

Where were the damn rescue ships?

Or the islands? Weren't there supposed to be islands scattered all over this area?

He slept. He woke. He listened to the sea and the creaking raft. He talked to the seed. He told it about his dead mother and boring job and empty life. He told it that wisteria was the only thing that would grow in his garden.

His lips chapped and split. The blood felt good coating his dry mouth.

The seed felt warmer. Was its magic failing? Was there something inside, dying?

Was there some way he could save her?

The shaman had said that any soil would do. There was dirt under all of this water. Maybe she'd be a mermaid. She'd be a beautiful mermaid.

Maybe one of them could live.

He thought about rescue, his back garden, his empty life. What if the ships came right after he dropped her?

What if they didn't?

He dropped the seed over the side of the raft and watched it sink through crystal water until the darkness claimed it. He'd never felt more alone.

He slumped against the thick rubber edge of the raft. His eyes were too dry for tears.

In his dreams, he was in his garden. A mermaid brought him tea.

•

The raft shuddered, and he scrambled to the edge. Maybe there was a ship? Finally? Rescue? But there was still nothing on the horizon.

He looked down.

The ocean glowed, then boiled beneath him, roiling and wild. The raft careened away on a steaming wave. He clutched at canvas straps with shaking fingers. Time grew meaningless. He held on, breathed when he could, and cursed the hot salt water that stung his eyes, his bloody lips, his cracked fingertips. The raft crashed into something solid, and his grip failed. He tumbled away and lost consciousness.

He woke on a fresh volcanic island. The ground—mercifully still—was uncomfortably hot against his skin, but it didn't burn him.

As he picked himself up, a golden flower erupted from the new earth. Hot lava glowed from the cracks it left as it burst free.

The petals opened, and his dream-woman emerged. She dipped her hands back into the flower and offered him nectar that dripped from her cupped fingers. The liquid soothed his lips, then his mouth, throat, and soul. Her soft, cool hands curled around his. Drops fell on the hot ground, and wisteria spread and bloomed around their feet. "Welcome home," she said.

"How?" Carl asked.

She smiled at him. "You saved me. So I saved you. Isn't that how love works?"

Carl touched her cheek. "I suppose it is."

GRANDMA'S SHOES

Originally appeared in *The Colored Lens*

Becca climbed out her bedroom window, grabbed a shovel, and ran to the graveyard. Becca's mother had ordered her grandma buried in Becca's favorite pair of shoes, and homecoming was approaching fast.

Becca figured she'd take the jewelry, too, while she was there. Her grandmother would have wanted her to have it. She didn't let herself hope for anything more.

The full moon illuminated the graveyard well enough for her to dig without any other light. The soil was loose, but she still worked up a sweat in the heavy late-summer air. She'd never done much digging before. Her arms burned and her back ached. She wished she'd thought to borrow a backhoe. She wished she knew how to use a backhoe. She wished that her mother wasn't so horrible, and that her grandmother was still alive.

After what felt like an eternity, her shovel thunked into the hardwood casket. She removed enough dirt to clear the top half of the lid, then she jerked it open. A thin stream of dirt cascaded down the side of her hole, onto her grandmother's waxy face.

The stink hit Becca like a bag of hammers, and her stomach lurched. She managed to turn enough to throw up on her own shoes instead of on her dead grandmother's carefully arranged gray curls.

She scowled down at her already-filthy canvas sneakers. They were going to be a total loss. But the shoes might have been a lost cause anyway, and it would have been wrong to throw up on her grandmother. Aside from the puffiness, she looked almost normal. And Becca had loved her grandmother.

That, more than homecoming, was why she wanted the shoes back.

She covered her mouth with her shirt and took a few slow breaths. She could do this. She reached in for the necklace, and her fingers brushed her grandmother's neck. The flesh was the same cool temperature as the dirt and too soft—like a foam mattress.

Her grandmother's eyes snapped open, she grabbed Becca's wrist. Her swollen fingers felt like refrigerated sausages. Becca yelped and tried to step back, but her feet slipped, and she fell to her knees. "What are you doing, Rebecca?" Her grandmother's voice was wet and distorted, but recognizable.

Becca's terror eased. Her grandmother wasn't mindless—she remembered who she was. The hope that Becca hadn't let herself feel spread in her chest, and she grinned. Even dead, her grandmother wouldn't hurt her.

"I'm here for the shoes," Becca said. "It's nice to hear your voice again, too."

Her grandmother blinked at her. "Which shoes?"

"The red pumps."

"I gave those to you," her grandmother said. "Why would I be buried in them?"

Becca shrugged. "Mom decided. I don't think she wanted me to have them. She always hates—hated it when you gave me things."

Her grandmother sniffed. "I raised her better than that." She released Becca's wrist and started wriggling around. She placed one red pump, then a second, on top of the casket. "Since you're here, you should take the jewelry, too."

She tried to pull off her rings, but they were trapped on her swollen fingers. She couldn't work the necklace clasp, either. "This whole dead thing is quite frustrating," she said.

Becca reached in and unfastened the necklace. The smell hardly bothered her at all now. "I can imagine." Becca put the necklace on and picked up the shoes. "Is there anything I can do for you?" she asked.

Her grandmother shrugged. "I can't think of anything. I don't really need much. I'm dead, after all."

Becca blinked back her tears. She'd already cried for her grandmother. "Okay. I love you."

"I love you, too, dear. It would be nice if you'd come and visit."

"I will."

"And don't worry too much about your mother. Things will get better. Eventually."

"I—I'll try not to let it get to me."

Becca reached for the lid. "Grandma?"

"Yes, dear?"

"What's it like?" Becca asked.

"What's what like?"

"Being dead."

"It's not bad. But it's not great either. It's certainly not something you should rush into."

"Right. Thanks Grandma. I'll remember."

"You do that."

Becca closed the lid. It took less time to fill the hole back in. She left her vomit-covered shoes next to the headstone and walked home in the red pumps.

Her mother noticed when she wore the shoes to homecoming, but neither of them mentioned it.

FOR LOVE OF THE STARS

Originally appeared in *Lakeside Circus*

Changó first came to me in a dream when I was six years old. The Orisha appeared as a huge red and white striped snake with scales shaped like double-headed axes, and he coiled himself around my body. He was smooth and hot and he smelled like air after a storm. He rested his head on my shoulder and whispered in my ear, "Do you love the stars?"

I looked up. The dream-stars were bright overhead, and they sang. I couldn't understand the words.

I had often dreamed of the stars, so I nodded. "They are beautiful."

His coils tightened. "Of course they are beautiful. But do you love them?"

The stars' song wrapped around my heart, and I longed to understand. My chest ached. "Yes. I love them."

"Do you wish to visit them someday?" he asked.

I freed an arm from his grip and reached up. A star tumbled from the sky and landed in my hand. It made my palm prickle, and it twinkled at me. "I do."

"I will help you reach them if you promise to take me with you when you go."

I couldn't imagine a god needing me for anything. "Why can't you just go yourself?"

"I can only go where my people go. Your ancestors brought me here to Cuba from Africa. They carried me in their hearts. I want you to take me to the stars."

"Why do you want to go to the stars?"

"I love them, too," Changó said. "And I grow restless. I want to explore—to see someplace new." As he spoke, his mind opened to me, and for a moment, we were one. I could feel his longing, his wanderlust, his love.

Joined with him, I was a tiny part of an incomprehensible whole, a small reflection of his dreams made flesh, but his feelings echoed and resonated in my soul.

I'd never through of leaving Cuba before, but standing in Changó's embrace, I knew that I must. I'd have to leave everything I knew and loved behind to reach the stars, but in that moment, it didn't matter.

I patted his hot scales. "I will go to the stars, and I will bring you with me."

•

Changó visited me the next Friday. Instead of a snake, he came as a man. No one else could see him, but he was as solid as he'd been in my dream. The people of Cuba gave him strength. He was tall and smiling, and his skin was two shades lighter than his midnight black hair. He wore a faded red t-shirt and old blue jeans and a baseball cap with an axe on it. He picked me up after school and we went to the park.

He sat cross-legged on the dusty ground next to me. "Did you know that six is a perfect number?" he asked.

I shook my head. "What does that mean?"

"Six is the sum of all of its divisors."

I'd just started school, but I was fascinated by math. It was easy for me. "I'm six."

"I know." He tousled my hair. "You won't be perfect again till you're twenty-eight."

He came to me every Friday. He didn't tell me any divine secrets— he just helped me with my homework and taught me how to drum on the Batá. When I surpassed my high school teachers, he brought me textbooks and helped me unravel them. When he couldn't find any more books, I bounced ideas off of him.

•

My mother sat a plate next to my elbow. "Where do you get all these books?" she asked. "Do you really need to study so hard? You never play with the other children anymore."

"I like studying more than I like playing," I said.

She kissed my cheek. "You're going to do great things. I just hope you don't forget about us. I love you very much, you know."

Cuba didn't have a space program. I couldn't stay here. I stood up and hugged my mother. She smelled like cumin and the sea. "I love you too, Mama."

I met Changó on the dock after school. He sat and stared out across the water, tapping out a rhythm on his Batá.

"Why are you helping me learn about math?" I pulled off my shoes and plunked down next to him. The water was cool against my skin.

"All of the secrets of the universe are math," he said, still tapping on his drum. "Math and magic are different ways of looking at the same thing. There is magic in music, in how it gets in your head and makes your body move. But there's also counting. Rhythms without structure aren't music." He handed me his drum, and I took up his beat. "There is math in everything. The limbs on a tree, the petals on a flower—math is life. The world without math is just noise. I'm training you to be a wizard. Formulas are your spells."

I don't know what strings he pulled to get me accepted into an American college. He told me he didn't pull any—that they saw my test scores and snapped me up. There was a scholarship waiting for me.

I just had to get to America. I packed my Batá, favorite books, and a picture of my family. I stood on the sand, between my homeland and the black ocean. The raft was a dark smudge against the water.

Changó stood beside me, his hand on my shoulder. "You will never be able to come back," he said.

I'd known that the government would never let me back in the country, but hearing him pronounce it made it real. Tears slipped down my cheeks. I looked back inland, where my family slept, where I'd left them nothing but a note on my pillow. My mother would cry. "Will you be with me in America?"

He tapped my chest. "Only if you carry me with you." He grinned. "It's not the stars, but it's a good first step."

I hugged him, and he whispered a blessing into my hair.

•

I missed my family, but even more than that, I missed Changó. Carrying him in my heart wasn't the same as seeing him every Friday. I'd never had many friends, and now I had a language barrier to add to my social problems. My English wasn't terrible, but it wasn't great either.

I threw myself into my studies. At least numbers were the same in America.

I stood outside and stared at the stars for hours. They weren't quite the same, but I still loved them.

Mitch, one of the guys from my advanced electromagnetic theory class stopped next to me one night. "What do you look at out here?"

"The stars."

"You know, they're not going anywhere."

I laughed. "That doesn't make them any less beautiful."

Mitch shook his head. "If you say so." He stood next to me for a while and looked up at the stars. "It's getting cold."

"I hadn't noticed." I liked the cold. It made the air feel cleaner. And the stars brighter.

•

I tapped on my Batá and missed Changó. I was alone in my faith, so he was weak, here. I tried to hold him in my heart, but I wasn't sure if I was strong enough. And if I couldn't even bring him to America, how could I carry him to the stars?

Tears dripped onto my drum.

I felt hollow.

•

I was failing Advanced Nonlinear Wave Equations. I just didn't understand it.

In Cuba, when the ideas were difficult, I would talk with Changó, and everything would make sense again. I needed Changó more than I ever had before, but I couldn't even feel his presence. I'd never felt so alone.

I sat in the library, staring at numbers that refused to mean anything. "Why have you abandoned me?" I whispered.

There was no answer. I asked Mitch to tutor me.

•

I dreamed of the stars, distant and cold. Their silence cut through me. Changó stood with his back to me, staring up at them. I called out and ran toward him, but I couldn't get any closer, and he didn't turn to me.

•

"What do you want to do after we graduate?" Mitch asked.

I shrugged. "I don't know."

"Didn't you say something about NASA? Going into space?"

"I'm not sure if that's what I want anymore," I said. "It seems like a sort of silly dream, now."

"I don't think it's silly. You shouldn't give up on your dreams," Mitch said. He squeezed my shoulder. "I've always respected your goals. And you never look up at the stars anymore. Maybe you should give them another chance."

•

I stood in the snow and stared up at the night sky. The stars still shone, bright unchanging. They would never abandon me. My heart ached with love for them. How could I not strive to reach them? Mitch was right. I couldn't give up on my dreams, even without Changó's help.

A hot breeze caressed the back of my neck. I turned around, and Changó was there, a shadow against the stars. He touched my cheek.

"Where have you been?"

His lips moved, but his voice didn't reach me. He tapped my chest, over my heart. My eyes filled with tears. He hadn't abandoned me. I'd locked him away. His touch was hot and real against my cheek. I kissed his palm, and he vanished.

That weekend I rode the bus out of town and camped in the park. I played my Batá, and if I closed my eyes I could feel Changó with me. I could almost hear his voice in the echoes of my drum.

•

I stared down at the computer screen in front of me. I'd figured out how to fold space. It still needed rigorous testing, but deep down, I knew that it was right. I'd done it. I'd never felt more like a wizard. Changó squeezed my shoulder. "Congratulations," he said. His voice sounded tinny and distant, but it was good to hear.

I turned my screen toward Mitch. "Check this for me."

"Why? I've never found a single error..." he trailed off, starting at the math. He read for a while, then shook his head and read it again. "Is this right?"

"I think so."

"Holy crap," he said.

"Want to come to the stars with me?"

He shook his head. "The stars are nice, but they're not for me."

My throat tightened, but I forced a smile. Changó would always be beside me.

•

I stare out the tiny window. The earth hangs in the blackness below, a vibrant blue marble, and it hurts that I'm leaving it behind. But the stars are brighter, out here, like the stars in my dream, so long ago. I can almost hear them singing.

Floating 100,000 miles above the earth, I tap out a rhythm on my Batá, close my eyes, and hold my god in my heart.

Tomorrow, we're taking each other to the stars.

JIGSAW PIECES

Originally appeared in *Plasma Frequency Magazine*

Betty sorted through her mother's belongings, separating and stacking a lifetime's worth of accumulated crap. Clothes and acrylic yarn and expired canned goods, books and an army of ceramic chickens and years and years of Christmas cards.

She heard her mother's irritated sigh every time something landed in the trash can.

She drove a carload to the local Goodwill, and the clerk scanned her offerings. "We only take complete jigsaw puzzles," he said. "Can you verify that these don't have pieces missing?"

Betty glanced at the stack. Her mother had really taken to puzzles, at the end. There had to be at least a hundred of them. "I'm sure they're fine."

"I'm sorry, miss, but that's not good enough."

"They were my mother's puzzles. I don't even know if she finished all of them."

He picked up the top box. "Take this one home, complete it, take a picture, and bring it back. If it has all its pieces, we'll take them all. If not, you take them back home or they go in the trash."

Betty clutched the box to her chest. She imagined the look on her mother's face if she'd seen her puzzles in the trash. "Fine."

•

She sat at her mother's dining room table and spread the puzzle pieces out in front of her. The box showed a spring landscape, complete with a pond and songbirds. Betty rubbed her forehead. "At least it's not Thomas Kinkaid."

She put on one of her mother's Brahms records and opened a bottle of wine that she'd given as a Mother's Day present. She started with the top edge, piece upon piece of bright blue sky. The feel of cardboard pieces clicking together soothed her aching heart.

The wine helped, too.

She finished the puzzle, but there was a piece missing. "I can't believe this," she muttered. She searched under the table and in the box. She glanced at the oddly-shaped gap in the middle of the scene. She ran her fingers over its edges.

The missing piece had to be somewhere in this house.

She left her glass, took the bottle, and started searching. She scoured the rooms that she's already been through, then the basement, then finally she pulled the ladder down and scrambled up to the attic.

The bare bulb flickered overhead, casting long shadows across the plywood floor, and she sneezed at the smell of dust and forgotten memories. The ceiling was too low to stand, so she crawled along, still clutching the now-empty bottle, feeling for cardboard with her empty hand.

"Come on, Mom," she whispered. "I know you didn't throw it away. You never threw anything away."

Her fingers touched a flat plane of cardboard, and she pulled it into the light.

Pieces from a hundred different puzzles fit together like they were made to. Their edges formed perfect seams, and the bits of sky and grass and feathered wing and castle wall came together to paint her mother's face. Not as she was at the end, but the way she'd been when Betty was growing up. Strong and beautiful and smiling, with a strong jaw and piercing eyes.

The familiar eyes blinked.

"There you are," the puzzle said. "I was starting to worry that you'd never make it to the attic."

"I've always hated it up here," Betty whispered.

"I know, dear."

"This can't be real."

"I wanted to let you know that I love you, Betty. That I appreciate all the things you did for me, that even when I didn't recognize you, I still knew that I loved you."

Tears slid down Betty's face and plopped on the bright surface.

"There, there, sweetie. I wish I could hug you."

The resentment of the past months, along with the stress and the heartbreak and the anger, all eased their grip. She looked into her mother's clear eyes. "I love you, too."

"It's okay to let go," her mother said. "You can throw out anything that you don't want to keep, and I really won't mind."

Betty sniffled and wiped her eyes. "Thanks."

She felt warm fingers on her cheek, then the puzzle was nothing but a confusing mishmash of colors.

She took the puzzle apart, piece by piece. Then she put the last piece from the spring puzzle in its place and took a picture. "Goodbye, Mom." She looked around the empty room, then slid the pieces into the box and closed the lid. "Goodbye."

THE STRAW-MOTHER

Originally appeared in *Triangulation: Parch*

When it rains, she walks with face bare into the wet wind. Her straw stuffing soaks and plumps and her burlap skin smoothes and knits. The resentment in her dusty heart unspools and floats away like clumps of dandelion seeds in the river.

She leaves the pans sticky in the sink, the laundry piled on the floor (she doesn't know why it is so hard to toss it in the hamper), the cups scattered throughout the house—the glass unpolished, the shelves undusted, the floors scuffed and sullied—and she walks in the rain. When the drops slow, she stretches out in a meadow filled with tiny white flowers that only bloom in the moments after a shower. She breathes their scent as the last gray clouds scuttle toward the horizon.

She goes back to her work refreshed. She smiles at the family's hungry faces and whips potatoes and carves the roast and juliennes thin strips of carrots and bakes the fluffiest of cakes.

Spring falls away into muddy memory, and diamond-bright summer days string together, each dryer than the last. Not even wispy white clouds touch the hard blue sky or golden-hot sun. She cooks and cleans and tidies. The counters gleam and glasses glisten. She puts fresh flowers in crystal vases, and they paint false rainbows on the walls. She makes sandwiches and wraps them in waxed paper, then later finds the papers crumbled in a corner, crumbs ground into the rug, and a pair of ants creeping along the wall. She has asked them a million times not to leave crumbs, to put garbage in the bin, to put dishes in the sink.

She finds another ant in the bottom of a coffee mug, swimming in thick black sludge.

Her dry limbs crackle when she hauls the rug out to beat it with her broom. Her fingertips fray as she scrubs down the walls, her straw slips out and floats with the ant in the gray dishwater.

She soaks in the copper washing tub while the family is away—she climbs in with the linens and they swirl around her like ghosts. The water soaks in, but it doesn't soothe the constant ache. She drags herself out, heavy and disappointed.

Worry edges out resentment in her sun-baked heart. What will happen to her if it doesn't rain?

She pulls bread out of the hot oven, and tiny sparks settle along her arms, leaving smoking black spots. She runs to the sink as wisps of orange flame lick down to her wrists.

The water hisses as she plunges her arms in.

She takes to wearing long sleeves to cover the ugly black streaks, and the scent of smoke trails behind her.

No one notices.

Her joints ache and lock and her limbs snap and creak as she moves. Dust bunnies gather in the corners. Ants creep in at the baseboards.

The father frowns at her and shakes his head sadly.

He leaves his coffee cup on his nightstand, and she leaves it there as well. Soon, the surface is crowded with cups.

Three course meals shrink to salads and fruit. Touching the oven dial fills her with dread.

The family complains, so she makes toast and spreads butter and jam in thick layers. They grimace and pull the bits of snapped-off straw out of their teeth.

The boys smear jam on the wall, and the ants rejoice. The father knocks a coffee cup over, and it cracks against the dirty floor.

He yells and threatens, and she cowers. But he seems far away. It is hard to focus on his red face with her dusty eyes.

She spends the night in the rocking chair, banned from her bed.

The sun rises, bright and clear in the cloudless sky.

She stands, and her straw snaps with every movement. Her burlap unravels as her feet scrape along the ground.

She finds her meadow, dry and brown and hot, almost unrecognizable. She falls in the dust then rolls to face the blue sky.

Ants crawl inside her collar, carry away bits of broken straw.

She stares up at the sky and waits for rain.

THE BUILDING-KING OF PITTSBURGH

Originally appeared in *Triangulation: Steel Cities*

Cold rain falls on mounds of dirty snow, and gray buildings loom over faded pavement. Cars hiss by, and Tallie huddles in the flimsy shelter of the bus stop, cowering under an oversized, overconfident, two-dimensional lawyer. She dislikes the way he points at her, and distrusts the printed promises at his feet, but she can't move away and stay out of the wind. She closes her eyes and tries to forget that he's there.

He's not real, anyway.

She is though, and so is the rain and the cold and the snow.

Overhead, the buildings murmur to each other. They blink their sad window-eyes, and old black soot seeps down their stone sides like cheap mascara.

They are real, but also not.

"I feel the cold seeping into my foundation," an old skyscraper grumbles.

"The winter of '42 was worse," the hulking stone courthouse says.

"Everything was worse in '42."

Tallie doesn't remember the winter of '42. She refuses to remember anytime when things have been worse.

There is a warm room with a locked door waiting for her. A shelter. A prison. She pushes the thought away and hugs her wet coat tighter.

"The king can help with your foundation," the library whispers. "He helped me fix one of my broken windows."

"Shh!" a matronly cathedral with trim stained glass windows and a barred gate says. "She's listening again!"

"What do we care?" asks a gruff old office building with carved lions flanking its glass doors.

"Well, it's just unnatural," says the cathedral.

"I wish I couldn't hear you," whispers Tallie. While she's at it, she wishes for a cup of coffee, a sandwich, a hot shower, a warm bed, and just for good measure, world peace and a pony.

She gets precisely none of it.

"Humph, imagine that. She eavesdrops on private conversations, then tries to excuse herself by wishing she was deaf? How utterly low class."

Tallie has never liked the cathedral. "I could put a rock through one of your precious windows," she says.

"You just try it, missy," the cathedral's stones groan as she leans over the street. Her shadow swallows the bus stop. "I will crush you like the insect you are."

"Now, now," says the office building. "She's not the type to cast stones, and we all know it."

The cathedral sniffs, but subsides back to her normal place.

"Why don't you come on in," says the office building. "I'm well heated, and the lobby has one of those new-fangled single cup coffee machines."

"Security will find me," Tallie says. "They'll throw me back out."

The office building shrugs. "Maybe. But you can warm up a bit, first. Have some coffee. We might even be able to find you a sandwich."

Tallie wonders if the buildings can read her mind. She glances up at the lawyer on the poster. What if he can read her mind, too? She edges away. His eyes bore into her, brimming with want.

She bolts into the office building.

•

She makes her coffee—two creams and three sugars, the real stuff in the rough brown packets. The elevator dings and hisses open behind her. She ducks behind the couch. "It's fine," the office building says. "I sent it. You can hide in one of the executive offices."

The elevator is small. The walls are lined with deep velvet. Soft. Padded. "I can't," she says.

"You can trust me."

Tallie doesn't trust him. She can't trust anyone. But she likes his lions. She steps into the elevator and the doors close. She gasps in tiny breaths until the doors hiss open again.

"The second door on the left."

There's a beautiful view of the city and a green dress hanging on the back of the door. And a private bathroom.

She stares at the shower. And the thick, soft towels.

Tallie weighs her options. The building offers no advice.

"Do you have eyes to close?" Tallie asks.

"No."

She peels off her clothes. They are heavy with cold rain, and the layers that were closest to her skin stink. Goosebumps cover her bare skin.

106

The soap smells like roses.

Tallie stands in the shower for a long time, waiting for something terrible to happen. She flinches at every noise. It takes her ten minutes to work up the nerve to wash her hair.

The water at her feet turns gray.

She wraps up in one towel and dries her hair with another. She finds a comb and counts 100 strokes, till her tangled hair falls smooth. She rubs scented lotion into her skin. She braids her hair.

The dress fits. She finds unopened panty hose in a drawer, and three pairs of shoes in the coat closet along with a long fur coat. In one pocket, she finds a clean lace handkerchief and a pair of sparkly green earrings.

The building is still silent.

She goes back into the bathroom and wipes faded steam off of the cold mirror. She slides the earrings into her long-empty earlobes. She struggles a bit with the right ear, but they sparkle so beautifully in the low light.

It has been a long time since Tallie has worn anything beautiful.

She stands by the window and looks at her ghost reflection over the city. Three rivers reflect the shimmering lights. Love for the city tugs at her heart—it is the one beautiful thing that she has never lost. "It's a nice view."

There is a couch against the far wall.

She locks the office door and uses the coat as a blanket and an extra towel for her pillow.

"There are sheets in the closet," the building says.

But Tallie's eyes are already closed, and she sleeps.

•

She leaves the next morning, and no one sees her. Their eyes skip over her like she belongs. She stops for another cup of coffee on her way out. Someone has brought fresh doughnuts, and she eats one. She licks lemon cream off of her fingers. People smile at her without meeting her eyes.

"You love this city."

Tallie shrugs. Of course she does.

"You should go see the building-king," the office building says.

Tallie's knees shake at the thought, but they're hidden by her new coat.

Outside, the winter air is still cold, but sun peeks through the buildings.

Tallie stops and puts a hand on a stone lion. "Thank you," she says.

The building rumbles.

Tallie's new shoes are simple black flats, and surprisingly comfortable to walk in. She strolls down the streets and sips her coffee. She watches pigeons move in iridescent feathered waves, and lets the ocean of foot traffic pull her along.

She arrives at a square, surrounded by turret-topped glass walls. The building-king of the city. He regards her.

She sits at a table where someone has abandoned half of a bagel. She shares it with the pigeons.

"I would repair our city, and I have need of subjects," the king says. Its voice is deep, and it rumbles in the sidewalk.

Tallie watches the pigeons. "Did you do this to me?"

"No. But I can use you, if you're willing."

Tallie almost believes him. Why would he single her out? But he's the only magic that she knows of. She strokes her fur coat and finishes her coffee. She thinks about wishes, then about world peace and a pony.

It had been a long time since she worked. She misses functioning.

"What will it cost me?"

"The more you interact with us, the less they will see you."

Tallie thinks about eyes sliding past her. She's already lonely.

The glass walls are beautiful in the morning sunlight.

"What if I change my mind?"

"You won't."

Tallie doesn't want to freeze, and she doesn't want the locked room. "What do I need to do?"

•

She carries messages and magic for the building-king. The magic curls around her bones, crackles at her wrists. It is uncomfortable. He sends her uphill, away from the steel towers and hulking fortresses. She walks on cracked sidewalks, and the buildings around her weep. They mourn their crumbling porches, their cracked foundations.

Some are too far gone to cry. The dead buildings pull at Tallie's heart. She wonders how long it will take for the whole neighborhood to fall silent. She wonders if the building-king can stop it.

She wonders if she can help.

She reaches the YMCA. Its sign flickers, but the building greets her. "Welcome, welcome! Yours is a new face! Do come in!"

Tallie sits on the cold steps and turns her face to the weak sun. "I have a message."

The YMCA trembles with anticipation.

"The king is pleased with you."

"I—I didn't even know he knew about me."

"You do good work. Spread cheer in this sad place. You're a place of learning and safety. He sends this reward."

Tallie pressed both hands to the concrete steps. She feels distant and dizzy and very hot. Her bones tingle. Then the moment passes, and the cold wind sweeps the feeling away.

The changes to the YMCA are subtle. Its sign glows steadily now, and tiny cracks and fissures have sealed.

"Thank you," the YMCA says. "Please come in. Have some coffee."

She sits in the computer lab and watches videos of running ponies. She watches their babies take their first trembling steps. The man at the computer next to her smiles at her, and she smiles back. She reads an article about mental illness, then one about the history of downtown.

She wonders how much of what she sees is real.

She types her old address and looks at the house from above, then from the street. Her mother is trapped in the picture, weeding her tulips forever.

Tallie touches the screen. There is so much gray in her hair.

She wonders if her mother's house can talk.

•

The building-king sends her to every corner of the city. The busses stop for her now. They make low purring noises when she sits, and the drivers never see her. She sleeps in a different building every night. They all seem happy to have her.

The Laundromats supply her with new clothes every morning, and the ever-present hunger slowly fades as kitchen after kitchen opens up to her.

She is proud of the help she gives. Proud to be the building-king's messenger. Human eyes ghost over her in a different way, now. It is both better and worse.

She returns to the YMCA, and the man at the next computer doesn't smile at her. "Hello," she says.

He looks around, then scratches his head.

She cries when she repairs a crack in the kind office building's lion. "Thank you," she whispers to him.

He opens his doors, and she sips coffee while he tells her stories about his youth.

She avoids her mother's neighborhood for as long as she can. Her mother's house is desperate and lonely. It begs her to come inside, to stay forever, or the night, or at least for a glass of water. The cupboards are full of things she once loved.

But she knows that the doors all lock, and she doesn't trust it.

"She misses you," the house whispers.

"I miss her, too."

•

"Don't think I don't know what you're doing," the cathedral says the next morning.

"What do you mean?" Tallie asks.

"You fix his lion. That tiny, stupid crack—did the beast even need a tail, honestly? And you ignore my broken window. You're holding a grudge, and I don't appreciate it."

Tallie hadn't noticed the window, and the building-king hadn't mentioned it. He hadn't given her any magic for the cathedral.

"Let me in," Tallie says.

The cathedral sniffs, but her gate creaks open and her heavy wooden door groans. Tallie slips inside. Early morning sunlight paints colors on the far wall, except for one ragged, sun-drenched spot. Tallie's footsteps echo on the marble floors. She kneels in that spot of un-colored sun and presses her palms to the floor.

The feeling is familiar now, but harder, since the magic comes from inside her. Something wrenches open in her, and the light turns purple.

Her knees buckle and she collapses on the floor.

The cathedral is silent for a long moment. "Thank you, child."

Tallie nods. Her skull aches, and her joints feel loose and wobbly. She thinks of running ponies.

"You are safe here," the cathedral says.

A woman pushes through the heavy door. She walks within an inch of Tallie's leg, then kneels next to her on the floor. "Keep my daughter safe," she prays. "I'd give anything to see her again."

The cathedral sighs. "This woman comes in every week," she says. "I do wonder if she'll ever find the girl."

Tallie stares up at her mother. Her mother turns and her eyes brush past her. Her throat aches. "I don't think so," she whispers.

The building-king gleams his approval at her from a thousand silver-black windows. "You did not have to help the cathedral," he says.

"It's too late for me to go back now, isn't it?"

"You are completely invisible to them, now. Your voice cannot reach their ears."

"Because I used my own magic on the cathedral."

"Yes."

"So it was a test?" Tallie asks.

The building-king rumbles. "Not one to pass or fail. One for you to see into yourself."

Tallie watches a flock of pigeons explode into a gray-rainbow cloud. She thinks about her mother, praying alone every week. She thinks of the purple feel of her own magic. "I haven't been happy with what I see in myself for a long time."

"Perhaps you were looking in the wrong places."

Tallie leans back and looks up at buildings in the city skyline. They are her family now, and she will take care of them. "Can I ask for one thing?"

The building-king winks his agreement.

"I don't like the lawyer posters. The ones on the bus stops."

The building-king laughs, and the lawyer disappears. Tallie's not sure if he's really gone, or if she just can't see him.

She knows it doesn't matter.

The building-king fills her with magic, and she sets off to help fix the city.

THE TASTE OF THE STORM

Originally appeared in *Daily Science Fiction*

Clouds gathered on the horizon, even though no wind churned the smooth face of the gray-green ocean.

Marlene scowled. "The weather witch is angry again."

"This is the third one this week," I said as lighting flickered between the clouds. I looked at the boats docked in the still water. At my father's boat, still tied where he'd left it before the stroke. "This can't go on. Sooner or later, someone's going to get hurt."

"There's no way to control or predict her. We have to take it as it comes."

It wasn't worth arguing with Marlene about, but I was done taking things as they came.

I stopped on my way home and bought flour and sugar and eggs. I kissed my father on the forehead and listened to the beeping machines that kept him alive.

When the storm hit, I opened the kitchen windows and captured the smell of the rain, the crash of the thunder, the sizzle of the lighting as it lit up the dark sky. I collected the feeling of standing in the cold, driving rain, with mud swirling around my ankles and water dripping from my hair. The rain that streamed down my cheeks tasted like despair.

I baked all night. I folded the captured storm into stiff-peaked meringues and whipped it into frosting.

I drove toward the mountains in the gray dawn. The staccato rhythm of my windshield wipers, the hiss of wet wheels on asphalt, and the smell of cookies surrounded me.

I bumped along a muddy driveway and pulled up outside of a stone cottage.

I grabbed the bags of baked goods and stomped to the weather witch's door.

Her door knocker was cold and heavy and stiff.

"Go away!" she shouted. "I'm not buying anything!"

"I'm not selling anything, and I'm not leaving. Open up!"

The door swung open, and the weather witch glared up at me. I thrust the bags out. "I brought cookies."

After a moment, the witch waved me inside. "I'll make tea."

She rinsed a dusty, chipped cup and set it next to an unchipped mug, dropped a teabag into each, then poured hot water from a blackened kettle.

She waited till I ate a cookie, then gobbled one down. "What do you want for them?"

"No more than three storms per month. Little storms. So no one gets hurt."

"Agreed, on one condition. You'll become my apprentice."

"What?"

"There's magic in these cookies. You should learn to harness it."

I'd never dreamed of being a witch. "What can do you do, aside from make storms?"

"Lots of things."

"But it hasn't made you happy."

The witch shrugged. "Life is still life, even with magic."

I finished my tea. It tasted like loneliness. "I'll do it."

•

I stood on a mountaintop and pulled dark clouds to me. This time, the rain tasted like freedom.

UNDER THE SHIMMERING LIGHTS

Originally appeared in *Stupefying Stories*

Kirima's ice skates hissed as she glided across her frozen pond. Four smooth strokes, then three crossovers, her left foot over her right, then four more strokes. Her skates left gouges and a trail of ice shavings. Her hair clung to her temples, and her breath misted in the cold air.

She hated the cold and the short hours of thin gray sunlight. As a child, she'd dreamed of hot winds and brown mountains and regularly spaced days and nights.

But she had always loved the dancing lights, and she came home when her grandmother wrote to beg her to save them.

She accelerated. The sharp edges of her skates dug into the ice, and for a second, it felt easy. She flew, free in her normally-clumsy body, balanced perfectly on one thin blade. Joy fluttered in her belly.

On the next turn, her skate caught on the worn ice. Her ankle twisted, then she stumbled, fell, slid across the ice, and ended up in a crumpled heap. The cold seeped through her fur-lined pants. Her joy shattered into despair.

Kirima would never be able to carry the crystalline eggs to rekindle the fading lights. She would fall and crush them. She would fail.

But she was the only one left to even try. She picked herself up and skated.

She stopped when she could no longer feel her fingers. She sat on the frozen snow and fumbled with her laces. Her fingers were clumsy, and her bruised hips ached. She winced as she slipped her feet into her cold shoes and limped to her shack. Her ankles felt shaky without the skate's support, and the left was swollen again.

Inside, she stirred her fire and boiled water for tea. She scraped frozen honey into her earthenware mug and threw in a small handful of dried flower petals. When she added water, the steam smelled like spring.

The grandmother had been gone when she arrived, but the coals still glowed in the hearth, banked around the three precious eggs, each no bigger than her thumb.

Kirima turned the eggs. They burned the tips of her fingers and painted the tiny room with pink, blue, and green light, just like the lights that had once danced in the sky. "I'm almost ready," she whispered. "I only fell once today, and it was because of rough ice."

The eggs didn't reply.

She strapped her snowshoes on and tromped across the snowy field. A white hare huddled in her trap. She sank her fingers into its thick fur. Its frantic heart thudded under her fingers, and its eyes shone with fear. She broke its neck with a sharp twist and carried it back home.

She skinned the rabbit. As the scent of roasted meat filled the drafty room, she gathered snow and packed it around her swollen ankle. She curled on her bed to sew the uncured rabbit hide into a pouch with her bone needle. Maybe with the soft fur padding them, they'd be able survive if she fell.

The days were growing short—down to a handful of hours of thin sunlight—and she didn't want to attempt the trip in darkness.

When the snow on her ankle melted, she wrapped it tight and edged close to the fire. Smoke curled around her, and she slept bathed in the eggs' rainbow glow.

•

The cold woke her. Sharp pain spiked up her leg when she put weight on it, and her ankle was hot and swollen.

"I should get some more snow and stay off of it," she told the eggs. "I won't be able to practice today."

Their glow seemed dim in the morning light.

•

Her ankle still ached two days later, but she didn't want to wait any longer. She imagined her grandmother's dark eyes, her twisted frown, her sharp disapproval and the muttered word, "Excuses."

"Maybe she was right about me," Kirima told the eggs. "Maybe I don't try because I am afraid of failure. But you should fear my failure, too."

She boiled the hare's bones in melted snow and drank the thin broth down. She heated all of her remaining honey. It was thick in her throat, and filled her with warm energy. She tucked the eggs into their fur pouch then slipped that into her anorak, just over her heart. She laced her skates tight, tied her hood close around her face, and set out toward the northern horizon.

116

She glided across the long ice. She concentrated on her balance, on every line and angle of her body. White ice stretched ahead of her, fading into the gray sky. The wind whispered in the distance, and her skates hissed.

As she moved, heat spread through her muscles. The pain in her ankle faded to a dull ache. Sweat beaded on her back and under her arms.

The gray horizon darkened, and the wind shifted.

"Oh no," Kirima whispered, but she skated into the storm. Stinging snow pelted down from the sky and pressed cold kisses against her exposed skin.

Her grandmother would have smelled the storm coming, but Kirima had refused to learn her ways.

Her world narrowed. She tucked her chin to her chest and skated. The cold clawed through her clothing, and exhaustion weighed at her muscles.

She could hear her grandmother's disappointment in the wind, but the eggs were warm over her heart.

She couldn't feel her feet.

She would save the only thing she loved in this frozen wasteland. She would not fail.

Darkness spread across the ice.

She wondered why her grandmother had left without saying goodbye.

Weak green light flickered through the storm ahead. She turned toward it, numb to any feeling of accomplishment.

The wind slapped against her face. Her balance faltered, and she flailed wildly, desperate to keep her feet. She planted both skates on the ice and bent her knees.

Her momentum carried her to her destination. A faint coil of light curled, limp and still, around a jagged black rock that thrust up from the ice. She'd reached the heart of the ice.

She pressed her palm to the light, and it wrapped itself around Kirima's wrist.

She pulled the first egg out of the fur-lined pouch. It was still warm against her palm, and it painted the snowflakes blue.

A blue wisp burst out of the egg and flowed up Kirima's body. It joined with the green coil. She pulled out the pink egg, and it hatched and followed its brother. The light grew, stretched beyond the stone's deep shadow.

She pulled out the final egg. It was cool, and its glow stuttered like a heartbeat.

Kirima held it close to and breathed on it, willing her warmth into its thin, fragile shell. "I got you here. Now it's your turn," she whispered. "You can do it."

The green wisp burst free and joined with the coil. Light exploded across the sky. They pushed the storm clouds away, and stars twinkled behind them.

Three wisps trailed down and caressed her cheek. Warmth spread from their touch. The pink and blue floated away, but the green lingered. It wrapped around her ankle, and the pain faded.

She skated back home under the shimmering lights, and joy danced in her belly.

FOR A SONG

Originally appeared in *The Colored Lens*

The ocean's whisper filled the night air as Lydia walked across the cold sand. But she wasn't here to listen to a whisper. She was looking for a song. She kicked off her shoes, left her clothes in a crumpled pile, and waded into the dark water.

Her skin instantly ached from the cold, and shivers wracked her body. She forced herself forward, one step at a time, till she was deep enough to throw herself into an oncoming wave. She gasped when her face hit the water, and the salt burned her throat.

She struggled forward. She wasn't a strong swimmer, and the cold made her limbs heavy and listless. "I will do this," she said, and choked on another mouthful of water.

•

In her senior year, Lydia's homeroom desk was near the middle of the room, fourth row, third seat back. Donna Harrison sat in front of her. Sometimes, Donna's long brown hair would brush against Lydia's desk.

Lydia loved Donna's hair. And her always-perfect nails, and the way her eyes crinkled when she smiled. Donna was on the basketball team and dating Tommy Miller. She'd been in Lydia's class since second grade, and they'd never talked. No one ever talked to Lydia. But sometimes, Donna would smile at her when she handed papers back. Lydia always smiled back.

•

Lydia caught lilting notes over the sound of the waves and the hammering of her heart. The song pulled her now, her legs kicking, her arms pulling her forward without effort.

The siren sat on a rock, knees tucked up to her chin, singing up at the moon. Her eyes were shadows as she stared down at Lydia.

She finished her song and started another. Lydia couldn't feel her fingers, though she could see that they gripped course rock.

Finally, the siren finished her second song. "Why are you here?" she asked, in a voice like shattered dreams.

Lydia knew just what that sounded like.

•

She'd asked Donna to sign her yearbook. It was a small thing, hardly out of the ordinary. Donna had spent a long time with her head bent over the blank page, her pen motionless in her hand.

Eventually, she wrote, "Lydia, I'm sorry. I wish we could have shared more. Goodbye, and good luck out there." She signed her name with a big, loopy D.

Lydia reached out and ran her hand over Donna's hair, just once. Donna didn't pull away, and Lydia gathered up her courage. "I think you're perfect," she said. "I've always thought that."

Donna's smile was sad. "Only God is perfect, Lydia."

•

"Why are you here?" the siren asked again.

Exhaustion tugged at Lydia's limbs. The water felt warmer than the air, now. She thought about letting go, about letting it wrap her in its liquid embrace. Her teeth chattered as she answered the siren. "I loved someone, and she—she didn't love me back."

"That is what happens when you love," the siren said. "But many people face unrequited love and do not seek me out. Why are you here?"

•

Lydia usually walked home from school. But one day, she didn't. Tommy Miller dragged her into his Buick. His eyes were glazed and he smelled like rum, but he was still strong. "Donna says you're a dyke," he said. "You know that's wrong, don't you? I can help you. Like I helped her."

"What do you mean?" Lydia said. Her head spun and her throat ached. Donna had said that about her?

"She told me about her impure thoughts, begged me to get them out of her head. I did, but then you put them back. But I can help."

"I don't want your help," Lydia said. She punched him in the throat, scrambled out of the car, and ran. She ran to the beach, the one that nobody ever went to, because sometimes, when the wind was just right, you could hear the siren there.

•

"I don't belong there," Lydia said. "I don't want to go back."

"Don't be foolish, girl," the siren said. "You are angry, but it will pass."

"Aren't you lonely?" Lydia asked. "I know what that is like. Don't send me away."

The siren's face was beautiful in the moonlight, her long hair as dark as the water. "What do you want?"

"I want you to teach me to sing," Lydia said. "I'm here to learn your songs."

The siren stared at her for a long time. "You don't have the strength to swim back, do you?"

"I wouldn't go, even if I could," Lydia said. "I've made my decision."

The siren took Lydia's hand and pulled her up onto the rock. "Stubborn child. Very well," she said. "I will teach you my songs."

MUSIC FROM THE AIR

Originally appeared in *Stupefying Stories*

Lavinia stepped onto the terpsitone's eight foot by fourteen foot metal stage. She faced the twin antennae that reached just above her head and switched the machine on. The boxy console between the antennae hummed and the instrument's electromagnetic field pulsed around her, responding to her movements with sound. She went en pointe, and the instrument responded with a clear C. Eerie tones, almost like wordless voices, but somehow alien, wove into ethereal music that filled the air as she danced.

She'd managed to scrape together just enough money to buy the ancient used instrument—she'd gotten a deal because the old woman who sold it to her, Mrs. Washington, needed the money to help her grandson move back home from California. Lavinia had sold most of her furniture to afford it, so the terpsitone was the only thing in her studio, aside from a bookshelf filled with books about ballet and a nest of blankets where she slept.

It was almost impossible for a junior dancer to get any time on the company's terpsitone, and Lavinia needed to practice.

She pirouetted and twirled, pliéd and leapt. Her song soared. The notes flowed from the air around her. She felt like the universe was singing to her.

She didn't stop until her legs cramped and trembled. She had to master the terpsitone if she ever wanted to be the prima ballerina with the American Negro Ballet, and she wanted that very badly. She hadn't wanted anything else since she'd started dancing when she was five.

Her deep brown skin glistened with sweat and wisps of her curly black hair clung to the back of her long neck. As she toweled herself off, the terpsitone started to hum. It sounded like someone else had stepped onto the stage, but there was no one there.

A sudden chill raised goose bumps on her arms. She wrapped the towel around her shoulders and approached the instrument. She twirled the knob to "off" and the sound died.

She turned it back on and the humming resumed. Something must have slipped loose in a vacuum tube. She grimaced. Mrs. Washington had warned her that it was very old—her beau had built it for her just as terpsitones were becoming popular almost forty years ago.

The hum slid into a glissando, and suddenly the terpsitone was singing. The raw longing in the otherworldly tones brought tears to Lavinia's eyes.

Loose vacuum tubes didn't make music like that. A cold breeze brushed Lavinia's cheek, and a form—a transparent man—started to materialize on the stage. The ghost held his hand out to her, inviting her to dance with him.

Lavinia fled.

·

Lavinia's heels clicked on the New York Public Library's stone floor. Her heart was still pounding. The library was the only place she ever went, aside from her studio and the theater, and the theater was closed on Sundays.

She needed to get her mind off of the thing that was waiting for her in her studio. She wandered through the stacks and picked up a newspaper. She read a story about President Webb's prize sheepdog. Lavinia had never had a dog. She wondered how they reacted to ghosts.

She put the paper down and rubbed her temples. She could check and see if there had been any mysterious deaths in her studio. She wasn't sure if the ghost had come in with the terpsitone, or if it had always been there.

The librarian smiled at her from behind the circulation desk. He looked like he was about her age—somewhere in his early twenties. His skin was burnt umber, and he had pretty amber eyes behind wire-rim glasses and a wide, expressive mouth.

"Hey, there, miss. Anything I can help you with?"

"I'd like to look through some old newspapers."

"Let me set you up with a projector. You looking for anything specific?"

"I'm looking for obituaries. Of male dancers."

The librarian raised his eyebrows. "No names?"

Lavinia shook her head.

"I'll see what I can do." He led her to a desk and flipped on a projector. Nothing happened. He sighed. "Ah, progress. We've got zeppelins that can do a hundred miles an hour, but we can't get projectors that work even half the time. These things are brand new." He pulled a screwdriver out of his back pocket, leaned over her, and removed a panel. He smelled good, like soap and old books and maple syrup. After a few moments a light flickered on in the view screen. Lavinia was very aware that his chest was only inches away from her cheek. "I'll go find you some microfilm."

Hours later, Lavinia stared at the never-ending boxes of information. Reading off of microfilm was better than digging through the actual newspapers, but her eyes ached from the glare of the projector. She still hadn't found a single clue about her ghost's identity. She wasn't even sure what she was looking for.

She was afraid to go home.

But she wasn't going to find any answers in the library. If they were there, they were buried too deep for her research skills to find. She shrugged her suit jacket back on, tugged her blouse sleeves back into place, smoothed her skirt, and adjusted her hat.

"Find what you were looking for?" The librarian called as she walked past the circulation desk.

Lavinia shook her head and tried not to remember how he smelled. "I don't think there's anything to find."

"Need help with anything else?"

"No, thank you."

The librarian walked beside her as she headed for the exit. "I'm Peter."

"My name is Lavinia Jones."

Peter adjusted his glasses. "Would you care to get coffee sometime, Miss Jones?"

For a moment, she considered saying yes. It would at least give her something to do instead of going home to face her ghost. She smiled at him. He was very handsome, in a quiet way. Lavinia liked that. But she had rules. She couldn't let social commitments get in the way of her dreams. "I don't date. I'm a ballerina, so I spend most of my time either practicing or performing."

"My grandma was a ballerina," Peter said. "She never made it sound so lonely."

Lavinia kept her smile bright and didn't think about her studio, empty except for her haunted terpsitone. "It can be lonely, sometimes. But I love what I do, and I'm happy. I appreciate the offer, but I really need to be getting home. Thanks again for all your help with the microfilm." She touched his hand. His skin was warm and smooth, and a shiver shot through her arm. She didn't allow herself to look back as she walked away.

•

Lavinia stared at the terpsitone for a long time before she turned it on. Her hands trembled on the knobs.

Something cold brushed her neck, and she shuddered. "I need to practice," she said. "This is my home, and my terpsitone, and you don't scare me. Go away. There's nothing for you here."

The chill touch withdrew, but Lavinia still felt like she was being watched. She took a deep breath. She needed to get used to dancing on the terpsitone for an audience. If she could dance in front of a ghost, she could dance in front of anyone.

She closed her eyes. She'd planned to practice all day. She'd lost hours at the library. She wasn't going to lose any more. Ghost or no ghost, there were solo auditions in two weeks, and she needed to be prepared.

She started slowly. The ethereal music swirled around her as she warmed up.

Her mind emptied as she danced. She forgot about Peter, the auditions, the ghost. There was only the dance and the terpsitone's otherworldly voice.

Then she wasn't alone on the stage. Ghostly hands gripped her elbows and lifted her, twirled her, threw her into the air—caught her, all faster than Lavinia could draw breath to scream.

She stumbled. For an instant, she could see her ghost's face, inches from her own. He was a little older than her, and oddly familiar. His eyes shone like copper pennies.

The ghost vanished, and she was alone. Her arms were still chilled from his embrace. But he hadn't hurt her. He was trapped and lonely, and a beautiful dancer. Lavinia wasn't afraid of him. She understood him.

He danced with her again the next day, and the next. She'd never had someone to dance with before, and she found that she liked having a partner. It felt good to trust someone to catch her. He grew stronger every day. He was a talented dancer, and Lavinia found herself welcoming his presence.

He was teaching her how to make the terpsitone sing. And it was better than being alone.

•

Lavinia looked out into the crowd. She'd landed her first short solo, and the house was packed. Excitement thrilled in her belly.

She spotted Peter in the third row, sitting next to Mrs. Washington. He looked dashing in his black suit, and she looked regal in her dark green gown, with her white hair gathered in a bun high on her head. His tie matched her dress. The two of them had their heads bent over a single program. He was holding her hand, and they were smiling at each other. The old woman was obviously his grandmother.

Lavinia's legs almost crumpled beneath her. She realized why the ghost had looked familiar. He looked like Peter. The ghost had to be his grandfather.

She had to tell them. They were a family, and they deserved to be reunited.

But what if Mrs. Washington wanted the terpsitone back?

Lavinia shuddered. She couldn't part with it. She needed it.

Her heart ached at the thought of losing her ghost.

One of the other dancers hissed at her. It was almost time for the show to begin.

She'd tell them after she danced.

•

Lavinia steeled her resolve and stepped out into the audience.

Mrs. Washington beamed at her. "Lavinia, sugar, you were terrific. I'm glad to see my old terpsitone is working out for you." She took Lavinia's hand. Her skin was like fine paper, cool and dry. "I want you to meet my Peter, back from California."

Peter looked sheepish.

Mrs. Washington pressed Lavinia's hand into Peter's. She was surprised by how warm he was. He kissed the back of her hand, and her breath caught.

"He rode across the whole country on freight trains, looking for work. I was so relieved when a position opened up in the library and I could get him to come back home."

"You were a hobo?" Lavinia asked.

Peter's lips twitched. "For a while."

"Isn't that dangerous?" Lavinia imagined falling off of a fast-moving train and shuddered.

"It is, indeed!" Mrs. Washington said. "I didn't want him to go, but he's stubborn, this one." She took his elbow, and he smiled down at her. "This is for you, sugar." She handed Lavinia a single red rose. "You danced beautifully. Did this old heart good to see it."

"Thank you, Mrs. Washington." Lavinia couldn't tell them. Not now. They wouldn't believe her anyway.

"Call me Ellen. You should come by for dinner sometime. My Peter spends too much time with old people and books. He needs a lovely young lady like you in his life."

"That sounds nice," Lavinia said. She'd ask her ghost if he wanted her to tell them, and if he did, she could do it then.

A look of surprise flashed across Peter's face. "Grandma, I'm sure Miss Jones doesn't need you playing matchmaker for her," he said.

Ellen laughed. "But you do, sweetie! You haven't had a date since you got back in town."

Peter looked away, his face carefully blank, and Lavinia's heart lurched. "I'd be happy to come by for dinner, really," she said.

"How's Sunday afternoon work for you?" Ellen asked.

Lavinia nodded. "I'll be there."

•

The instant she was back home, she regretted her rash promise. She stared forlornly at her rose. She didn't have a vase to put it in. Or a table to put a vase on.

She switched her terpsitone on, and her ghost appeared. "I saw your wife tonight. Ellen Washington."

A look of pure joy flashed across his face. Lavinia couldn't believe that she hadn't noticed his resemblance to Peter before. "I didn't tell her about you. I wasn't sure if she'd believe me." Lavinia crossed her arm over her chest and glanced away. "Do you want me to tell her?"

She wanted him to shake his head and hold his hand out to her. She wanted him to choose her. "Do you want to see her?"

Her ghost took her hands between his. His touch was so cold. He nodded, his eyes pleading with her.

Lavinia's heart broke. "I'll tell her. I'll get her here somehow, I promise," she whispered.

•

Ellen roasted a chicken. Her apartment was cozy and smelled like garlic, lemon, and vanilla. Lavinia perched on the edge of her chair and ate slowly. Peter kept his eyes on his plate. Ellen carried the conversation through dinner. She chatted about church socials and bake sales at the fire hall. Lavinia made encouraging noises and waited for an opportunity to tell them about her ghost.

Ellen poured two cups of coffee, then stood up and stretched. She still had a dancer's figure, long and lean. She smiled down at Lavinia and Peter. "It's this old lady's bedtime. You two go out and enjoy the stars."

"But—" Lavinia reached for Ellen's hand, ready to blurt out her secret.

Ellen chuckled. "Now, now, sugar. Peter's gonna think you don't want to look at the stars with him, and that'll crush his poor heart."

Peter rolled his eyes. "You don't need to concern yourself with my heart, Miss Jones."

"Don't listen to him. He's got it bad for you. You can't hide that sort of thing from old ladies." She tapped the side of her nose. "We can smell romance."

"For heaven's sake, Grandma!"

Ellen kissed Peter's cheek and squeezed Lavinia's shoulder. "You're welcome to come again for dinner next week, sugar."

"Thank you," Lavinia managed. Ellen vanished into her bedroom. Lavinia stared at the closed door and blinked back frustrated tears.

"Hey, now. What's wrong?" Peter asked, his voice gentle. "Looking at the stars with me isn't that terrible of a thought, is it?"

The pain in his voice pierced her heart, and Lavinia shook her head. "Oh, Peter, no! That's not it at all. Any girl would be happy to look at the stars with you."

"Ah, so it's the coffee, then."

Lavinia laughed. It hurt her chest.

Peter took a step closer to her and took her hand. "You have a pretty laugh. You should do it more often."

His fingers were so warm, and he smelled so nice. He traced her cheek, and a shiver raced through her whole body.

One corner of his mouth twitched up into a tentative smile.

Lavinia wanted him to kiss her. His grandfather hadn't chosen her, but maybe he would. He wasn't a dancer, but he was fascinating. And he was alive. She was tired of being alone. She closed her eyes.

His lips brushed hers, and she melted into his arms. She felt like she did when she danced, like she was flying, like the universe was singing through her.

She opened her eyes and met his eyes—eyes that were just like his grandfather's—and crashed. Guilt churned in her stomach. "I—I have to go." She turned from him and fled into the night.

Lavinia paced back and forth outside the library. She needed to tell Peter about the ghost. She needed him to understand. And she needed him to convince his grandmother to come to her studio.

She didn't want him to think that she was crazy.

What if she was crazy? What if the whole experience was one long hallucination? She almost left, but she remembered the pleading look in her ghost's eyes and the feel of Peter's lips against hers.

She took a deep breath and walked inside.

Peter sat at the circulation desk. His smile looked forced. "Miss Jones! Good to see you again. I was worried that I'd scared you off."

Lavinia's stomach twisted. "Peter, I have a confession to make."

Peter's fake smile faded. "A confession?"

"When I saw you at my performance last week—"

"My grandma wanted to watch you dance," Peter interrupted. "She had the tickets before we met, I swear."

Lavinia shook her head. "Your grandmother sold me her terpsitone."

"She told me that."

"The terpsitone is haunted."

"Haunted?" Peter scoffed. "You're trying to tell me that my grandma's terpsitone is haunted? What, do you want your money back?"

"No, I don't want my money back! I'd happily keep my terpsitone, and my ghost too! But he's not happy, and he's your grandfather."

"My grandpa? That's impossible. He died thirty years ago, in The Great War. I'm sure grandma would've noticed if his ghost came home."

"Did she ever dance on the terpsitone after he died?" Lavinia asked.

Peter blinked. "I—I don't know."

"You could come see him. Please. He wants to see your grandmother. I think—I think that's what he's waiting for."

"I can't think of any reason why you'd make up a story like this."

"I'm not making it up! Please, Peter." Lavinia blinked back tears. "Please, I need you to trust me."

He sighed, but nodded slowly. "I suppose it can't hurt to go and see."

"Thank you," Lavinia said. "I'll be home all day tomorrow."

"Lavinia, it took my grandma a long time to get used to the idea that he was gone. If you hurt her, I'll never forgive you." Peter's voice was as cold as his grandfather's ghostly touch, and Lavinia shivered.

"I swear, I'm telling you the truth."

"We'll see."

Peter took his grandmother's coat. He looked suspicious. Ellen looked nervous. Their eyes flicked over Lavinia's studio, and she winced. Peter's eyes rested on her nest of blankets, and she wanted to sink into the floor. The rose that they'd given her was wilting in a coffee cup on her windowsill. It was the only bright color in the room.

"Let's see this ghost of yours," Peter said.

Lavinia met Ellen's eyes and smiled at her. She didn't know what to say. She couldn't look at Peter. She switched the terpsitone on, and her ghost materialized.

Peter gaped, and his grandmother took a startled step forward. Her look of joy mirrored the ghost's. "Jonathon!"

"He doesn't speak," Lavinia said. "But he can dance."

Jonathon held his hand out to Ellen, and Lavinia squeezed Ellen's fingers. "He wants to dance with you."

Ellen trembled as Lavinia pulled her toward the stage. "I haven't stepped on a terpsitone since Jonathon died. I couldn't even bear to look at this one."

"Don't worry. He's a strong partner," Lavinia said.

Ellen smiled. "He always was."

Years seemed to melt off of her as she and Jonathon danced. Their song was bittersweet, filled with longing and love. As the last note lingered in the air, the ghost lowered his lips to hers and vanished.

Lavinia reached for Peter's hand, and his fingers closed around hers.

PROTECTION FROM THE DARKNESS

Originally appeared in *Triangulation: Morning After*

Tommy found Scraps at the bottom of a pile of frozen kittens. We heard him mewing under the porch, and Tommy slipped underneath the worn boards and pulled out the whole sad heap.

I started crying when I saw them. They had huddled under our porch and piled together for warmth, and only the kitten in the middle had survived the night. If we'd heard them the night before, maybe we could have saved all of them.

Tommy peeled away twisted, frozen bodies until our kitten poked his tiny face out. His eyes were glued closed by thick yellow puss, and his orange and black fur stuck to his skin in matted patches.

"Mom!" I shouted. "Come here!"

Our mother peered out through the screen door, her thin face shadowed by her dark tangled hair. "What is it, Dolly?"

"I found a kitten!" Tommy said, holding up the tiny body that nestled in his cupped hands. "His name is Scraps."

Our mother pressed a palm against the screen. For a second I thought she was going to come out. She hadn't come outside since Dad died. She pulled her hand back. "Bring him in."

Tommy scrambled inside, and I gathered up the other kittens to bury in the back yard. I couldn't get the shovel into the frozen ground, so I buried the kittens in a snowdrift. The coyotes would probably get them, but at least I'd tried.

I made breakfast while Tommy and Mom tended to Scraps. I made tea with bags I'd already used three times, spread butter and jam over burnt toast, and scraped underdone oatmeal into almost-clean bowls. I wanted to be better at cooking, but Mom wouldn't teach me.

I heated up the last of the milk for Scraps. I took trays into the spare bedroom, where Mom was singing one of her weird songs over Scraps' tiny body.

Tommy was clutching Mom's hand and staring, his blue eyes almost as wide as the teacups that clattered in their saucers when I set them down on the bed. The song sounded like the same one she'd sung when

133

Tommy fell down the stairs and scraped his knee. I'd seen Tommy's knee get better, but the song didn't seem to be working on Scraps. He flinched away from Mom and tried to hiss.

I was glad. Mom's magic made my skin crawl. It used to be okay. But since Dad died, it had gotten all dark and twisted.

I took Scraps from her and washed him with a warm cloth while Mom and Tommy ate their toast. The kitten's eyes cracked open, and he stared up at me. One of his eyes was dark green, and the other was deep gold. They seemed too bright and wise and deep for kitten eyes. He grabbed my index finger in his toothless mouth, and my heart melted. When he let me go, I dipped my finger in the saucer of warm milk and dripped some onto his pink tongue. When Mom offered to take him back so I could eat, I just shook my head and kept dripping milk into Scraps' mouth.

I hadn't saved his brothers and sisters, but maybe I could help him.

•

He was Tommy's kitten. Tommy found him, after all. As soon as he was healthy enough to get around, Scraps started following Tommy around all day. They kept each other out of trouble. Scraps avoided Mom, so Tommy started avoiding her, too.

At night, Scraps came to my bedroom, and he'd stay with me till dawn. He hated the night. I think it reminded him of the cold and how his brothers and sisters had all died around him while he survived. Even though Scraps loved Tommy, he didn't trust him to protect him from the darkness. That was my job.

I was glad to do it. And sometimes, when I had a nightmare, Scraps would curl on my chest and purr so hard he woke me up. It was like he was protecting me, too.

It was nice to feel protected.

The winter wore on, and Mom slipped farther and farther away. She would go days without saying a single real word. She stopped eating. She still muttered in her weird not-language, still sang creepy songs, but she'd turn her too-thin face away from me when I'd ask her if I should go to the store and buy more milk.

When she didn't get out of bed, I had to go up to her room. I hated her room. Dark spider webs clung in the corners, heavy curtains covered the windows, and the close, musty air smelled like dust and lavender.

It made me sleepy, and I was afraid to sleep in Mom's room.

I pressed a mug of honeyed tea into her hand, and she stared at me with eyes that were almost black. Her eyes scared me. They'd been blue before Dad died. Before her magic had spiraled out of her control. "Who are you?" she whispered. "Where's my husband?" I blinked back my tears and told her to drink her tea.

We started to get letters from the school about me and Tommy not coming anymore. I wrote back that we were very ill and forged my mother's signature. I didn't know what else to do. I couldn't leave her alone, and I couldn't trust Tommy to keep his mouth shut at school. He thought Mom's going crazy was cool. He liked her weird songs and her words that didn't make sense but sounded like the summer wind.

Sometimes I liked them too, and that scared me even more than Mom's eyes did. Anytime I caught myself listening, maybe understanding, I'd grab Scraps and drag him and Tommy out to make snow angels.

Our yard was covered with angels.

•

The school sent a man to check on us. He was tall and thin and he carried a briefcase. Mom heard his car turn into our drive, and she actually got out of bed to answer the door.

For a minute, I thought maybe things would be okay.

But when she saw the man on our porch, she cried out in joy. "Henry!"

When my mother's hand touched his arm, the man's eyes turned black, and his face changed. His pinched, cold expression broadened and warmed. My mother was right. Somehow, this man was my father. Or she'd put something that looked like my father inside of him. He swept my mother up in his arms and twirled her around.

She laughed and kissed him. "I missed you so much. Promise to never leave me again."

"I promise," he said with my father's voice.

"Tommy, your father is home!" Mom called. "Come down and give him a hug!"

Tommy barreled down the stairs with Scraps at his heels. The kitten froze in the doorway. Tommy flung himself into the man's arms. "I knew you'd come back!" Tommy cried.

The stranger smiled at me over Tommy's head. "I'd like to hug you too, Dolly."

I wanted to go to him, to feel his arms around me. I'd always felt safe in my father's embrace. Instead, I knelt and scooped Scraps into my arms. He buried his face against my neck, and I knew that what my mother was doing was wrong. "Shhh, it's okay, Scraps," I whispered.

"Dolly." My father's voice brought tears to my eyes, but I refused to look at him. I was afraid that if I looked at him, I'd start to believe that he really was my father, and not some stranger with a briefcase that my mother was doing something horrible to. "It's okay, Peanut," he said. No one had called me that since he died.

"Mom, you can't do this," I said. "I—I won't let you."

Black eyes bored into me. "Don't be silly, Dolly. Give your father a hug," she commanded.

One of my feet moved forward on its own. I imagined her magicking up another Dolly and putting her in my body. A happy, hugging, fake Dolly.

My other foot moved toward the man who wasn't my father.

I looked down at Scraps. "Help me," I whispered with a wobbly voice that didn't want to obey me.

Scraps looked back up at me. One of my tears rolled down my cheek and plopped onto his forehead, and he blinked his mismatched eyes. He nipped my finger, and my feet stopped moving. The man in the doorway didn't look like my father anymore.

We were both immune to her magic, now.

Scraps twisted himself out of my arms. He puffed up and hissed, then launched himself at the man who thought he was my father.

The man backed away a step, and my mother started to wail. The sound was inhuman and horrible. Tommy covered his ears and started crying.

Scraps drove the man back another step, and he was out the door.

When his foot hit the porch, the blackness faded from his eyes, and his face lost all traces of my father. He stared at the kitten for a moment, then collapsed.

My mother was still screaming, and she launched herself at Scraps. "No! I can't lose him again!"

Her emaciated arms stretched, and her face twisted into something inhuman. Her fingernails glistened like talons. I threw myself in front of her.

It was my job to protect Scraps from the darkness.

My mother's nails raked across my cheek. The cuts burned, and I cried out in pain. Scraps darted between my ankles and sprang at my mother. He sank his teeth into her leg and clung there.

Her screams changed in pitch, and she kicked Scraps off. Hard. He flew across the room, but Tommy caught him.

Maybe, since Scraps bit her, Mom would be immune now, too. Maybe she could come back. I stepped toward her. She raised her hand to hit me again, but slowly, like she was underwater. Recognition and confusion flittered across her face. Her scream wavered. I rushed in and wrapped my arms around her. She tried to pull away, but I wouldn't let her.

Eventually, the anger in her voice transformed to sadness. She slumped back in my arms, and her eyes swirled blue and black.

I draped her on the couch and held her hand. The black took a long time to fade.

Finally, my mother stared at me through the bright blue eyes that I remembered. "Dolly?" She touched the cuts on my cheek, and I winced away. "Did I—what did I do?"

I squeezed her hand. "It's over now."

She fainted. Scraps scrambled out of Tommy's grip. Tommy looked up at me. "Daddy's gone for good now, isn't he?"

I nodded. "I'm sorry, Tommy."

Tommy sniffled and hugged Scraps. "Is Mommy going to be normal again?"

"I hope so."

Tommy stared at the unconscious stranger on our porch. "I hope so, too."

I emptied the stranger's wallet and sent Tommy to the store for more tea and fresh milk. I figured my mother and the man from the school would want something warm when they woke up.

CHRISTMAS LIGHTS

Originally appeared in *Cast of Wonders*

Jenna stared out the car window and watched snowflakes cling to the glass. They glistened like tiny strings of Christmas lights. She wished she could be like them, bright and beautiful and free.

"I think we're lost," her mother said.

Jenna had felt lost since they pulled out of the driveway, leaving Grandma and Grandpa's warm house filled with presents and cookies. She didn't answer.

"Is this the silent treatment?" her mother asked.

Jenna shrugged.

"I just couldn't be there," her mother said. "With all the lights and forced smiles. She even made his favorite cookies."

The catch in her voice would have made Jenna feel guilty if wasn't so common. "You could have left me," Jenna said.

"That's not fair. No one wants to be alone on Christmas."

Jenna sighed. She wanted to spend Christmas with a tree and music and lights. Home was dark and cold.

Jenna spotted a sign. *Christmas Trees. Entrance Ahead.* Christmas carols drifted in the wind. "Let's stop there."

Her mother sighed and pulled into the dirt entrance. "We're just getting directions, not getting a Christmas tree. I don't want a tree, you know that."

Jenna crossed her arms tight over her chest. She knew. Just like she knew that what she wanted didn't matter.

"You folks looking for a tree?" a man in orange overalls asked.

"We just need directions," Jenna's mother said, her voice tight and cold.

Jenna hopped out of the car. "I want to look at the trees."

"Jenna, get back in the car."

"She'll be fine." He winked at Jenna. "These trees can grant wishes. You just wander till you find one that feels right," the tree-man said. He turned to her mother. "Where're you heading?

139

Show crunched under Jenna's boots. It collected on her eyelashes and reflected invisible colored lights. She wandered, looking at the trees.

Her mother hated Christmas, and Jenna understood. Or at least she tried. Losing Uncle Mark hadn't been that big of a deal for her—she'd only met him once—and last year was a long time ago. But her mother had loved him. Jenna just wished that she'd act like she loved her, too.

The air smelled like pine, but she caught a hint of Grandma's orange spice cookies.

She wasn't cold, not even when the wind blew snow into a glowing whirlwind that whipped her scarf away. It fluttered in the air, then drifted onto a tree.

As soon as Jenna saw it, she loved it. It was tall and green and perfectly shaped, with dark flat needles. "I wish I could take you home with me," she whispered.

All of her wishes curled together in the center of her chest. She just wanted to belong somewhere, just wanted to be important.

Uncle Mark's favorite cookies—the orange spice—were Jenna's favorite, too. She wondered why her mother never remembered that.

Her fingers glowed as she reached toward the tree, and the smell of cookies curled around her. When her bare fingers touched the cold needles, she exploded into a thousand tiny lights. She settled into the branches and clung like the trapped snowflakes. She was part of the tree. Part of a perfect Christmas. She could hear the carols clearly, now.

Her mother wandered by. "I don't really have space for a tree," she said. She shook her head. "Was I looking for something else?"

"Just directions," the tree-man said.

She pulled Jenna's scarf from her tree. After a moment, she wrapped it around her neck and walked away. "Thanks again. I should get back to my folks—I don't want to be alone on Christmas."

FOAM AND YELLOW SAND

Originally appeared in *Penumbra*

Wet, gritty sand caked under Ellen's fingernails and the surf tugged at her ankles as she dragged herself out of the water. Fragmented memories cascaded through her mind. Where was she? Why had she been in the ocean?

Where was Nick?

She raised her head and stared out at the endless blue expanse, and terror tugged at her belly. She remembered salty water filling her mouth, burning down into her lungs, its heavy resistance hampering every movement.

A foam-topped wave rolled in, and the spray misted her skin.

She scrambled away from the water, over the hot yellow sand. Her rubbery, weak legs protested, but she ignored them.

The wind caught the sound of voices, and she turned toward them.

"I now pronounce you man and wife. You may kiss your bride."

Then a familiar voice, "Who's that?"

Shouts, and the sound of running feet. "The poor thing's stark naked!" Faces swam around her, and hot hands wrapped around her arms. "And freezing!"

"Give me your coat, sweetheart." A woman in a white dress pushed forward and wrapped a black jacket around Ellen's shoulders.

Ellen clung to the woman as the scent of Nick's aftershave tugged at her mind like an undertow. The woman in white was solid and warm—she was the only one who seemed real. "Help me," Ellen whispered. Her voice vanished into the burble around them, and the sound of the surf threatened to consume her.

"You poor thing. Of course we'll help you. Let's get you inside," the woman said.

"Stop!" That familiar voice again. A woman.

"Grace?" Ellen tried to focus. The world swam around her, then her mother-in-law grabbed her shoulders.

Grace's hands were ice cold, even through the jacket, and the world solidified around them. "Oh my god," she shouted, "It's Ellen!"

The woman in white froze. "That's not possible."

"I swear, it's her! Nick! Nick, come look!"

Ellen blinked. Nick was here?

The crowd parted, and Ellen stared at her husband. Unfamiliar wrinkles crinkled the skin around his eyes, and silver strands shot through his black hair.

A wave of possessive yearning filled her. She pulled away from Grace and stumbled toward him.

He caught her. She buried her face in his chest, and his heartbeat drowned out the sound of the waves. "What's going on?" Ellen asked.

"You—you've been missing for five years. I thought—everyone thought you'd drowned."

Memories of blue-tinged blackness bubbled in the back of her mind, but she forced them down.

"Come on, we should get her inside," the woman in white said. "We can sort everything out later."

"Hold on to me, darling," Nick whispered, then picked her up. She breathed him in. He was warm and solid. Real, and hers.

She tried not to see the pain on the woman in white's face, tried not to recognize the wedding dress or notice the fact that Nick was missing the jacket to match his black tuxedo pants.

She clung to Nick, and the feeling of his arms around her was enough.

●

Nick carried her to Grace's suite and set her gently on the bed. He touched her cheek. "I can't believe you're real," he whispered.

"You should go talk to Bianca," Grace said. "I'll stay with Ellen."

Ellen didn't want to stay with Grace—she didn't want to let Nick out of her sight. She clung to his hands.

"Let him go, Ellen. He'll be right back."

Ellen's fingers relaxed, and Nick pulled away. He kissed her forehead.

Ellen stared down at her traitorous hands. What was going on? She pulled the tuxedo jacket tight and wished for a robe.

Grace sat next to Ellen, overwhelming her with the scents of baby powder and fresh perm. "I'm sure you've realized what's going on."

"I interrupted Nick's wedding."

"Yes."

The confirmation was a punch to her stomach.

Grace patted her shoulder. "Don't worry, dear. It's not too late to fix it. Nick loves you more than anything, and I'm sure you'll be able to win him back."

"Yes. I—I have to win him back." Nothing else mattered but Nick.

"Come, dear. Let's get you dressed. You'll need to look your best." She pulled one of Ellen's dresses out of her suitcase. The floaty blue one—Nick's favorite. "This should do nicely, don't you think?"

Ellen ran a finger along the soft, cedar-scented cotton. "Why do you have this?"

"That doesn't matter. Why don't you get a shower, then get yourself made up? I'll lay this out for you."

"It does matter. What's going on, Grace?"

"If you want to win Nick back, you're going to have to trust me, Ellen."

Ellen didn't trust her. "Tell me what's going on."

"You've been gone for years. Things have changed. Nick has changed. Without me, Bianca might be able to take him away from you. You don't want that, do you?"

"I—I don't." She couldn't imagine living without Nick.

"Go get a shower."

●

Ellen dried and curled her hair. The cosmetics spread on the sink matched her complexion, and wouldn't have worked at all on Grace. The powder made her sneeze, and the lipstick was heavy and greasy.

Grace dressed her like a doll, then led her down to dinner.

Nick and Bianca sat together at a long table. The other guests were scattered around small round tables. Soft candlelight filled the room, and a string quartet played softly in a corner.

"This should be their wedding reception," Ellen said, pausing in the doorway. Doubts and questions swam in her mind. How had she missed five years? Why didn't she remember anything? What were the odds of her washing to shore here, at the very moment of Nick's wedding?

Grace squeezed her arm with fingers like icy bones. "They shouldn't be having a wedding reception. Come on, dear."

The command pulled her forward and drowned her thoughts.

Nick stood up and hurried over to them. "You—you look amazing. It's like you stepped right out of my dreams." He took her arm and led her to a seat next to Bianca, who'd changed out of her wedding dress. She looked up at Ellen and Nick, then quickly away.

"So, Ellen, where have you been for the past five years?" Bianca asked.

Grace and Nick both glared at her. "Now's not the time," Nick whispered.

"I—I don't know where I've been." Memories sparked like sunlight on waves. "I remember the plane. The noise it made as we fell and the pilot repeating over and over again to remain calm—then after we crashed, the way the water rushed into the cabin, all white peaks and foam. We all scrambled for the rafts—I remember holding Nick's hand, but there was so much water—" She remembered the salty tang of it in her mouth, remembered the moment that his hand pulled out of hers—she shook her head.

"It doesn't matter now," Nick said. "We're all just glad that you're alive."

Waiters brought them each a salad. Ellen wasn't hungry. She couldn't remember what hunger felt like.

"I thought about calling your mother, but then I thought it might be better if you do that yourself," Nick said. "She's living in a new place now—a little bungalow in the country. I think you'll like it."

Ellen struggled to remember her mother's face, but the image was like a sand castle in the surf—soft at the edges and collapsing.

Nick took a bite of his salad and gave Bianca a pleading look. Ellen recognized that look—it was the one he used to give her when he couldn't think of anything to say.

Bianca closed her eyes. "What are you going to do, now that you're back?" she asked, her voice brittle with false friendliness. "Nick told me that you used to paint."

"I—I did." She remembered the scrape of the brush against canvas, capturing the fall of sunlight on bare skin.

"And I'm sure you'll want to catch up with your friends and family and everything."

"Nick is her family," Grace snapped.

Ellen tried to think of the names of old friends, or feel a desire to paint, or remember the things she'd wanted other than Nick. The memories were there—distant and muted and faded, like old videos played on a black and white TV—but she couldn't feel anything.

She looked at Nick. He was her anchor, her one thing that mattered.

But what she felt for him wasn't love. It was ownership. And that possessive, greedy need made it hard to catch even the wispy memories of her feelings from before.

"She's going to have a rough time settling back into her life, and she needs someone to take care of her," Grace said.

"Mother's right," Nick said. "She is going to need someone, and I am her family."

Bianca stood up. Her chair clattered to the floor, and the quartet stopped playing. Everyone froze.

The sound of the ocean filled the silence, and terror crept along Ellen's skin.

"I'm sorry. I can't do this," Bianca said. "I—I just can't." She ran from the room, and Ellen was grateful for the noise of her shoes against the marble floor.

Nick took Ellen's hand. "I'm so sorry about all of this, darling. But don't worry, I'll set it right. Everything will be just like before. You'll see."

Grace smiled at Bianca's fleeing back.

•

The waiters kept bringing food, and Ellen pushed it around her plate. "Would you like something else?" Nick asked.

Ellen shook her head. "I'm not hungry."

"I have to run to the bathroom. I'll be right back."

He kissed her cheek before he walked away. His absence ached.

Grace ran a cold finger along Ellen's cheek. "I knew you were the key to getting rid of her."

"What have you done to me?" Ellen asked. "Why don't I care about anything other than Nick?"

"What else should you care about? He is your husband."

"I remember caring about other things."

Grace sighed. "His is the one thing in the world that you want, and he's yours for the taking. Don't be a fool."

Nick slid back into his seat. "How are my two favorite ladies?"

"I think Ellen looks a bit tired, don't you?" Grace asked. "You'd better get her to bed."

•

Nick led Ellen to the honeymoon suite. Bianca's things were still inside, and he ran around, stuffing clothes into her suitcase while Ellen stood in the doorway. His hands hovered over the crumpled wedding dress, and he stopped. He pushed his fingers through his hair, and Ellen caught a glimpse of his confusion and pain. "Why don't you go freshen up, and I'll deal with all this?"

Ellen nodded and went to the bathroom and locked the door behind her.

She stared at her reflection. Pushed her hair back and bared her teeth and stuck her tongue out. She still had the scar on her cheek from when she fell off her bike as a kid. Her eyes were still just the same shade.

She didn't have any extra wrinkles or gray hairs.

Bianca's toiletries were lined neatly on the sink—her toothbrush and hairbrush and curling iron and a whole bag of make up. Ellen flicked the curling iron on. The metal ticked as it heated.

The plastic handle felt fake—like a thing in a dream. Ellen pressed the curling iron into her forearm. The hot metal hissed against her skin.

The skin around the curling iron dried and cracked, then a rivulet of yellow sand tumbled down over her wrist and into the sink. Foamy seawater started to bubble up from the wound.

She pulled the curling iron away. The gash looked like a hole in the sand. Its edges crumbled.

It was a relief to see proof of what she felt inside.

Proof that she was dead.

Proof that she was a monster.

She looked out the window, at the moonlight on the ocean. It was beautiful, and it filled her with terror.

She didn't want to live, caring only about possessing one other person. She didn't want to be Grace's tool. She wanted to want to call her mother or paint or watch the sunrise over the ocean.

But she only wanted one thing, and it was so hard to fight against that feeling.

She turned on the shower and climbed out the window. The fall didn't even hurt.

"Oh my god, are you all right?" Bianca rushed out of the shadows, then froze when she saw Ellen's face. "Ellen?" Bianca's eyes were red and her skin blotchy from crying, even in the weak light that spilled out of the hotel lobby.

"Promise me that you love him," Ellen said.

"I—I promise," Bianca held out her hand. "What's going on? Are—are you okay?"

Ellen shook her head. "No. But you can be. I—I think I can fix it. I shouldn't be here, Bianca. I'm sorry that I ruined your wedding day."

She ran toward the ocean. Bianca screamed her name, but Ellen couldn't stop. She wouldn't have the courage to start again. Her feet splashed into the surf and dissolved. She fell forward, and water filled her mouth.

It didn't taste like anything.

SILENT COMMANDS

Original to this Collection

Shandra squeezed through the loose boards beneath the basement stairs and hugged her knees to her chest. She slowed her breathing and hoped that the thunder of her heart wouldn't give her away.

"Come on, sweetie. It's time to go." Her mother clomped down the steps and gray dust settled in Shandra's dark hair. "I know you're down here."

Shandra held her breath as her mother strode back and forth. The basement was empty—the movers had taken all the familiar mildewed boxes and loaded them into a huge yellow truck.

Her mother sighed. "This isn't cute anymore, Shandra. Come here, right now."

Shandra's toes twitched, ready to obey the command in her mother's voice, but she managed to hold the rest of her body still.

"Have you found her?" her father called down the stairs.

"I don't see her."

"Maybe she's not down there."

"I swear I saw her come down here."

"We need to be leaving right now," her father snapped. "If we don't, we're going to get caught in rush hour traffic."

"Do you think I don't know that?"

"Leave me," Shandra commanded. Her voice, as always, made no sound. "Forget me."

"Are you done down there?" her father called.

Her mother stopped on the steps, her feet right above Shandra's head. "I just feel like I'm forgetting something."

"The movers already took anything important."

"You're right. Let's go."

•

Shandra sagged in relief as the sound of their footsteps faded. She grinned when their ancient sedan coughed to life. She wriggled back out into the basement and danced across the cold cement. The house was hers! She could stay! Stay in the dark and be alone forever! No demanding voices, no confused and hurt faces, no need to stand in the burning sun. Her silent laughter echoed from the rough, mildewed walls.

Then a car door slammed, and the unwelcome sound of running feet interrupted her celebration. She sprinted back toward the loose board.

But hands grabbed her even as her fingers brushed the cracked wood. "Oh my God, Shandra! I can't believe that we almost left you!" Her mother buried her face in her hair, and sneezed gray dust. "Oh honey, I'm so sorry."

Her mother carried her up the stairs, and silent tears slipped down Shandra's cheeks. Her father kissed them away. "We're both sorry, honey. We'll stop and get ice cream to make it up to you, okay?"

Shandra reached for the door frame, the doorknob, anything, but her arms were too short, her grip too weak. Nothing she did slowed her mother's inexorable stride.

Shandra wished she could scream.

They buckled her into the backseat so tightly that she couldn't even turn to watch her home vanish behind them. Morning sunshine stabbed her eyes.

Her father bought her a chocolate ice cream cone, and she ate it. She wished she understood why the command had failed. Eventually, her fingers sticky and her stomach aching, she slept.

•

They sent her to a special school with other children who couldn't talk. It was better than the old school, where everyone had screamed and chattered and giggled, but she didn't understand their hand talk, and didn't care to learn it. "I'm sure that head is just full of ideas you want to share," her pretty young teacher urged. "Signing will allow you to communicate, just like any other little girl."

Shandra frowned. She wasn't like any other little girl. She never would be, and she didn't want to try anymore. She'd already tried, and failed. Now wouldn't be any different. She just wanted her basement back.

The new house didn't even have a basement. Shandra dug a hole in the hard, hot dirt in the backyard. She dug till it was was deep enough to hide her from the sun, she huddled in it till her mother dragged her inside and plopped her into the bathtub.

Her mother's hands fluttered like clumsy birds as she spoke. "Did you have a good first day at school?"

Shandra recognized the hand talk for school, and realized that her mother was trying to sign along with her speech. She sighed silently, but responded in the hand talk with a simple, "No." It was one of the only ones that she'd bothered to learn.

But even that negative response thrilled her mother. Her face lit up like Shandra had given her a gift, and tears glittered in the corners of her eyes. "Honey, Shandra just answered my question!"

Her father poked his head into the bathroom. "Really?"

"I asked if she had a good day, and she said no."

"Oh. Well, I'm sorry you didn't have a good day, sweetie. First days are always hard."

"Remember to sign it," her mother said. She flapped her own hands. "I'm so proud of you, sweetie."

Shandra imagined a face in the white bubbles around her knees. She smashed it. She hated when they were sweet. It made her feel hollow and broken. "Go away," she commanded.

Her mother stood, and she and Shandra's father walked down the hall together. Shandra floated in the tub and imagined that it was an underground river. The water chilled around her, and the skin on her fingers and toes crinkled. She climbed out of the tub and into her bed, still wet and naked. Bubbles clung to her hair.

The moon shone bright and sliver outside her window. She glared at it, but didn't have the power to command it to leave.

·

The school did have a basement. She made the janitor give her a copy of the key, then hid there during gym class. She did not want to run in circles in the sun while sweat soaked into her hair and clothes.

She leaned back against the water heater and listened to the metal tick. The basement smelled like bleach and window cleaner, which wasn't right, but at least it was better than her sad little hole.

For a long time, she'd wished that she could be normal. She'd tried so hard. She'd stared into her reflection and commanded it every morning. Her mother deserved a daughter who loved her. She supposed that her father did, too. She'd tried to pretend, hoping that eventually she'd feel it out of habit, but it just made things worse. Instead of love, she started to feel resentment.

All she wanted was to stay in her basement. Alone in the musty dark. "Be my basement," she commanded the darkness around her, and for a second, it was. The familiar smell brought tears to her eyes.

Then the overhead light flicked on, and the pretty young teacher glared down at her, hands on her narrow hips. Then, her hands moved along with her voice effortlessly. "What are you doing down here, Shandra?"

Shandra didn't know the hand talk to answer her. She shrugged. She opened her mouth to command the teacher away.

"I don't think you appreciate how lucky you are," the teacher said. "There are lots of little girls out there who don't have two parents who love them, and even fewer have parents who'd be willing to uproot their whole lives so their daughter could have the best possible chance at learning."

Shandra blinked. They'd come here for her? They'd pulled her away from her home so that she could come here and learn to talk with her fingers? No wonder she hadn't been able to make them forget her. The idiocy of it made her eyes sting.

"Oh, don't cry!" The teacher ran forward and wrapped her arms around her. "It'll be okay. I promise. I know it's hard at first, but you'll pick it up. Just remember how lucky you are. Your parents love you, and you're able to hear. Lots of other kids here don't have either of those advantages."

Shandra listened to the teacher's heartbeat and decided that she'd learn the hand talk, after all.

•

Shandra watched the other children and tried to learn which ones didn't have parents. It was hard—she could only give commands, not ask questions, and she still couldn't follow their rapid hand talk. And none of them wanted to be her friend—they could all sense the difference in her. But she learned. And as she did, her parents did, too.

And eventually, she found a girl with no parents. She was close to Shandra's age. Her hair was blonde to Shandra's black, but they were close enough in size and height. The other girl's feet were a bit small—Shandra's shoes would rub, but she figured the rest of her clothes should fit.

The girl laughed with her friends but couldn't talk. She was deaf and had been at the school for years. Shandra followed her home one night.

Her house was filled with people, but none of them signed when they spoke. The other girl drifted through her evening in silence. She ate with her head down then went to her room to read and work on homework. The others piled into a room around a television, but didn't even bother to turn on the closed captioning.

The next day, Shandra approached the other girl at recess. "Come with me," she commanded. Her fingers flickered along.

The girl followed without question, which was a relief. She hadn't commanded anyone who couldn't hear before, and she needed it to work for what she had planned.

They went to the basement. "Why are we here?" the other girl asked with her fingers, looking around in alarm. "Why did I follow you? Are we allowed to be here?"

Shandra cupped the girl's face between her hands and looked deep into her eyes. This command was big—bigger than any she'd tried before. "Be Shandra." She imagined the Shandra that she wished she could be. Loving and sweet and happy. Responsible and hardworking and studious. The Shandra her mother deserved. A Shandra who could be happy living in a house without a basement.

The girl blinked. Confusion flickered across her face. She opened her mouth, but no sound came out.

"Be Shandra," not-Shandra-anymore repeated.

New Shandra blinked again, then looked around the basement. "Who are you?" her fingers asked. "What are we doing here?"

"It doesn't matter," not-Shandra signed.

New Shandra rubbed her head. "I feel strange."

"It will pass."

"If you say so. I should go. I have class."

Not-Shandra just nodded, then curled up in the corner and slept.

•

She woke in the darkness, then padded out into the night. She crept along the streets to Shandra's house. The moon lurked over her shoulder, mocking her with its sickle smile.

Had her command reached her parents? Had they accepted new Shandra as their daughter? She peeked into the rooms and saw them all sleeping. New Shandra was a blonde lump on her blue pillow. The moonlight glinted on her hair.

Not-Shandra waited by the open window till morning, when not-her-mother came in to shake Shandra awake. "Morning, sleepyhead," she said, kissing Shandra's forehead.

New Shandra smiled at her and sat up. Her hands raced so fast not-Shandra could hardly follow them. "Good morning, Mom! What's for breakfast? What are we doing today? I love you!"

Tears of joy flowed down Shandra's mother's cheeks. "Honey! Shandra just said she loves me!" Her fingers spelled the words, as natural a habit as breathing.

Her father poked his head in. "Really?" he both said and signed.

"I love you, too, Daddy," Shandra said.

Not-Shandra had never seen that look on his face before. "Let's go get ice cream," he said.

"Right now?" her mother asked.

"Yeah."

"Yay! Ice cream for breakfast!" Shandra signed.

Not-Shandra examined the feeling in her chest and realized that it was pride. She'd fixed things for everyone. She'd finally done something completely right. She grinned and walked to the hole in the backyard. "Take me back home," she told it.

Then she opened a door in the earth and passed through it. She danced around her basement and laughed.

UNHAPPINESS IN HEAVEN

Originally appeared in *Roar and Thunder*

Harlan folded his suit jacket and draped it over the kitchen chair. The table was covered with sympathy casseroles, and the stack of unread Hallmark cards teetered on the counter.

He poured himself a scotch and pulled his hunting rifle out of the gun cabinet. The worn stock felt good in his hands. Smooth. Familiar. It reminded him of countless trips with his dad, hunting pheasants and ducks and rabbits.

He'd dreamed of taking his own kid hunting. But that'd never happen, now.

An unfamiliar voice broke into his thoughts. "That's not the best thing to kill yourself with."

A white man leaned against the doorframe between the kitchen and the living room. The summer sun from the windows behind him threw his whole body into shadow.

Harlan hadn't heard anyone come in. And he'd locked the door behind him. "Who the hell are you?"

The stranger laughed. "Fair question." There was something odd about his voice, aside from the accent that marked him clearly as not-from-around-here. If Harlan had to guess, he'd peg him as from New England. "I'm the devil."

Harlan snorted. "Sure." The guy was probably high.

Then the devil stepped into the room, and Harlan saw his face. And he believed. No mortal man looked like that. Golden eyes bored into his. "Also known as Lucifer. Angel of the Morning Star. You can call me Lou if you'd like."

Harlan pulled the rifle to his shoulder. It probably wouldn't do much good, but it made him feel better. "Get outta my house."

The devil smirked and took a few steps forward. "That's no way to treat a guest. Where's your southern hospitality, Harlan?"

"You ain't no guest of mine."

"Aren't I?"

"I didn't invite you in, didn't wish for your company. I had other business on my mind."

The devil picked up Harlan's scotch, sniffed it, and winced. "How can you possibly drink this?"

"The same way I drink anything else," Harlan snapped.

The devil laughed again. Harlan heard a tinny sound, like distant, broken bells in it. "See, this is why I'm here. You don't want to kill yourself. You're too good for that."

"That don't mean much, coming from you."

The devil downed Harlan's scotch. "Not true. Who else could actually offer you what you need?"

"And what's it I need?" Harlan asked.

"Companionship. You don't want to be alone. Your wife's dead, after all. And the baby with her."

"I hadn't forgotten," Harlan growled.

"Oh, but you did. For an instant, at least. I'm very distracting. And I can help you forget again."

Harlan lowered the gun. "Why don't you want me to kill myself? Won't I end up in hell if I do?"

The devil shrugged. "Hell's full of people. We're won't miss one more."

"How exactly are you gonna help me forget?"

The devil's smirk stretched to a leer. "Oh, I have a million ways."

Harlan's skin crawled. "Not interested."

"You want a child," the devil said. "Someone to love, to teach, to share your life with now that your wife is gone."

A spark of interest pulled at Harlan's heart. "So?"

The devil shrugged. "I can give you that."

"What's your price? My soul?"

The devil sighed. "Everyone's so obsessed with souls. No. I'll give you your son, but I want your heart."

"My heart? Will you cut it out and keep it in a box? Like in some horror movie?"

The devil shook his head. "No. You'll give me your heart, and you'll love me."

"Hell no."

"Why not? You'll still be able to love other things. Hunting. Football. Your son. Before I came in, you were planning on shooting yourself, Harlan. Is loving me really worse?"

"You're the devil."

The devil shrugged. "And you'll always remember that. But it won't matter to you."

Harlan couldn't imagine that not mattering. "If I give you my heart, what happens when I die?"

The devil shrugged. "That depends on you."

"What's the catch?"

The devil shrugged. "There's no catch."

"They don't call it a 'deal with the devil' for nothing. There's gotta be a catch."

The devil shrugged. "If you go to heaven, a tiny part of you will still miss me."

"You wanna to use me to corrupt heaven?" Harlan asked.

The devil shook his head. "I just like to remind Him that I'm here, sometimes. That it's possible to love me. It's between me and Him. It won't affect you."

"Except I'll be in heaven and sad forever."

"Or you could end up in hell with me," the devil said.

"Or you could get outta my house."

"The boy will have his mother's eyes," the devil said. "He'll be the son you would have had, miraculously saved from the accident. No one will remember anything different."

Harlan's wife had had the prettiest eyes. "Will giving you my heart hurt?"

"Of course it will. Love always does."

Harlan touched his chest. Love did always hurt. But if he loved the devil, he'd never lose him in a stupid car crash.

"I'll throw in a monthly supply of scotch. Good stuff, not the crap you're used to," the devil said.

Harlan nodded. "Okay. Okay. I'll do it."

The devil moved forward, till Harlan could feel the heat radiating off of his skin, like from the highway in the middle of summer. He smelled faintly of burning leaves, sulfur, and Harlan's cheap scotch. "Close your eyes," the devil whispered.

Harlan hesitated. He imagined taking his son hunting, teaching him how to shoot and track, taking him to boy scouts and high school football games.

He imagined an empty life, alone.

He closed his eyes.

The devil's lips burned against his. "I'll be back next month."

When he opened his eyes, Lou was gone. There was a new bottle of scotch on the table.

Harlan poured himself a scotch. It was better than any he'd ever tasted before. Harlan's chest ached. He missed Lou. But he'd be back in a month.

And there was a bassinette in the living room. Harlan walked over to it and picked up his son. The boy burbled in his sleep and nuzzled into Harlan's shoulder. He smelled like baby powder and clean skin.

It was worth a little unhappiness in heaven.

THE TRAVELING CAROUSEL

Originally appeared in *EGM Shorts*

Judy wandered through the park, past joggers and couples walking their dogs. Her back ached from sitting in her office chair all day, and she just wanted to go home. But Ken had his friends there, helping home move. Taking his half-packed boxes and all of their furniture and leaving the apartment something alien. She remembered how it had echoed when she first moved in.

She wandered into the trees. She tried to let the whisper of their leaves sooth her, but she'd never been one for the soothing power of nature. She glanced at her phone. No messages, and Ken would be another hour, at least. He'd promised to call when he was done, but he'd promised so many things. She kept walking.

Cheerful music floated on the breeze, and she followed it, weaving through tree trunks and hopping over a small stream. As she grew closer, she expected to find a crowd, but the woods remained deserted. She came into a clearing, and in the center stood a carousel. Bare green lightbulbs twinkled from its blue canopy, and chiming music chorused from its barrel organ. Fresh paint gleamed on the leaping horses and silver bars, and the body of the carousel was lined with bright mirrors.

It was perfect.

A tiny old woman smiled and waved her over. "Hello there, child. Would you like to ride the carousel?"

Her dark face was creased with smile lines, and she smelled like funnel cake and powdered sugar. Her eyes were the same green as the carousel lights.

Judy nodded—she loved carousels. "How much is it?"

"For you, just a smile."

"Oh," Judy said. "I'm not sure if I can manage that. It's been a bad day."

"That happens to the best of us. You can pay after, dear. Hop on."

There were no other riders and no reason for the carousel to be there, but Judy stepped up onto the platform anyway. If things could fall apart for no reason, then maybe she could just have this. Maybe there was a tiny bit of balance in the world.

The wood creaked beneath her feet. She wandered among the wooden mounts, trailing her fingers along slick paint. She chose a gray horse with purple flowers twined into its darker mane and tale. She swung herself onto its back and rested her cheek against the cool metal pole.

She closed her eyes and the carousel moved. Her horse leaped forward, up and down, and around in the neverending loop. The music surrounded her, twinkling note upon twinkling note.

She glanced into the mirror, and saw her reflection distorted by the curve of the carousel's body. The boots that she bought because Ken liked them, the jeans she wore because they'd been a gift from his mother. The purse that his sister had made.

She used to wear sandals and skirts and only carry what fit in her pockets.

She ran her fingers over her horse's painted neck and realized that she wouldn't have any trouble filling the space that Ken would leave behind.

Her horse slowed, then stopped. She dismounted. "Can I go again?" she asked.

"Of course."

She chose another horse, this one deep black with a red saddle and ribbons in his mane. She examined the blue sky painted on the canopy's underside. She reached out to touch the fluffy painted clouds, but never got quite close enough.

She rode until the green lights lit and fireflies flickered in the trees. She stepped off of the platform smiling.

"There now, that's better," the old woman said.

"Who are you?" Judy asked.

"Just a traveling carousel, dear."

"Will I be able to find you again?"

"If you need to. Just follow the music."

"I will. Thank you."

When Judy looked back, the carousel was gone. But if she listened, she could still hear twinkling notes on the breeze.

Judy went to her apartment, and set to making it a home.

THE IMMOBILE GOD OF SECRETS

Originally appeared in *Cast of Wonders*

Jun slogged through the rice paddy, muddy water swirling around her calves. She glanced behind her, checking again to make sure that Reiko and her friends hadn't chased her. The only figure in sight was a lone scarecrow, wearing a tattered yukata.

Jun bowed to it. "Thank you for your hospitality."

"You are welcome anytime."

Jun started back and almost fell. She looked around again, then walked around the scarecrow. Even the water was still—the only ripples were from her own passing. She remembered her manners and bowed again. "Thank you."

"If you would stay and keep me company, I will share a secret with you."

Jun's socks were soggy and the sun was sinking in the west. If she was late for dinner, her mother would worry. But she liked secrets, and she'd never met a talking scarecrow before. "I'll stay."

"Thank you. Tell me, child, what brings you to my field?"

"There is a girl at school who hates me. I ran away from her."

"You must have run very fast to find this place."

"I am fast. That's why she hates me—she used to be the fastest girl on the track team."

"Maybe she only chases you because she wants to catch up."

Jun remembered rocks whistling past her ears, and the sting of a stone clipping her calf. "I don't think that's the case."

"Maybe not."

"I don't know why it bothers her so much. She's better than me in every other way. She has tons of friends and is top in our class and her parents buy her anything she wants."

"I will tell you her secret, if you wish to know it."

Jun hoped she could use the secret to stop Reiko from tormenting her. "I do."

"Her parents do not love her, and she knows it."

"But they're her parents."

"Yes."

Jun frowned. She didn't want to feel sorry for Reiko. "How do you know that?"

"I know many things," the scarecrow said.

"Do you know about me?"

"Yes, I know everything about you, Shuuichi Jun. You love pork cutlets and math class and running makes you feel free. You want to take care of your mother and you worry about your grades, but have a hard time making yourself study."

"How do you know all that?"

"That is my secret, child."

"I need to get home—my mother will be worried."

"Yes. And she made you your favorite dinner."

"Will I be able to come back?" Jun asked.

"The future is always uncertain. But it would please me to see you again."

Jun bowed again. "Thank you for the secret." She walked back toward the path. When she turned around, the field was empty.

•

Jun had no idea how to use the scarecrow's secret. She couldn't imagine her parents not loving her. Had Reiko done something horrible? Or had they not wanted a daughter in the first place? If they didn't love her, why did they buy her so many presents?

Reiko glared at her during track practice, just like she always did. Then she and Reiko raced, just like they always did. The coach believed they pushed each other.

Jun won, like she always did. "Good race," she said.

Reiko's face darkened. "Don't patronize me."

Jun tried to keep her pity off of her face.

Reiko's hands tightened into fists. "What is up with you today?"

Jun shrugged. "Why does it bother you so much?"

"Why does what bother me?"

"That I'm faster."

"You bother me because you're ugly and stupid. I don't care about track. I'm only here because my father made me join a team."

"Is he going to come to any of the meets?"

"Don't talk to me, Shuuichi." Reiko snapped, then stormed off.

Reiko and her friends weren't waiting to torment Jun after practice, and she couldn't find the path to the scarecrow's rice paddy.

●

Jun stared down at her homework, but she'd read the poem a dozen times and it still didn't make sense. She padded out to the kitchen, where her mother was washing dishes. "Mom, do you know anything about poetry?"

"No, sorry. Have you tried asking one of your classmates for help?"

"Good idea," Jun said. She went back to her room and flopped onto the floor. She pulled her phone out of her pocket and stared at it for a long time. Reiko was top of their class. She probably understood poetry. What would she do if Jun asked for help?

Jun climbed out the window and ran. The ground was hard against her bare feet.

The scarecrow's rice paddy was different in the moonlight. Silver and black and clearly magical. Mud oozed between her toes.

"Hello," Jun said, bowing.

"It is dangerous here at night," the scarecrow said.

"What will Reiko do if I ask her for help?"

"I do not know what the future holds, child. I only know the now."

"Well, what do you think she'd do?"

"She might help you. Or she might lash out. She is not a happy girl."

"Why don't her parents love her?"

"Do you think she would want you to know that, when she herself doesn't?"

"No. I suppose not."

"I will tell you another secret, instead."

"Okay."

"There is a monster hiding by your path."

Chills ran along Jun's skin. "A monster?"

"It is strong, but you are fast."

"What will happen if it catches me?"

"I do not know the future."

"What does it normally do when it catches someone?"

"It eats them."

"I will run."

"Good. I hope to see you again, child. In the daytime."

Jun sprinted down the path. Her bare foot caught on a rock, and pain spiked through her. She felt hot breath on her neck, but heard no sounds

161

but the pounding of her own heart, the rhythm of her feet hitting the path, and the ragged cadence of her breath.

A shadow engulfed hers and spread before her on the path. It was huge, with two tapered horns.

Jun pumped her arms faster. Icy claws ripped through her hair and sliced the back of her left arm.

She saw a streetlight ahead and managed one last burst of speed.

The shadow faded, and she burst onto the road. She collided with someone, and tumbled to the ground.

Jun stared up at the sky and panted. Blood dripped down her elbow.

"What is wrong with you?" Reiko loomed above her, scowling. "Do you run everywhere?"

Jun blinked up at her. "Would you help me with my poetry homework?"

Reiko rolled her eyes. "No."

Jun sat up and winced. Her whole arm ached, and it felt like she'd plunged it into an icy river.

"Are you bleeding?"

Jun nodded.

"Are you okay?"

"I don't know. Could you—could you help me home?"

Reiko rolled her eyes again, but gave Jun her hand and pulled her to her feet. "Just don't bleed on me, okay? This is a new top."

The cold spread up her arm and to her chest. She started to shiver.

Reiko pulled Jun's good arm over her shoulder. "There's something really wrong with you, isn't there?"

"I—I'll be okay." It was difficult to speak through her chattering teeth.

Her home was an oasis of light and warmth. Reiko dragged her to the door. Jun saw her mother's worried face, then darkness took her.

•

She woke tucked into her futon with a clean bandage around her arm. A hot water bottle was nestled into the crook of her elbow, and another warmed her feet. Her arm hurt, but she felt warm all through.

Her mother had dragged her own futon in and was sleeping beside her. "Mom?"

"Oh, thank goodness. Are you okay?"

"Yeah, I'm feeling much better."

"What happened? Why were you out without your shoes?"

"I went to visit a friend," Jun said.

"The girl who brought you back? She seemed very worried. She offered to bring your schoolwork by today."

"No, I met her on my way home."

"Was it a boy? Did he hurt you? You can tell me sweetie, I promise I won't be mad."

"No. I—I was running from a monster."

"A monster."

"I found a rice paddy with a scarecrow, and he could talk, and he told me secrets, but then there was a monster—"

Her mother pressed the back of her hand to Jun's forehead. "Why don't you lie back down. I'll make some tea."

Her mother didn't ask what happened again, but she brought a steady stream of hot drinks and made pork cutlets for dinner again.

Reiko arrived with a stack of books just before dinner. "I'm so sorry," she said, bowing. "I didn't think—"

"Come on in, dear!" Jun's mother said. "I was hoping you'd get here for dinner. I made enough for everyone—I wanted to thank you for getting Jun home last night. That is if your own family won't miss you—"

"They won't," Reiko said. "Thank you, Mrs. Shuuichi."

"I do hope you like pork cutlets. They're Jun's favorite."

"They're mine, too. Thank you."

After dinner, Reiko followed Jun to her bedroom. "I'll help you with your poetry, but only if you tell me what happened last night."

"What if I tell you and you don't believe me?"

"I'll believe you."

"When I was running from you the other day, I found a rice paddy with a scarecrow. The scarecrow can talk, and he knows things."

"A scarecrow that knows things? Like Kuebiko—the god in the stories?"

"I didn't ask—I thought it might be rude. Anyway, I went back there last night, and then a monster chased me."

"It must have been a pretty fast monster."

"I guess."

"It probably would have caught me."

"The scarecrow told me not to come back at night."

"Why did you go at night, anyway? And without your shoes?" Reiko asked.

"I had a question."

"Was it about me?"

Jun looked down at the floor. "Yes."

"What did he tell you?"

"He told me that your parents don't love you."

Tears welled in Reiko's eyes. "Oh. That."

"I'm sorry," Jun said.

"Did he tell you why?"

"No." Jun reached out and took Reiko's hands between hers. "Do you want to ask him?"

Reiko blinked and two tears slipped down her cheeks. "Yes."

"Let's go tomorrow, right after school."

"Okay."

•

"We can only find the path if we run," Jun said. "Sometimes, I can't find it at all. Stay as close to me as you can."

"Don't push yourself too hard," Reiko said. "You're still recovering, and I don't want to have to carry you again."

"Let's go."

They ran. The path opened up under her feet, and she splashed into the rice paddy with Reiko close behind.

"Hello, children."

Jun bowed.

"The scarecrow really can talk," Reiko said.

"I can." It sounded amused.

"Go ahead, ask your question," Jun said. "I won't listen."

She turned away and covered her ears.

After a while, Reiko tapped her shoulder. Her eyes were red. "I'm done."

"Are you okay?" Jun asked.

Reiko shrugged. "Thank you for bringing me here."

"You're welcome."

"I'm sorry I was such a jerk to you."

"It's okay."

"I didn't mean to hit you with that rock. We were trying to miss. I won't do anything like that again, I promise."

"Yeah? Okay."

"I can keep helping you with your homework, if you want."

"I'd like that."

"It is safe to walk down the path now," the scarecrow said. "And your mother is finishing up your dinner."

"Thank you. We'll be going." Jun asked.

"Can we come back?" Reiko asked.

"I do not know what the future holds," the scarecrow said. "But I will never shut you out."

"What is her mother making for dinner?" Reiko asked.

"A hot pot."

"Is there enough for me?"

"Of course."

Reiko grinned. "Awesome. Let's go."

They walked down the path together, then Jun stopped. "Wait for me here just sec, okay?"

"Sure."

Jun ran back up to the rice paddy and splashed out to the scarecrow. "Did you plan all this? Or did it just happen?"

The scarecrow chuckled. "How can I control anything? I cannot move from this spot."

"Well, I just wanted to say thank you."

"You are welcome, Shuuichi Jun. You deserve to be happy."

"And Reiko does too, right?"

"You've already answered that question."

Jun bowed, then ran back to her friend.

HILLSIDES OF FORSYTHIA, YELLOW IN THE RAIN

Original to this Collection

The winter lingers on, reaching its gray fingers through March and deep into April, but ads on the bus stop already warn of the approaching beach season. Tamalyn dislikes the beach, but she is fond of the neighborhood pool, with its clear water and soothing blue paint. She goes in the mornings, when the shade keeps the concrete from scorching bare feet, when there are fewer people about see if her body is beach-ready or not.

But the pool feels a long way away. Cold rain spits sideways into the meager shelter, and her shoes are soaked through.

Still, she thinks. Still. She'll try out that new diet.

•

Her mother got her a diet book for Christmas, and she finds it in the middle of her kitchen table when she gets home. She doesn't remember the cover being soft gray leather or the pages smelling just like the cold rain. But the holidays can be overwhelming, maybe she just didn't notice.

She flips to the first page.

The first step, she reads, *is to let no food pass your lips while the sun is in the sky. You may drink tea brewed from bruised flower petals and rainwater.*

She skims through the explanation of why this works—burning ketones and mystic resonance and distancing the body from the material realm. But she doesn't really care why it works, if it works. She puts out her biggest mixing bowl to catch the falling rain and goes to bed.

•

She wakes after sunrise, so she dips out a mug of rainwater and throws in some bruised petals from the neighbor's forsythia bush. The taste is bitter, bracing. She empties her mug, then thinks to check if forsythia is poisonous.

167

It isn't, so she fills a thermos with tiny yellow petals and rainwater. It is still gray and drizzling, so she puts all of her clean mugs on the picnic table, along with her other mixing bowls.

She doesn't pack a lunch, and she's pleased that she's saving both calories and money with this diet.

At work, not eating is easier than she expected. She is hungry, but not painfully so. She sips her tea and does her job and feels normal. No one notices that she doesn't eat, and she's grateful that she doesn't have to explain.

At home, she cleans the house to distract herself, till the sun finally slips below the gray horizon and she eats two poached eggs and dry toast.

She's still hungry, so she sets her alarm early, so she can eat breakfast.

•

There is a food truck the next day at work, so everyone around her is eating and the scent of fried food hangs in the air.

But she's never been able to afford to go to the food trucks, and she doesn't miss her peanut butter and jelly. She sips her tea, and her hunger is peace and strength.

It is all so much easier than she expected.

•

Weeks pass, and the forsythia should be fading, should be giving way to dogwood and lilac and azalea. Green should be creeping in to replace the gray and brown. But the yellow forsythia remains the only splash of color.

Tamalyn eats less and less at the ends of her fasts, which grow longer and longer as the gray days lengthen. Her fridge and cabinets are empty, and she doesn't bother to go to the grocery store.

The diet book sits in the middle of her kitchen table.

She opens it and flips to the next section.

•

Next, you must watch for the moon and dance to it when it peers through breaks in the clouds.

The book gives very specific instructions on the dance steps. Tamalyn reads it and nods. It makes sense to add in some exercise to the routine.

Staying awake through the night to watch the sky is harder than not eating during the day. Tamalyn spends the first week nodding off while the ever-present clouds mask the moon, then jerking awake when the pale light caresses her face.

The ground is wet and cold beneath her bare feet, and the grass in her back yard is slippery. During that first week of groggy dancing, she often slips and lands with a squelch in the mud.

But the moon doesn't judge her mistakes, so she gets up and starts again.

By the third week, she has new long, lean muscles, hard under her skin. Her body is free and graceful and light. Maybe even beach-ready.

•

The final section is a fold out map, labeled in thin, spidery script. At dawn, the sky has been clear for hours, and Tamalyn is warm and ready. She follows the map, turn by turn. At first, it is hard to understand, but she catches the trick of it quickly and arrives at the end without trouble.

Her destination is a volcanic beach. Rounded gray-black pebbles give way to soft black sand. The waves crash white, and the gray water stretches to the pale horizon.

This place is impossible, the ocean is hundreds of miles away. But that doesn't matter, and the water is calling her. The waves are the rhythm of her heartbeat, and the sun crests the horizon and she feels its touch on her skin for the first time in what might be forever.

The sunlight reminds her of picnics with friends, of waking after a long nights sleep, stretched out under warm blankets in a soft bed. But she no longer feels hungry or tired, has no need for the sunshine's promises, and when the clouds roll back and the soft ran falls, she is grateful for it.

She takes off her shoes and socks and dances into the surf. And behind her, clinging to the hillsides behind the volcanic cliffs, the forsythia blooms, yellow in the rain.

ELECTROMITRA
Original to this Collection

Electromitra started her life as a stuffed storm cloud with a cheerful yellow zigzag of lightning jutting out of one gray side. She might have had a stitched-on face at one point, but I can't remember for sure.

She was my favorite thing, and I carried her with me everywhere.

She came with me the first time my parents took me to the zoo. I held her up so that she could see the lions, I hugged her tight when the tiger yawned and I could see all of its long, sharp teeth. I clutched her in one hand while I happily devoured the strawberry soft serve that my mother bought me for being so good.

And that's when I dropped her. She bounced twice before I lost sight of her. My parents helped me search till the zoo closed, but she was gone.

I cried myself to sleep.

•

I woke up to cold fingers poking my cheeks. My eyes were dry and my chest ached. I made a small noise of protest and buried my face in my pillow. The poking changed to tentative petting, the cold fingers stroking my tangled hair.

Then I yelped as a static shock sparked through me. "Oh, sorry!" said a voice that I'd know anywhere, even though I'd never heard it before.

I sat up and stared. Electromitra stared back. She was mostly girl-shaped, now, with arms and legs, though both were short for her cloud-shaped head. She was gray and fluffy at the edges, but solid when I reached out and touched her shoulder.

Tiny sparks arced through her here and there, as beautiful and unpredictable as distant lightning.

"You came back," I said, the words catching in my throat.

"Of course I did," she said. "I love you."

I hugged her, ignoring the pain from the tiny shocks. "I love you, too."

"I know," she said.

When I told my parents that Electromitra was back, my dad smiled and said, "That's nice, honey."

But my mother frowned. "You lost Electromitra, sweetie. Pretending that she's still here doesn't change that. You need to take responsibility for your actions."

I looked back at Electromitra, who was hesitating in the doorway. "But she's right there!" I said, pointing.

Both of my parents looked, but their eyes skimmed past Electromitra as she floated into the room. "Oh no," she said, her soft voice alarmed. "They can't see me."

My mother reached down and took my hands between hers. "Sometimes we lose things, and we can't get them back. And that's okay. As long as you remember Electromitra, she won't be really gone."

"And we can get you a new toy," her father said. "Maybe a new doll."

My mother glared at him. "Or maybe a truck?" he added.

"You can't just replace things anytime you lose them," my mother said.

My father rolled his eyes. "Of course we can. That's how capitalism works."

Electromitra took my hand and pulled me back up to my bedroom. "I'm sorry," she said. "I didn't know that they wouldn't be able to see me." Her soft gray body darkened, so that she was almost black, and she drew her knees up to her chest. "What if you stop being able to see me someday?"

"You can just shock me till I remember," I said.

She laughed, and turned back to her normal color, and we played in my room till my mom called me back down for breakfast.

•

The next few years passed in a happy blur. I started going to school, and I even made a few friends. Electromitra helped me study for tests, and prompted me if I froze up when I had to talk in front of the class.

Then I fell down a hill in the woods behind our house. My feet slipped in the wet leaves, and I tumbled, crying out as the world spun around me.

Then it came to a sudden stop, and I screamed. I looked down at my arm and saw white bone.

My breath came in harsh pants, and everything started to go black. "I'll get help," Electromitra said, her voice distant and thin. "Hold on, please. I'll be right back."

•

I came to in a hospital bed, the pain in my arm a distant throbbing and my mind feeling floaty and disconnected. My parents were both standing next to me, their faces haggard. Electromitra floated on my good side, and I reached my hand toward her. "You did it," I said, my words slurring together.

"Teresa Allen was biking past, and I shouted and shocked her till she saw me," she said. "I think she can still see me."

"S'okay," I said. "Teresa's nice."

"Who are you talking to, sweetie?" my mother asked.

"Electromitra," I said, forgetting that they couldn't see her. "She saved me."

"Maybe you should go back to sleep," my father said, reaching across my body and pulling my hand away from Electromitra's. "You gave us all a scare, and it's gonna be a while before you're back to 100%."

Electromitra floated around the bed and took my bad hand. Her cool fingers felt nice, and I smiled. I let the dreamy feeling pull me away, into strange dreams where I fell up a long, slippery hill that never ended.

•

When I woke up again, Teresa Allen was in my room, glaring at Electromitra. "Hi," I said. I felt hot and itchy and achy, but she'd helped save my life. "Thank you for helping me."

"Hi." Teresa crossed her arms over her chest. "The monster says that you can see her, too."

I tried to sit up in outrage, and only managed to flop over, which hurt. "Electromitra's not a monster!"

"She looks like a monster to me," Teresa said.

I took a deep breath. "That's not very nice," I said. "First off, you can't judge people by how they look. And secondly, she doesn't look at all like a monster! She doesn't have teeth or claws. And she's pretty."

"She's a raincloud shaped like a person. Who can talk. It's weird."

Electromitra sniffed. "Your face is weird."

"Electromitra, be nice!" I said.

"She called me a monster!"

The pain in my arm spread to my head, where it throbbed in time with my heartbeat. "Well, you can't stoop to her level."

"You sound like your mom," Electromitra grumbled.

"Good, my mom's cool and smart." The pain kept growing, and it was hard to listen to Electromitra and Teresa bicker.

They kept at it, and I let my eyes drift closed.

•

The next time I woke up, my arm ended just below the elbow. I thought I was alone, till I spotted Electromitra floating high in the corner by the window. "Hey," I said. "What happened?" My voice was high and tight, and it didn't sound like me.

"They had to operate on you again," she said. "You almost died. Again."

Tears blurred my vision. "I'm sorry," I said, my voice twisting into a sob.

"Teresa had to call the nurse. I couldn't do anything. I couldn't even shock anyone into seeing me, because I was afraid I'd fry the machines keeping you alive."

The frantic pain in her voice cut through my growing panic. I had to be strong for her. "Teresa wouldn't have been there if not for you," I said.

"You can't leave me," Electromitra said. "I can make new people see me, but no one else will want to."

"I don't believe that," I said. "After I get out of here, we can pick someone else, someone nice, and you can introduce yourself in a nice calm situation."

"You thought Teresa was nice."

"Well, she did come and help, even though she thought you were a monster."

"I guess that's true."

"This whole thing has probably been hard on her, I bet she's not at her best."

"You sound like your mom again."

"Do you want to try again?"

Electromitra shrugged. "Maybe. We'll see. Just get better, okay?"

I looked back down at my arm and blinked away tears. Thinking about Electromitra's problems had distracted me from my own. "I'll do my best."

174

My mother settled into the chair next to me. She took my remaining hand between hers, and how hot they were surprised me.

"You're going to have to stay in the hospital a little longer," she said. Her voice was soft and steady, but a slow stream of tears crept down her cheeks. "When they found you, the doctors were so focused on saving your arm that they missed some damage to your spleen and kidneys. And then you got an infection and it tore through all of your defenses." She squeezed my hand. "They couldn't save your arm the second time around. The doctor said that it's a miracle that you're still alive."

I had no idea how to process that. "Am I dying?"

"No, sweetie. But your immune system will probably always be a little weak, and your arm will probably hurt, at least a little, for a long time. I—" her voice broke, and she took a ragged breath. "I'm so sorry, sweetie—your arm—"

I'd been strong for Electormitra, I could be strong for my mom, too. I squeezed her hand. "Sometimes we lose things, and we can't get them back. And that's okay."

•

My father got me flowers, and I liked them so much that he got me more when they started to wilt. Electromitra spied on all of the doctors and nurses and told me all of their secrets. They weren't nearly as exciting as TV doctors and nurses—mostly they were just tired and sneaking naps in weird places.

But eventually, after physical therapy and regular therapy and picking out a prosthetic—I picked a two-pronged hook that made me feel like a pirate—I was ready to go home, then after a bit longer, it was time to go back to school. "You should spy around school for possible new friends," I said while I slung my backpack over my shoulders.

Electromitra sighed. "I'm afraid. What if everyone but you thinks I'm a monster?"

I hugged her tight, even though it sent tiny shocks through my prosthetic. "You're not a monster." I buried my face in her cold chest. "I'm afraid to go back," I said. "All of my friends are a year ahead of me now." I looked down at my hand and my hook. "And then there's this."

Electromitra stroked my hair. "If anyone is mean to you I'll shock them," she said.

175

I laughed. "We want to make new friends who can see you, not enemies."

"Teresa said she thinks your hook is cool. And she's still your friend, even if you're a grade behind now."

I nodded.

Electromitra sighed. "It would be easier if she wasn't ever nice."

I still didn't understand now Teresa could possibly see Electromitra as a monster.

I couldn't really blame Electromitra if she didn't want to try again. I decided to stop mentioning it. If it was something she wanted to do, I'd have to let her do it in her own time.

●

After I'd been back for about a month, I dragged Teresa into one of the bathrooms. "How come you haven't told anyone else about Electromitra?" I asked.

"I'd sound like a lunatic," Teresa said. "And anyway, she's your monster, not mine."

"You know she's not a monster."

"What is she then? An alien? Some kind of magic fairy creature?"

"Why does that matter?"

"How are you so weird, of course it matters."

I shrugged. "Not to me."

"Look," Teresa said, "I won't tell anyone. I don't have anything against your monster."

"Her name is Electromitra."

Teresa rolled her eyes. "Well, she creeps me out. But I'm glad you're alive, so I guess I'm glad you have her."

"You should tell her that," I said.

Teresa shrugged. "Maybe."

●

"I have no idea how I'd pick someone new to see me," Electromitra said. "I wish I was just a normal person, like you and Teresa."

I took her cold hand and squeezed it. I couldn't think of anything to say that wouldn't sound stupid.

"I get lonely sometimes," she said. "Even though you spend so much of your time with me."

I had to say something. "I love you. I love you just the way you are, and I'd love you if you were a normal person."

Electromitra was quiet for a long time. Then she squeezed my hand back and said, "I know."

•

"Anthony Smith is going to ask you to prom," Electromitra said.

Even though she'd never picked another person to reveal herself to, she had taken to spying around the school. She liked knowing what was going on.

Anthony Smith was cute. And nice. But if I dated someone, I wouldn't have as much time for Electromitra. "Hmm." I said.

"It's just prom," Electromitra said. "It's not like you'd be marrying him."

"I don't need to date in high school," I said. "I have too much else to focus on."

"You know, most people wait till they're old to turn into their mothers."

I shrugged.

"You should go if you want to," she said. "I don't like you holding yourself back for me. And don't say it's not about me, I know it is."

"Maybe I just don't like him," I said.

Electromitra rolled her eyes. "I know you better than that."

I pulled an SAT prep book off of my shelf with my hook and opened it to a random page.

"If it goes well, maybe I'll reveal myself to him."

"You can't do that just because I like him!"

"So you admit that you like him!"

I sighed. "You know I do."

"So go to prom."

"No! You can't just decide that for me! It doesn't matter if I like him! You're more important!"

"Teresa said that I'm the reason you don't have more friends."

"Teresa is full of crap! I have as many friends as I want. Do you think I don't have enough to deal with?" I waved my hook at her. "I have dealt with everything life's thrown at me. I can make my own decisions about prom and about dating!"

"But you want to go! And it's just one night! I can take you choosing someone else, just once."

"But what if it's not just once?" I asked. "What if it goes well, and then he meets you, and we're all friends. But then you start feeling like a third wheel. What if he replaces you as the most important person to me? Do you really think you'd be okay with that?"

"I want you to go," Electromitra said.

"What if it changes everything?" I asked.

Electromitra reached out and touched my cheek. "Maybe change is what I need."

"I'm afraid," I admitted. "I don't want to lose you."

"Everything will be okay."

"Are you sure?"

She shook her head. "Of course not. But you should go, anyway."

"You know I love you, right?" I said.

Electromitra smiled. "I know."

·

Anthony brought me a corsage, which made my dad tear up. "I guess I'm not the only guy getting you flowers anymore," he said. I hugged him, and then he took about a hundred pictures while my mother pulled Anthony aside. Probably to lecture him about my curfew and the dangers of my weakened immune system.

At the dance, Teresa leaned close to me during one of the fast songs. "I'm surprised to see you here without your monster," she said.

In that moment, the lights stuttered, just like lightning. Static sparked through the room, leaping from one dancing body to another.

Electromitra stood in front of the DJ, her tiny hands clenched into fists, shedding tiny sparks.

Everyone was staring.

The music stuttered and died, and I pushed through the crowd, desperate to get to her side. I grabbed one of her clenched fists.

To my surprise, Teresa grabbed the other one, and the three of us stood there together.

Electromitra smiled out at the gaping crowd. "Hi," she said. "I'm Electromitra."

THE GIRL IN THE GLASS BLOCK WINDOW

Originally appeared in *The Colored Lens*

My grandfather shoved me into the basement and locked the door behind me. The cold, damp smell wrapped around me, and thin sunlight slipped in through glass block windows set high into the walls.

He didn't like having me underfoot, so I spent a lot of time in the basement.

In the summer, I could sit on stairs and read. But it was late January, and too cold to be still, even wrapped in the cedar-scented wool blanket that I'd stolen from the dusty room where he stored the other things that my mother had left behind.

I jogged around the rotting workbench, hugging the blanket tight.

Between one step and another, I saw her, fragmented into a thousand pieces by the panes inside the glass blocks. A girl, older than me, with long black hair and shadowed eyes.

I dragged a broken chair over to the wall and balanced on it, face even with the window.

She stared back at me from a hundred angles, her face twisted into a plea for help.

I fell off the chair.

•

She was always there, after that. Maybe she'd always been there, waiting for someone to see her. But I'd seen horror movies, and I knew that I couldn't trust her. She probably wanted to steal my body. She couldn't have a body herself, trapped inside that window.

Still, it was hard to face her.

•

I snuck into the closed room and stripped the sheets off of the bed. I pulled the quilt back over the bare mattress and smoothed it out.

179

I pictured my mother's hand, smoothing the same spot.

The sheets made serviceable curtains. The basement was darker, but I felt better with the windows covered.

•

I dreamed that my mother came back for me, but she had the girl from the window's eyes.

•

Time slipped by. My grandfather sent me to the basement anytime he noticed me, so I made myself quiet and small. I didn't try to make friends—it didn't seem worth the effort. And trusting people had never worked out for me.

I ran away on my 15th birthday. I took the wool blanket and $400 that my grandfather had hidden in a pickle jar. I hid in the woods for a week and lived on food I bought in the gas station. I should have gone to the city, should have had a destination. My mother knew where she was going when she left.

But I didn't have anywhere to go, so I slept under the stars and felt giddy with freedom.

I was standing next to the Hostess rack, trying to decide what snack cake I wanted for breakfast, when a friendly voice said, "I imagine there's someone looking for you, honey."

I bolted, but the cops were already outside. They put me into the back of their car, and I wept all the way back to my grandfather's house.

He pushed me straight into the basement.

I tore the curtains down and stared at the girl in the window. She hadn't aged—hadn't changed at all since I'd covered her up.

"If you want my life, you can have it," I said. She pressed a distorted hand to a hundred surfaces inside the glass block. Her dark eyes glittered like stars.

My grandfather had a battered set of golf clubs in one corner, and I swung one at the window. The club bounced back, leaving a single white chip in the middle of the center block. I swung again with a cry of frustrated rage. The window cracked, a splintered spider web that spread across the panes. I waited for the girl to flow into me, to take over my body and thrust me out.

Nothing happened.

I stared at the window, at each place where I'd seen her pleading face and bottomless eyes.

She was gone.

She was free.

And I had freed her.

I slumped beneath the broken window and cried.

The next day, I saw a glimpse of her, reflected in Tina Thompson's glasses. Maybe—maybe I could try trusting someone. What else did I have to lose?

I met Tina's eyes and smiled. "Hey. Did you do the homework? What did you get for number 4?"

She smiled back, and told me.

THE PULL OF THE WAVES

Originally appeared in *The Colored Lens*

The first letter came in a bottle, bobbing in with the tide. My older sister and I had gone out before sunrise to stand with our toes in the ocean. It was so big, so loud, so strong. I was already overwhelmed when the bottle tapped against my calf.

The glass was turquoise—my favorite color—and it was shaped like an old-fashioned coke bottle, long-necked and elegant. I picked it up without thinking and hugged it to my chest.

Denise laughed and danced across the wet sand. Her hair billowed in the wind and shone in the early morning light. I stood and hugged the bottle and shuddered at the feeling of the ocean pulling at my feet.

•

I didn't notice the letter until after breakfast. Everyone else was excited to go swimming, but I stayed in the cottage, searching for pliers to pull out the cork.

The letter was folded in half, then curled tight. A pale purple flower was pressed flat inside it.

It took another moment to realize that the letter was actually addressed to me.

"Dearest Lindy," it read, "You don't know me yet, but I wanted to send you a token of my regard. I know that the upcoming months will be difficult for you, but know that I care deeply for you already. If you ever have need of me, simply stand in the water and call. I will come. Yours forever, Elzin."

"Elzin," I whispered. It wasn't a name I'd ever heard before. I left the flower in the letter, put it back into the bottle, and tucked it into my suitcase. I was young enough to not question, to just believe in this tiny magical moment, but old enough to know that it wasn't something to mention to anyone else.

I sat on the porch and read my book till Denise came and dragged me down to the ocean for our picnic lunch.

·

Denise's cough started soon after we got home from vacation, and she faded quickly. The doctors did what they could, but it wasn't enough.

When there was nothing more to do, they sent her home. I sat next to her in her dark room, holding her hand as it grew thinner, day by day. I read to her, using a single strip of sunlight that fell through the curtains to see the letters. Books about the ocean always made her smile. I tried not to remember the fear I'd felt looking out at its vastness, and smile at the bits of trivia that my sister loved.

After the funeral, I found a wooden box on my bed with a seashell nestled inside. When I held it to my ear, I could hear my sister's laughter.

·

Time passed. Anytime I was lonely or sad, Elzin would send a note or a gift. I treasured each one, but questions started to nag at me. How did he know when I needed him? And why me? I was intimately aware of just how average I was. Elzin was the only magic in my life—he was the only magic anywhere, as far as I knew. He was special. He deserved to love someone special. But I didn't want him to stop loving me.

So, I decided that I would become special.

I wandered into my mother's sewing room. "Mom, how can I be special?"

"Oh sweetie, you're already special," she said.

Which was a sweet answer, but useless. I hugged her, then went to ask my father.

"Well, I suppose that depends on what you mean by special," he said. "Your best bet is to find something that you're already good at, then devote yourself to practicing it till you're the best at it."

"You think being the best at something will make me special?" I asked.

"Yeah, don't you?"

"I guess." It was certainly more useful than my mother's answer. But what was I already good at? What could I practice enough to be the best at?

That night, in the bath, I wrote a note that just asked, "How can I be special?" I held it under the water, half expecting something to happen, half not.

The paper disintegrated between my fingers. A few minutes later, an origami swan floated up to the surface.

I unfolded it carefully, taking note of each fold. It said, "Just be yourself."

It was just as sweet, and just as useless, coming from Elzin. Still, I refolded the swan and put it with the rest of my collection.

I focused on cooking, playing the piano, and swimming. Cooking let me spend time with my mother, the piano had been Denise's and felt like a good way to honor her memory, and swimming made me feel close to Elzin.

I became very good at all three, but I wasn't the best. My mother worried that I didn't have any friends. My father came to all of my swim meets and piano recitals and raved about the food I made.

Elzin sent me a book of piano music that reminded me of the ocean. My fingers shook when I played the songs, but I loved their haunting beauty.

I found that I was happy. I felt special enough.

•

Elzin sent me three tickets to the movies along with a note encouraging me to take my parents.

They were surprised when I invited them—I didn't really watch movies—but they were happy to go on a family outing. I spent the entire time feeling restless and wrong. The story was simple, but I couldn't follow it. My parents were enthralled.

I wanted to know what was going on at home—what it was that Elzin had sent us away from. But still, I didn't rush back. I trusted him.

It was raining when we left the theater. Heavy sheets that shut out the world around us as we dashed to our car. My parents chatted about the movie. I wondered if I called Elzin if he could come through the rain.

I thought more and more about calling him. I wanted to see his face, to touch his hand.

My parents decided to wait out the worst of the rain at a diner. We ordered pie and coffee and I tried to ignore the creeping worry in my belly.

"Hmm," my father said, poking at his coconut cream pie.

"What's up?" I asked.

"Maybe you should start baking more. I bet you could make a mean coconut cream pie if you set your mind to it." He winked at me.

My mother rolled her eyes. "If she's going to start making pies, clearly she should start with lemon meringue," she said, taking a big bite of her favorite.

I laughed. "You're both crazy. If I'm going to start making pies, I should make chocolate ones."

Chocolate pies had always been Denise's favorite.

My father smiled. "Well, I suppose those would be a good start."

"Chocolate, then lemon," my mother said.

My father rolled his eyes, and they argued as we headed home.

We sat in the car in silence for a long moment after my father turned off the engine. The only sound was the steady drum of the rain on the car roof. The oak tree behind our house had blown over and landed squarely on our kitchen.

"It's lucky we weren't home," my mother managed.

"I'll—I'll make some calls," my father squeezed her hand. "We're all okay. Everything will be okay."

"I'm going to go look around," I said.

"Be careful," both parents said in unison.

As soon as I was out of sight, I found a puddle and stood in it. Cold water soaked through my socks and swirled around my ankles. "Elzin."

Instantly, I felt his presence. A moment later, I saw him, a shape formed out of raindrops. And then, there he was, standing in front of me.

"Lindy," he said. His voice was like the tide. "What is wrong? Were you in the house, after all?"

I shook my head and stepped forward. His arms surrounded me. He smelled like the sea on a cold, windy day. "What would have happened? If you hadn't sent us away?"

"You would have survived."

"But my parents?"

A scene floated into my mind, of my mother and father doing the dishes together, since I'd made dinner. She flicked him with a towel, then after chasing each other around for a few minutes, they started dancing, slow steps to the rhythm of the rain. Then a crash, then darkness.

"You've never changed anything before," I said, my face tight against his chest.

"Saving your sister was beyond me. This was not."

"I don't know how I deserve you," I said, my throat tight.

"You found me. You woke me from my long slumber."

"But I didn't—I haven't. What if I don't?"

"You have already. My existence... it does not follow the same rules as yours."

"I've always thought that you knew the future," I said.

"In a way, I do. I exist outside of time," he said. "You came to me in another reality."

"Was I happy? In this other world? Other time?"

"You were unhappy for a long time. You didn't deal well with the loss of your sister, and the loss of your parents was worse. But you were happy with me, once we were together."

"What happened to that other me? Why aren't you with her?"

"She is you—you do not exist outside of time. When I changed your life, I changed her."

"You sacrificed your version of me."

"I wanted you to be happy."

"I'm happy now," I said.

"I know."

"It's because of you."

He shook his head. "It is because of you. I have done nothing but support you."

"And save my parents' lives."

"I am only here because of you. Really, it is you that saved them."

I laughed at him. "You really are too sweet." I pulled away, wiped my eyes. "Did I love you? In your other world?"

His smile was the sunrise over the ocean. "You did."

"And you loved me?"

"I love you in all worlds and through all times."

"Can I be with you here, in this world?"

"Before, when you came to me, you left nothing behind. I will not blame you if you make a different choice." His hands stroked my hair.

"Will I be able to come back if I leave?"

He laughed. "Of course. Though you will be bound to the water, as I am."

"Can I have time to think about it?"

"Of course." His fingers trailed along my cheeks, wiping away tears and rain.

"I should get back, before they start to worry."

"Goodbye, then," Elzin said.

I reached out, touched his hand, tried to commit his face to memory, though I wasn't sure I'd be up to the task. "I will call you again," I said.

"I will come."

I studied music in college. My parents encouraged me to pick something more practical, but they supported me when I refused.

It was hard to be away from them.

Thunder rumbled as my composition class ended. Lighting flickered in the distance, and fat drops of rain speckled the pavement. One of the boys in my class pulled an umbrella out of his bag and smiled at me. "Want to share? Then maybe get coffee?"

He was cute, and seemed kind. But he wasn't Elzin. I shook my head. "I like to walk in the rain."

·

Elzin loved me for something that I hadn't done. He existed, somehow, apart from time.

He had saved my parents' lives and preserved my sister's laughter.

He assured me that all I needed to do to deserve his love was to be myself.

I had so many other options. I didn't have to be with him. But I wanted to. I still feared the ocean's pull, but there was an answering pull within me. Maybe it had always been there.

I left the gifts that Elzin had given me and a long letter for my parents. I told them that they could step into the water and call on me anytime.

Then I went down to the ocean. The waves pulled at my feet, and I stepped forward.

LAKE MONSTERS

Originally appeared in *Wild Musette*

Sheila first saw the monster in Uncle Jake's pond when she was seven. She'd pulled the dry-rotted canoe into the muddy water, climbed inside, and floated away from the shore. She imagined that she was lost at sea, that there was a reason for her to feel adrift and alone.

She ignored her cousins shouting at each other and playing tag in the field behind the house. It didn't matter that they hadn't invited her to play. She didn't want to play with them anyway. She'd have just as much fun in the canoe. By herself.

The canoe rocked, hard and sudden, and she cried out in fear. The boat rocked again, and she clutched the crumbling wood. Her cousins' laughter drowned her calls for help.

The boat rocked again, then flipped. The water was cold, even in the height of summer, and she could see nothing but hazy brown.

Then, she saw something else. A flash of blue scales, the glint of a huge black eye.

She woke up on shore, covered in dried mud and flaking pond scum and missing the smallest toe on her left foot. It was like she'd never had that toe—there was no pain, no wound. Her balance was shaky for a few days, but no one noticed the extra clumsiness on top of her normal lack of grace.

She sewed padding into her socks, and never went barefoot again.

No one ever noticed.

•

They didn't go back to Uncle Jake's till she was 18. It was Christmas, and the pond was frozen over. Her cousins went sled riding, then ice skating. None of them invited Sheila along, but she was used to that. She stayed inside with a cup of cocoa and her book.

But after everyone else had gone to bed, she snuck outside. Moonlight sparkled on the snow and glinted off of the smooth ice. Her breath misted in front of her.

She'd never even tried to ice skate before, but she snagged her cousin Mary's skates and laced them on. The blades hissed against the ice as she slid forward.

She managed to stop near the center of the pond. She stared up at the pinprick stars and shivered.

Coming back here was insane. She'd already lost a toe. What would it take this time?

But at least it wanted her. No one else did.

The ice creaked underneath her skates, then cracked. She tumbled sideways, away from the black water. Something hit the ice again and again.

She felt a tug in her missing toe.

She wondered how long it would take for them to notice she was gone. Would they notice at all? Would she vanish just like her toe?

She took a deep breath and slid into the crack.

This time, she woke in her bed, but there was ice in her hair. She ran her hands over her body, and found nothing missing. She could still see and hear, her tongue and voice were both intact.

The next week, she went to have her wisdom teeth taken out. But they were already gone. She smiled while the oral surgeon stared at her x-rays and mumbled to himself.

•

Sheila chose a college close to Uncle Jake's. At first, she hoped college would be different—that she could finally make some friends. But she had no place in the clubs and cliques, and her roommate dropped out after the first week.

She offered to watch Uncle Jake's place when he went to Florida in October. She drove out alone on Friday night and sat on the shore. She stared out at the water. Every once in a while, she saw something moving beneath the surface. She could feel it calling to her—feel its pull deep in her gums and in the empty corner of her sock. The monster was too big to leave, but how could it survive in this tiny pond? How had it taken her toe, her teeth? And why?

Was it even real, or was she crazy? Maybe she'd almost drowned when she was seven, and the whole rest of her life was a strange coma dream. Or maybe she had drowned, and she was dead.

She took her socks off and dipped her remaining toes into the cold water.

The sun dipped toward the horizon, and the red light reflected on the smooth pond surface.

She stood and took a step forward. Cold mud squished between her toes.

The monster reared its head out of the water, and Sheila got her first good look at it. Its scales were midnight blue, and its eyes solid black. It was just as she'd imagined it, with it serpentine neck and draconic face.

It loomed over her, holding a fist-sized pearl between its fangs.

Sheila held out her hands, and it dropped the pearl into her cupped palms. Today, it gave instead of taking. The pearl was flesh-warm.

Sheila realized that it wasn't a pearl at all, but an egg. The egg sang to her, a song of warmth and welcome.

It pulled at her, at all of her, and folding herself into its shell was as easy as slipping into the pond.

When she hatched, she'd be a lake monster. And neither of them would ever be alone again.

THE UNICORN'S COMPANION

Originally appeared in *Stupefying Stories*

Bennie pushed through the tall weeds, ignoring the sting of thistles and sharp-edged grass against her bare arms. Sweat dripped into her eyes, and she wiped it away with her wrist, still pushing forward.

She'd left the paved trail behind, and Lissy's texted directions were no help at all. Bennie was just following a feeling, a pull in her gut that she hoped would lead her in the right direction.

But maybe that feeling was just guilt over skipping debate practice.

The weeds thinned, and she found herself standing between two young trees. She had to duck beneath their lowest branches. Then, as she looked up, she finally saw the unicorn.

It stood under another young tree, its pure white coat dappled in shifting shadows from the tiny leaves overhead. Its spiral horn gave off a soft, opalescent glow, and its eyes were the deep violet of the late twilight sky.

After a long, silent moment, the unicorn huffed out a breath. "What do you wish of me?" it asked in a voice like distant bells.

"I don't want anything," Bennie said. That wasn't exactly true—she wanted lots of things. Just nothing the unicorn could grant.

"You are not dying of some mysterious illness? You are not in possession of an ailing mother?"

Bennie shook her head. "I'm fine. And I don't have a mother."

The unicorn rolled its eyes. "Then perhaps it is your father? Sister? Brother?"

"No one is sick!"

"Then why, pray tell, are you here?"

"I came to warn you! There's a monster hunter in town, bragging that he's looking for unique prey."

"And you instantly assumed that I am his quarry? I am no monster."

"He sounds kind of unsavory, so I'm not sure if he'd care. Plus, this town isn't exactly a hotbed of interesting fauna."

The unicorn cocked its head. "I must concede that is a fair point. Though perhaps his interest lies in the sphinxes near the railroad tracks or the host of pixies across the river."

"Just be careful, okay? I don't want anything to happen to you."

"Why not? Are you concerned that someone you care for will fall ill in the future?"

"No," Bennie snapped. "I just... I just like that you're out here, I guess."

The unicorn blinked slowly. "So, you came all this way just to warn me? With no ulterior motive?"

"Yes," Bennie said, even though she had been looking for some excuse to skip debate club—she hadn't wanted to spend another afternoon debating what the nation's most precious resource was. She didn't want anything from the unicorn.

"Did you inform anyone of your quest?"

Bennie frowned. "I asked Lissy Tyler where she met you."

"Which one was she? The girl with the bad teeth?"

Bennie nodded. "Not after you fixed them for her, though."

The unicorn sniffed. "Yes, well. I do exceptional work, with far less pain than an orthodontist. Anyway, I have never been hunted before, so this shall at least be novel."

A twig snapped in the weeds behind her, and Bennie realized just how silent it had become. No birds sang, no insects buzzed.

"I do sense a threatening presence. I suspect the hunter followed you," the unicorn said.

Bennie's stomach sank. "What—I didn't mean—I'm sorry—"

The unicorn stepped toward her. "You are not at fault. Quickly, climb on."

Bennie hesitated for half a heartbeat before she leapt onto the unicorn's back.

She'd ridden a fat pony once at the fair. This was nothing like that. The unicorn's mane was like silk between her fingers, and it moved like water—fast, smooth and sure. Its cloven hooves were silent on the forest floor as it ran back in the direction that Bennie had come. The weeds parted before her, bending out of her way like they were bowing away from the wind.

Bennie caught a glimpse of the hunter, his eyes narrowed in anger, but they left him behind in a moment.

They reached the edge of town in a handful of heartbeats, and the unicorn stopped.

"What now?" Bennie asked. She knew she should dismount, but the world looked so different—so much softer and farther away—from the unicorn's back, and she wanted to stretch the moment for as long as possible.

"I know not. I suppose I must hide until he moves on to more appropriate prey."

"Come stay in my room," Bennie said.

"Your room? Inside a house?"

"Yeah. I mean, it's not a huge room or anything, but I think you'll fit okay."

"I have never been inside a human home," the unicorn said.

"Never?" The unicorn had helped so many people, Bennie found it hard to imagine that it'd never been inside a single house. But then, maybe inviting it inside was rude, somehow. Maybe she'd overstepped her bounds. Bennie opened her mouth to apologize.

"It seems a good plan, for I doubt the hunter would think to look for me there. Where is this room of yours?"

Bennie slid off of the unicorn's back, back into the world all close and huge, and led the way.

•

"My father should still be at work," Bennie said. "So we shouldn't have to sneak you in. Though we should probably use the back door, just in case anyone is around."

"That seems wise," the unicorn agreed.

Bennie's room was different with a unicorn in it. The pink bedspread and lilac walls were somehow more soothing, and the dusty curtains shimmered.

It was strange. But nice.

Bennie perched on the edge of the bed, feeling awkward as the unicorn looked around. "Now what?" she asked.

The unicorn tucked its feet under it like a cat and reached its head up to rest it on Bennie's pillow. "We wait, I suppose."

A long moment passed while they both sat, unmoving. "Well, I guess I should do my homework," Bennie said. "Is that okay?"

"Yes," the unicorn said.

"Do you... want anything to do? Like a book to read? Or I could get my laptop and put on a movie or something?"

"What is a movie?" the unicorn asked.

"It's a story, I guess. Like a play, but recorded so you can watch it anytime you want."

"Hmm. Very well. Put on a movie."

"What kind of movie would you like?"

"What do you mean?"

"Well, there's all kinds of different types. Romance or science fiction or action adventure."

"I will watch your favorite one."

The Last Unicorn was just too embarrassing, but Bennie couldn't think of anything else.

A few silent minutes passed while Bennie's mind spun uselessly. "Do you not have a favorite?" the unicorn asked.

Bennie sighed. "I do. I'm not sure if you'll like it, though."

"I am uncertain as well."

Bennie sighed again, then started the movie. She tried to ignore both it and the unicorn while she worked on her algebra homework.

Her father came home about halfway through the movie. "You home?" he shouted up the stairs.

"Yeah, just working on homework," Bennie called back.

"How do you feel about frozen pizza for dinner?"

"Sounds good to me!" Bennie turned to the unicorn. "What do you eat?" she asked.

"Sorry, what?" the unicorn asked, eyes not leaving the computer screen.

"Food. Do you want any? And if yes, what?"

"I can subsist on starlight. But I would not turn down a handful of violets and some spring water."

"I'll see what I can do." Bennie hesitated in the doorway. "Will you be okay up here on your own?"

The unicorn nodded. "I have spent most of my years alone."

"Okay. Well, my dad is home, so just stay here. I'll bring your dinner up."

"Very well."

•

Bennie managed to find a handful of violets growing in the backyard, and she found a bottle of water that claimed to be from a spring at the convenience store on the corner. She also grabbed some lemonade to have with dinner.

Her father was pulling the pizza out of the oven when she got back. "There you are."

"I got us drinks."

He grinned at her. "That's my girl."

They couldn't agree on toppings, so they compromised on plain cheese. "How was your day? Do anything to celebrate getting through your first week of the new school year?"

Bennie shrugged. She wanted to tell her father the whole story—the hunter, the unicorn, even skipping out on debate practice. She didn't usually keep secrets from him. But he wasn't great with secrets himself, and she didn't want the whole town knowing where the unicorn was hiding. "I did my algebra homework."

"How did you get all those scratches on your arms?"

"Oh, I went out for a walk."

"Did you check yourself for ticks?"

Bennie rolled her eyes.

"You can't be too careful. You know that."

"I'll check when I go back upstairs, okay?"

The unicorn strolled into the room and nosed at the Bennie's grocery bag. "Ah yes. These will do nicely. Thank you," it said.

Bennie looked from the unicorn to her father, then back again.

"Oh, he can't see me," the unicorn said. "I can make myself invisible to most humans."

That brought up a lot of questions that Bennie couldn't ask the thin air while having dinner with her dad.

"The movie was interesting. Thank you for showing it to me. The unicorn in it was one of the better representations that I have seen. Not perfect, but certainly not offensive, which is where most plays generally rank."

The unicorn hummed the movie's theme song as she munched on her violets.

"Earth to Benjamina," her father said.

"Sorry, Dad."

"Just tell me that you're not thinking about boys."

"Dad!"

He frowned. "That's not a no."

"I'm not thinking about boys, Dad."

He gave her a long, suspicious glance. "If you say so. You remember the rule, right?"

"The ridiculous no dating till I'm thirty rule?"

"That's the one."

"Your father seems like a sweet man," the unicorn said. "He could see me, if I let him. There are those who cannot, you know."

197

Bennie wanted to know why the unicorn was so chatty. She shoveled pizza into her mouth.

"Is it just the two of you?" the unicorn asked.

Bennie nodded.

Her father started talking about his current case—his client was desperate to keep a beach house in the divorce. Her father was an engaging storyteller, and any other day, she'd be happy to listen. Instead, she finished her pizza and kissed her father on the cheek. "I'm going to go do some more homework."

"Okay, sweetie. I'll handle the dishes."

"You're the best."

"Don't you forget it."

Upstairs, she turned on the unicorn. "What was that? I asked you to stay up here!"

"I wanted to see your father. Why are we not informing him of my presence?"

"He's terrible with secrets."

"So, you do not think he would object to my presence. You just worry that he may inadvertently reveal my location to my pursuer."

"Exactly."

"I see."

"Why do you need to hide from the hunter if you can make yourself invisible?" Bennie asked.

"He almost certainly has his own magics. He would not be a very successful monster hunter if he could be fooled by simple illusion."

Bennie opened the bottle of spring water. "How do you want this? Should I pour it into a bowl?"

The unicorn sniffed at the bottle and wrinkled her equine nose. "Please."

After she got that sorted out, Bennie opened her biology book.

"Despite the inaccuracies of the movie, it has inspired me to examine my current situation," the unicorn said. "Certain things, like being transformed into a human and falling in love with a man, simply seem horrific. However, the thought of traveling with a companion is appealing. I have never had a human companion before, but you seem to be the clear choice for the role."

"Pardon?" Bennie had never been the clear choice for anything before.

"Your father can support himself without you, and you are the first human to approach me with only my interests in mind. You are special."

Bennie blushed. Traveling the world with a unicorn sounded amazing. But she couldn't just leave her dad, even if he could support himself without her. "Thanks. But I—I have school."

"How long does that last?"

"Three more years."

"Not long at all, then! Very well, we can wait until you finish your education."

"I have to go to college after that. Then law school."

"Why?"

"Well, my dad wants me to take over his law practice. And I'll need some way to support myself."

"As my companion, that will be unnecessary. We will have adventures, and the magic will provide."

"Where will we have these adventures, exactly? If we're going to leave the country, I'd need a passport. And money. Will the magic provide those?"

"If they are truly necessary, then yes. There is no need to make up your mind now. It seems that I have time to convince you of the idea's appeal." The unicorn turned to the window.

Bennie tried to work on her homework. "What are you doing?" she asked, after the unicorn had stood motionless for a good ten minutes.

"Contemplating the stars."

"I... see."

"They are very beautiful, you know."

Bennie looked out the window. How long had it been since she'd just looked at the stars? "They really are."

•

On Monday morning, she left the unicorn contemplating the fall of shadows in her backyard and tried to just have a normal day at school.

But the hunter had other ideas.

He sat down across from her at lunch, glowering. Bennie wasn't sure how old he was, but he could at least pass as a teenager. His shoulder-length hair was pulled back into a ponytail, and he wore fashionably distressed jeans and a leather jacket.

Bennie glared and tried to ignore her racing heart. "I'm pretty sure you're not allowed to be here."

"Where is the unicorn?"

"I have no idea," Bennie said. "I went to warn it, we escaped, it left."

He blinked, and a silvery film coated his eyes. When he blinked again, it was gone. "Why did you go warn it, anyway? I can't see any of its magic on you—it's never healed you, you don't owe it anything."

"Maybe it healed my mother," Bennie said.

"You don't have a mother, Benjamina." He gave a dangerous smile, all teeth and threat. "Just a father."

Pure terror curled in the pit of Bennie's stomach. "I don't know where the unicorn is."

"You found it once, you can do it again."

"If you think that I'm going out into the woods with you alone, you're insane."

"If you think I'm giving you a choice, you're naïve."

"You're bluffing. The authorities might look the other way when you go after magical creatures, but they're not going to let you travel around hurting people."

"People will pay lots of money for bits and pieces of magical creatures. And money will buy a lot of leeway." He leaned forward. "You know, when a unicorn dies, a new unicorn is created. No matter how many you kill, there are always the same number in the world. They're a renewable resource. Killing it doesn't hurt anything."

"I imagine it would hurt the unicorn," Bennie said.

He shrugged. "You can't even prove that much." He stood up, loomed over her. "I'll let you get to your lunch. Think about what I said."

Bennie called her dad, but it went straight to voicemail.

•

The unicorn was curled on Bennie's bed when she got home, hardly indenting the firm mattress. She didn't take up any more room than Bennie normally did the twin bed.

"You are distressed," the unicorn observed. "What is going on?"

"The hunter threatened my father. And now he's not answering his phone."

"Is that uncommon?"

Bennie shook her head. "He sometimes leaves it off for days. He's probably fine."

"But you are still worried."

Bennie nodded.

"Then let us go and check on him." The unicorn hopped off of the bed. "Open the window, and climb on."

"It might be a trap," Bennie said as she did as it commanded.

"Oh, almost certainly." The unicorn leapt out the window and landed half a block away, in Mr. Thomas's flowerbed.

No one noticed as they galloped past, dodging joggers and dog-walkers and the occasional car. "Am I invisible now, too?" Bennie asked.

"Indeed."

"That's pretty neat."

"There are many rewards to being my companion."

Bennie didn't bother to remind the unicorn that she hadn't actually agreed to be its companion. She just directed it toward her father's office.

Her dad was in a meeting with a client. Something in Bennie's chest loosened as they stood out in the hallway, watching him. He was smiling and talking and completely, utterly fine.

The hunter was waiting for them in the parking lot, his eyes glowing silver. He flashed his dangerous smile. "I thought you didn't know where the unicorn was, Benjamina."

Bennie glared at him. "I lied."

"I can't believe it's letting you ride it," he said. "It must really like you."

"She is an incredibly special girl," the unicorn said.

"Is that so? It would be a shame if something happened to her, then." He drew a long, curved knife that glinted dangerously in his hand.

The unicorn cocked its head. "Do you usually find these empty threats helpful in your quest for petty wealth?"

He snorted. "A couple million dollars is hardly petty wealth."

"Anything you touch turns petty beneath your fingers. You will not be satisfied, no matter how much you accrue. I see a hundred curses already upon you, each one draining any joy out of your heart, turning everything you want to ash as soon as you grasp it."

"Shut up," he growled.

"If you harm me, your path will be forever set. But if you do not, I could help," the unicorn said. "It is within my power to remove those curses."

"And why would you do that?" he asked.

"Unicorns heal the injured, cure the sick. It is our nature."

"So what's to stop me from killing you, getting my money, and then going to another unicorn?"

The unicorn cocked her head to one side. "There are some wounds that even unicorn magic can't heal."

"Don't bullshit me. Killing a unicorn isn't any different from killing anything else."

"You said yourself that unicorns are a renewable resource," Bennie said, sliding down from the unicorn's back. She didn't want to slow it down, if it needed to fight or run. "If that's true, there has to be some reason why supply can't keep up with demand." Bennie had no idea what that reason was, but she figured it would not be good for the hunter.

"There is a cost to bringing a new unicorn into existence," the unicorn said. "When one of us dies, the replacement is created from the soul of the creature that slays us."

"So you're saying I'll drop dead and my soul will turn into a unicorn?" the hunter asked. He looked skeptical, but not comfortable in his disbelief.

"No, you will live on. But your soul will be…" the unicorn hesitated, then continued. "Your soul will be harvested. Some portion of it will remain—enough to animate your body, enough for you to feel the torment of the other curses upon you. Not enough to ever feel joy, or even simple contentment. And if you approach another unicorn, they will know you, and know that you are beyond their help."

"And what if I kill a second one?" the hunter asked. "What happens then?"

"You would not be able to kill a second unicorn," the unicorn said. "No matter what damage you inflict, it would not die under your hand." The unicorn lowered its head, so that its horn pointed straight at the hunter's heart. "Choose your path," it said. "Ask for my help, or slay me."

The hunter raised his curved knife, and Bennie stepped between them.

"Get out of my way," the hunter growled. "Nothing bad happens to my soul if I kill you."

"But you will go to jail," Bennie said. "This parking lot has complete camera coverage."

The hunter glanced up, to where there were, in fact, cameras mounted.

"You're not the first person to threaten my dad," Bennie said. "He's a divorce lawyer." She spread her hands. "Look, there's no way that you're going to get what you want, here. I won't let you kill the unicorn without going through me. If you kill both of us, you go to prison, and you probably won't even get to sell the unicorn's body, so you'll get your soul harvested for nothing. You should accept the unicorn's generous offer, get your curses lifted, and move on with your life."

The hunter glared at her for another long moment, then he dropped the knife.

The unicorn stepped around her, glowing like the moon. It touched the hunter with its horn, and the glow slowly spread through his body.

Then the unicorn turned from him, and its eyes bore into Bennie's. "You truly are a worthy companion," it said, then it stepped forward and nuzzled into her cheek. "Let's go home," it said.

They walked side by side, the unicorn's feet not-quite-dragging.

"No one has ever saved my life before. It makes me… happy. Thank you."

"You're welcome."

The unicorn hummed. After a few bars, Bennie recognized the theme from *The Last Unicorn* again.

"What happens to you if you die?" Bennie asked. "Are you still there, in the new unicorn?"

The unicorn shook its head. "We die like everything else. I know not what lies beyond that veil." They walked in silence for a few blocks. "You will be a good lawyer, if that is what you wish," the unicorn said. "I have no doubts that you will be able to do anything you set your mind to."

"And if I set my mind to being a unicorn's companion?"

"Well, you did save my life today. I would be honor bound to give you a recommendation, if you seek it."

Bennie laughed. "You're willing to wait till I'm done with school?"

"Yes."

"College, too, if I want?"

"I am immortal. A handful of years are nothing to me."

"So, that's a yes?"

"Verily."

"Okay, then." Bennie took a deep breath. "I'll be your companion."

"It is good that you have seen the light."

Bennie laughed again. "It wasn't a sure thing."

They climbed the stairs up to Bennie's room slowly. "It took me literally a day to convince you."

"Yeah, yeah."

"So, can I meet your father today?"

"Sure. I think he'll love you."

"Oh? I thought he would be unhappy with me for taking you away from him."

"Maybe at first. But I've figured out how to win him over—he'll assume you'll keep me away from boys."

"I have no reason to do so—unicorns do not actually care about physical virginity."

"Well, don't tell him that."

The unicorn curled up on Bennie's bed, and she could just barely squeeze in next to it. It shouldn't have been comfortable, but it was.

The unicorn nuzzled its cheek against hers. "As you wish, honored companion."

WIND CHIME MEMORIES

Originally appeared in *The Colored Lens*

Gary had put quite a bit of thought into his last meal. He considered steak and lobster or some fancy four course feast. In the end, he requested blueberry waffles.

A tiny old woman came in with a covered tray. She was dressed in a ragged gray cloak, with a hood that shadowed her face. She placed the tray on the table in front of him.

"I told them I didn't want a priest," he said. He wasn't sorry for his crimes. He didn't want to talk to anyone. He just wanted to eat his waffles and be done.

The woman made a low, crackling sound that he thought might be a laugh. "I'm no priest."

"What are you doing here, then?"

"I'm here to make you an offer."

Gary took the lid off of his tray and the smell of blueberry waffles filled the tiny room. "I'm not interested."

"As things stand, when you are gone, you will leave nothing good behind."

He shrugged. "That's not really my problem."

"I understand that you are tired," she said. "I understand that you want your suffering to end. But no one wants to fade from history without a ripple."

Gary took a bite of his waffle. "I'm sure I'll be on a list somewhere. Maybe be a cautionary tale."

"That is not a legacy."

"And what legacy do you suggest in the hour I have left?"

"There is good in you, as there is in all people. I could take it from you and share it with the world."

They'd also given him orange juice and milk and coffee. He poured himself a glass of each. "If I just ignore you, will you go away?"

She reached out and touched his wrist. Her fingers were long and bone-thin, but warm against his skin. He looked up at her. Her eyes were deep summer green in her shadowed face, and her body looked like a thornbush forced into rough human form.

She drew her fingers away, and pulled a clear crystal prism out of his flesh.

Its facets reflected pieces of an almost-forgotten memory. A fishing trip with his grandfather. The smell of the water, the feel of worms wriggling between his fingers. The silver flash of scales in the cloudy water. His grandfather's calloused hand, showing him how to hold the pole.

Gary dropped his fork. "What are you?"

"There are a thousand tiny happy memories lost in the darkness of your soul. If you are willing, I will take them from you so that they do not end here."

"They're my memories. How could they exist without me?"

The woman shrugged. "I have made my offer. Now, if you want to refuse, I will go. If you accept, I will get to work."

"What will you do with them?"

She shrugged again. "Do you have any requests? Anyone you'd like to benefit?"

"I have a sister, Lisa. I think she has a son."

"Give me your hand."

Gary wondered if he was dreaming. It was the only thing that made sense.

He held out his hand.

She drew the memories out, one by one. His first kiss, under the slide at the local park. Watching a falling star on a hike in the desert. His father teaching him how to swim. His mother making blueberry waffles on Sunday morning. The time he skipped a rock and it bounced ten times.

"There are more than I expected," Gary said, his voice sounding distant and thin in his ears.

The woman smiled at him, and pulled memory after memory after memory.

Finally she released his hand. She reached down and picked up his forgotten fork. "I will take good care of these. You enjoy your waffles."

And then she was gone.

The waffles were still hot, and steam rose from his coffee.

Gary ate slowly, savoring each bite.

•

Lisa walked her son to the bus stop, where they stood beneath a lamppost and waited, hand in hand. She heard a sound like crystals chiming in the faint breeze, and a tiny rainbow danced across the pavement.

For some reason, she remembered a morning with her mother and her brother, when she was very young and things had been good. She squeezed her son's hand. "How do you feel about waffles for dinner tonight?"

THEATER CAT

Originally appeared in *Horror d'oeuvres*

Jordan crouched between Tim and Steve in the snow-covered shrubs, trying to figure out the best way to sneak into the boarded-up theater.

"Guys, seriously, this is a bad idea." Steve said. "I mean, look at that place. We go in there, we die. It might be zombies, or ghosts, or a serial killer, but no matter what, we're no match for it."

Jordan grunted. He didn't really want to sneak into the theater, but he was more worried about cops and permanent records than serial killers.

"You watch too many horror movies," Tim muttered.

"You sound like my mother," Steve said.

"Shut up. We're going in." Tim wiggled out from underneath the shrub.

"How?" Steve asked.

"There's a gap big enough for us to squeeze through right there." Tim pointed to a window near the corner of the building.

Jordan looked at the small opening in the window and almost sighed in relief. "Well, then I guess you're counting me out of this adventure, cause I can't squeeze through that. Plus, it's right on the front of the building, you'll get spotted for sure."

Tim grinned. "You lack both imagination and daring, my chubby friend."

Jordan glared at Tim. "Oh yeah?"

Tim dashed across the street. Before Jordan could react, Tim had wriggled through the window.

"He's so totally dead," Steve breathed. Jordan could tell that he was waiting for the screaming to start.

The front door opened. "Are you two wieners coming or not?" Tim called.

Tim'd never let it go if they didn't join him. Jordan cursed under his breath, then barreled across the street and through the door, with Steve on his heels.

"How'd you get the door open?" Steve leaned against the door, panting slightly.

"It's one of those doors that are only locked from the outside."

"That means we won't be locked in when we have to run away." Steve turned around and opened the door a crack.

The theater was dark and smelled like stale popcorn and cat pee. Jordan could barely see his friends' faces in the light that made it through the dirty windows and the gaps in the boards. Tim clicked his lighter on and held the tiny flame above his head.

Something moved on the edge of the flickering light. Glowing eyes appeared from the darkness and began to creep toward them. Steve screamed.

Tim started laughing. "Steve, it's just a cat."

"A black cat," Steve snapped.

"She's pretty." Jordan knelt down and held out his hand. The cat sauntered over and sniffed his fingers. After a second, Jordan started to scratch behind her ears.

"Black cats are bad luck," Steve said. "Stop petting the stupid thing."

"Steve has a point. It probably has fleas or something," Tim said.

"She doesn't have fleas." Jordan picked up the cat, and she promptly started purring. "I'm taking her home with me."

"How do you know it's a girl?" Tim asked.

"I dunno." Holding the cat made Jordan happy. He wished he could start purring, too. He kissed the top of her silky head.

"Oh my God." Steve started backing toward the door. "The cat is the monster."

"What?" Jordan hugged the cat tighter to his body.

"Back away from Jordan, Tim."

Jordan expected Tim to laugh, but he obeyed Steve's command. "You two are both being retarded," he said.

"We're leaving now, Jordan. And the cat stays here." Steve grabbed the door handle.

"Guys, come on."

"Put it down, dude." Tim said as he joined Steve by the door.

Jordan didn't want to put the cat down. She was so warm and he could tell that she loved him. She smelled like the cinnamon cookies that his grandmother used to make for him. She'd never let him feel lonely again.

"Jordan. Come on," Steve said.

It was hard for Jordan to bend down, and even harder to let go of the cat. He felt like he was letting go of Christmas. He felt empty and cold and completely alone. As soon the cat's feet touched the dusty carpet, Tim lunged forward, grabbed Jordan's wrist, and pulled him out through the door at a full run. Tim didn't let go until they were a good three blocks away from the theater.

"What the hell was that about?" Jordan demanded, almost doubled over from the run and from the pain of letting go of his cat.

Steve just shook his head.

"You started to look weird." Tim said.

"Weird? Weird how?"

"You started to turn into the shadows. Sort of—I don't know, Jordan. It was just weird," Tim said.

Jordan gazed back toward the theater. "I guess it doesn't matter, Mom wouldn't have let me keep her anyway. She's allergic. What do you guys want to do now?"

"Let's go to Steve's house and watch one of his movies," Tim suggested.

"A horror movie?" Jordan asked.

"Yeah. Next time I want to be prepared," Tim said.

"You two are both crazy." Jordan watched his cat slip out through a broken window and follow them. He didn't mention it to his friends.

THE WHITE STALLION

Originally appeared in *Beyond Centauri*

Joni slipped out of the dark house, careful to keep the hem of her nightdress out of the thick spring mud. She crept away from her sleeping family, and didn't look back.

Her father had promised her a horse for her birthday, but April had come and gone and all she'd gotten was a new dress and a sturdy pair of boots.

But she knew where she could get her own horse. A white stallion. They said that old George had seen it before he passed, and that's why no one was allowed in the woods west of town.

Joni couldn't figure how just looking at a horse could kill you. It seemed right silly. And she was twelve now, too old to be scared of silly stories.

She'd never been in the woods at night before. Branches covered with spring buds intertwined overhead, and thick roots caught her boot-clad toes. She looked back, and she could still see the moonlight on the path behind her. Ahead, the woods were dark as pitch. She wished she'd thought to bring a lantern.

She stumbled along the path, scraping her palms on rough-barked trunks. Brambles caught at her nightdress and tangled in her hair. She trudged on. She wanted that horse.

Wind gusted in her face, and her feet slipped out from under her. Cold mud seeped through her dress, and she stood up, shivering. All around her, invisible in the darkness, trees swayed. Their creaking branches sounded like dead voices. Stinging scratches covered her legs and arms, and she hugged herself against the sudden cold.

"Turn back," the branches groaned.

"No." Joni thrust her chin forward. "You're not the boss of me, trees. I'm here for the white stallion."

"You are too young to come here seeking death, child," the trees said.

"I'm not seeking death," Joni said.

"Death is all you will find here. Turn back! Turn back now!"

Joni thought about her family, sleeping in their warm, safe house. Maybe she'd get a horse for Christmas. Or for her next birthday. Waiting wouldn't be that hard.

Joni didn't want to wait. She stepped forward.

A white light appeared before her.

Joni glanced away, thinking again about her warm bed, about oatmeal for breakfast, about how her father's beard scratched her cheeks when he hugged her.

She looked back toward the light and saw the stallion. His white hide glowed brighter than moonlight. Joni held her hands out to him. He galloped up to her, then stopped just out of her reach, rearing and whinnying.

"You must be lonely," Joni said. "When you're my horse, you won't be lonely anymore."

The stallion took a hesitant step forward. The trees moaned.

"It's all right," Joni said. "I'm not afraid." She reached up and laid a hand on his neck, and the white stallion trembled at her touch. Joni stepped closer and buried her face in his mane. He smelled like the roses they'd put on her baby sister's grave, like fresh-turned earth, like the river after a storm. Joni twined her fingers through the stallion's mane and pulled herself up onto his back.

The stallion reared, but Joni clung on. Beneath her stallion's hooves, she could see a little girl's body on the ground, her white nightdress torn and muddy.

Joni mourned the girl, and the life she'd left. Cold tears crept down her cheeks. The stallion shifted beneath her, ready to be gone.

"Run," Joni commanded, and the stallion obeyed. They galloped through the woods, and Joni could see the path before her, lit by the stallion's glow. She ducked under branches, and was always ready when the stallion leapt over logs or streams. They ran until the moon set and the sun broke over the horizon. They reached the end of the woods, and the stallion hesitated. But Joni urged him on, and they rode into the sunrise.

They passed Joni's house. Joni waved once, but she didn't look back. She knew that they'd never come back to these parts. But that was just fine. There was a whole world for them to explore.

YOUR WEATHERMAN

Originally appeared as "The Prognostiquestiran" in *Bronies: For the Love of Ponies*

Max watched his girlfriend's daughter ride slow circles around the Kiddy Corral. It was one of her friend's birthdays. Or something. It wasn't his ideal way to spend a Saturday morning, but her mother wasn't feeling very well.

At least the weather was perfect.

Just like Max had said it would be, for once.

Minuette (Emily was amazing, but seriously, who named their kid Minuette?) waved at him from atop her dun-colored pony. He waved back.

He needed a smoke, and since Emily freaked if he smoked in front of her kid, he wandered around the barn. He stopped once he was out of sight, right next to the wooden fence that enclosed the farm's collection of miniature ponies. He pulled his smokes out of his pocket.

One of the tiny ponies trotted over. It was only a little higher than his knees. "Hey," it said.

Max dropped his cigarettes.

The pony was the deep gray of an angry cumulonimbus, and its mane and tale were lightning-white. "Don't think of making any Mr. Ed jokes."

"I was too busy thinking about psychotic breaks," Max managed. He was in TV; he prided himself on his quick recovery time.

"You're gonna want to put a pin in that thought, since I'm about to blow your mind," the pony said.

"I might actually prefer my mind unblown." Max picked up his cigarettes and lit one with shaking hands.

"Those things'll kill you, you know."

Max grunted and inhaled.

"You can call me Cap," the pony said.

"Cap?"

"It's short for Thunder Cap, but I've always thought that was a little pretentious."

Max wished he carried a flask. A drink might help.

"I've seen you on TV," Cap said. "You're a weatherman, right?"

"Meteorologist," Max corrected automatically.

Cap snorted. "Really?"

"I won't mention Mr. Ed if you don't call me a weatherman."

Cap shrugged. Max hadn't known that ponies could shrug. "I guess that's fair. Anyway, I can predict the weather."

"So can I."

Cap snorted again. "After a fashion, I suppose. But I'm never wrong."

Max imagined never being wrong. It would be... heavenly. His father called him every time he made a mistake and asked what exactly the money he'd spent on Max's big time education was worth.

"If you bust me out of this joint, I can guarantee that you'll be the most accurate weatherman in the Tristate Area."

"If you're never wrong, I'd be the most accurate meteorologist in the world."

•

He'd scribbled Cap's forecast on his hand. Now, looking at it under the harsh lights in the studio, the whole thing seemed ridiculous. Maybe he'd hallucinated the whole thing. Did he really want to stake his career on a talking miniature pony?

His planned forecast was different from Cap's. Max had predicted rain Thursday, then sun all through the weekend. Cap called for the rain to arrive later, then stick around.

Max washed his hand and went with his original forecast.

•

He hung up on his father halfway through the old man's predictable rant. He needed an excuse to go back out to the Kiddy Corral. He dialed Emily's number.

Minuette answered. "Hey, Max," she said. "My mom's in the bathroom." Her voice lowered to a whisper. "I think she'll be a while. She's sick."

Max winced. Emily had been sick a lot lately. "Is there anything I can do?"

"She just needs to be alone."

"Do you want to go back out to the Kiddy Corral? My treat."

"It's raining."

"Their website says that they're open, rain or shine."

"I'll ask my mom."

Emily beamed at him when he stopped by to take Minuette. She looked worryingly pale, and her cheek was clammy when he kissed it.

The kid yammered nonstop about horses while he drove. She really was a smart little thing. Max hadn't known that much about anything when he was her age.

He put her on a full sized horse this time. He admonished her to be careful, and not to tell her mom.

Cap was waiting for him by the fence. "You were wrong," the pony said.

"Yeah, I know."

"You want me to tell you about next week?" Cap asked.

Max pulled his raincoat tighter around himself and nodded.

"If I'm right, you promise to get me out of here? I need a jailbreak."

"Can't I just buy you?"

Cap shook his head. "They'd never sell me. They love me." He rolled his eyes and looked around at the other tiny ponies. "But no one here ever talks to me, and every day is the same. I'm going nuts. You've gotta help me, man."

•

On the drive home, Minuette finally ran out of horse-related facts. "If you want, you can call me Minnie," she said, staring at the dashboard.

"Okay. I'll do that." Max smiled at her.

"Why were you talking to that pony?"

Max drove in silence for a few moments. The windshield wipers swished back and forth. Confiding in his girlfriend's 10-year-old was probably a terrible idea, but he needed to talk to someone about all this.

He pulled over. "He says that he can predict the weather."

Minnie laughed. "Max, ponies can't talk."

Max shrugged. "This one does."

Minnie was silent for a long moment. "You're serious."

Max nodded.

"Well, can he predict the weather?"

Max nodded again. "I think so. And he wants me to rescue him from the ranch and bring him home with me."

"You'd need a bigger apartment. Even little horses need space."

"Do you and your mom have enough space? Would you be able to keep him for me?"

"Maybe," Minnie said. "But my mom won't like it. And what if we get caught? I don't want to take the fall for you."

"Maybe I can move in." Emily had asked him to, months ago. He'd put her off.

Minnie closed her eyes, then nodded. "I think mom would like that." She nodded again. "I would like it, too."

•

When they got back, Emily still looked exhausted, but she'd put on some makeup and ordered pizza. She remembered to order ham and pineapple. No one ever remembered that Max loved ham and pineapple.

"So, Minnie and I were talking," Max said, scooping up two slices. "And we think that I should move in."

Emily gaped at them. "That—that's great!" She jumped up and hugged him, hard. "Oh, Max. I—" she blinked and wiped away a tear. "When?"

"This week," Minnie said. "I can clean this place up while he packs."

Max nodded. "And we'll pay movers, and you won't have to worry about a thing."

Emily cried some more, then they finished the pizza and watched reruns all piled together on the couch.

It almost felt like family.

•

Cap's predictions were right. Max wasn't surprised. He and Minnie snuck out of the house at midnight that Saturday.

"You really should stay home," Max hissed at her as they closed the car doors as silently as possible. It wasn't nearly as silent as he'd like. Luckily, Emily slept like a log.

"Not happening," Minnie said. "And anyway, you need me."

"Do I?"

"Do you have a plan?" she asked.

"Sure. Go in, grab the pony, drive home."

Minnie sniffed. "My plan's better."

"Okay, what is it?"

Minnie shook her head. "I'll tell you when we get there."

Max pulled over a mile away from the corral.

"Will you still bring me back to ride after this?" Minnie asked. "If you don't, it might be suspicious."

Minnie really did love riding. "I guess you're right."

The farm was completely dark, but Cap's bright white mane shone in the starlight. He was waiting for them by the fence. "Glad you could make it," he said. "Now what?"

"We break off that limb," Minnie said, pointing to a dying tree. "It'll bust the fence, and then it'll look like you escaped on your own."

Max stared at her. "That's brilliant."

She shrugged. "I read a lot of Nancy Drew."

The tree was sturdier than it looked, but with both of them hanging on it and bouncing, the limb eventually gave way. It was wretchedly loud, and they just managed to dodge out of its path.

The fence wasn't so lucky.

Cap clamored over the broken slats. "Come on, before someone comes to investigate the crash."

They ran all the way back to the car.

•

Max's reputation for flawless weather reporting started to grow, and he was even getting better at understanding why the unexpected elements in Cap's forecasts happened. His own predictions only differed from Cap's once every month or so.

He liked coming home to Emily and Minnie more than he would have believed. He helped Minnie with her science homework, and he got accustomed to falling asleep to the soft rhythm of Emily's breath. They went to the movies every Friday night and ate grilled cheese sandwiches every Tuesday.

Max called his father every couple of weeks, and he quit smoking.

Emily was sick more days than not, but she insisted that she'd be fine. Max and Minnie cooked and cleaned and let her rest.

She never even noticed Cap, who spent his time in the basement or out in the backyard. When Max asked how he kept himself hidden, he just shrugged and said, "I'm tiny. And she's distracted."

Max and Cap spent hours discussing weather, baseball, and the meaning of life while Max folded laundry.

But eventually, they had to face the fact that Emily wasn't getting better.

The doctor's office was cold. Max took off his blazer and draped it around Emily's shoulders. They seemed thinner than they had a few months ago. He kissed the top of her head.

She squeezed his hand and smiled at Minnie. "You two will see. Just wait, I'm sure the doctor will tell you that I'm fine."

The doctor didn't tell them that Emily was fine. She sent them to an oncologist, who diagnosed Emily with stomach cancer. She stared radiation and chemo. She grew thinner and paler every day.

The treatments failed.

Max asked her to marry him.

●

"How far out can you see?" Max asked as he dumped a capful of detergent into the washer.

"Why?" Cap asked.

"I want Emily to have a perfect wedding day."

Cap closed his eyes. "June 14th. You should get married on June 14th."

●

Emily took Minnie dress shopping. Max took her horseback riding. He never saw her cry. But he did find her down in the basement more and more often, curled up on a pile of laundry and combing out Cap's tail.

Emily was brave and strong, most of the time. She had bad days, and afterwards she'd cry and apologize and beg him not to leave her.

He didn't have the heart to ask her not to leave him.

●

"Is there some way I can save her?" Max asked. "You're magic, right? That means that there is magic. And magic has to be able to cure cancer. Could you—could you save her?"

Cap shook his head. "I'm not the right kind of magic."

"There's got to be a way."

Cap hesitated.

"Tell me," Max said. "Please."

"The blood of a dragon can heal anything," Cap said.

"How do I find a dragon?" Max asked. He pulled his phone out of his pocket to call in to work for the next few days. Finding a dragon couldn't take that long, could it? Not with the internet and airplanes.

"Max."

"What?"

"I can see more than the weather. I—I see the future. All of it. If you go looking for a dragon, you'll find it. But it will kill you. And Emily will die anyway."

Max buried his face in his hands. "And Minnie will be left alone."

Cap nodded. "That's her biggest fear, you know. That after Emily dies you'll leave, too."

"I would never do that."

Cap nodded. "I know."

Max started to cry. "I don't want to lose her, Cap. I want to save her."

"You can't."

"I would give up anything," Max sobbed.

"I know."

"I've never felt so useless."

"You're not useless. So you can't kill a dragon for her. You're making her last days happy, and you're going to take care of her daughter."

"That won't save her."

Cap shrugged.

Eventually, Max cried himself out. "It's not enough," he said. His throat ached.

"Max, it is. Sometimes, all you can do is enough. This is one of those times."

Minnie came down the basement stairs, comb in hand. She spotted Max, his face still wet with tears, and froze.

"Hey," Max managed. He held his arms out to her.

She hesitated for a second, then she ran to him and buried her face in his chest. He held her while she cried. "I'm here," he whispered. "I'm here."

•

June 14th dawned a perfect day. Emily looked almost ghostly, but she was still radiant in her wedding dress. Minnie was the only bridesmaid.

They had the ceremony outdoors, beneath an apple tree.

The next day, Max took Emily and Minnie to Disney World. They spent a week there, then came home. The weather was perfect every day.

Emily died on August 1st.

•

The house was full of casseroles. Max wasn't sure if he'd ever be able to look at a casserole without wanting to cry ever again.

It was Tuesday. He and Minnie made grilled cheese. Cap came up from the basement and stood in the kitchen with them.

"I'm sorry I couldn't save her," Cap said.

Max wondered if he'd have ever moved in if Cap hadn't come into his life. He wondered if he'd have stuck around, or left for greener pastures when Emily was diagnosed.

He didn't really want to know.

He looked at what was left of his family. "I love you. Both of you," he said.

"I love you, too." Minnie hugged him.

"You're the best friends I've ever had," Cap said.

Max handed Minnie her grilled cheese. "You can call me Dad, if you want."

She managed a tiny smile. "Okay. I'll do that."

SEASONS OF FRIENDSHIP

Originally appeared in *Silver Blade*

If Verna didn't find a flower soon she wouldn't make it through the night. The icy wind blew snowflakes in her face and buffeted against her iridescent wings as she flitted from one window to another. She hated Pittsburgh's winters. She could have moved to Hawaii with her mother, but Pittsburgh was home, and she refused to leave. Plus, the city deserved at least one fairy.

Where were all of the poinsettias? There'd been one in every other window here just a week ago. She should have stayed at the conservatory, but she always had bad dreams when she slept there. Something strange happened to flowers that knew their scientific names. She avoided the florists' shops because flowers that knew their prices were even worse.

Verna spotted an African violet in a pot inside a tiny third story window. She heaved a sigh of relief and flitted up to it. Energy surged through her as she pressed her fingertips against the window, leaving tiny fingerprints. She curled up on the tiny shelf of window ledge with her back pressed into the frigid glass and drifted into restorative sleep. She dreamed of spring—of fields of lush grass dotted with dandelions, of resting in the branches of a fragrant blooming lilac, of beds filled with daffodils and tulips.

•

"Hello."

Verna jerked out of her dreams and nearly fell off of the window ledge. Her wings fluttered for balance.

"Are you a fairy?" A little girl's face peered out the window at Verna. She tugged the window open, and her breath formed a silver cloud in the morning sunshine. Her eyes were the dark brown of freshly turned soil, and her hair was a mess of short blond curls.

"I am," Verna said. Children often saw her. Most of them pretended that they didn't, though. They didn't believe their eyes.

"What's your name?" the little girl asked.

"Verna," the fairy answered. "What's yours?"

"Angelica, but everyone calls me Angie."

"It's nice to meet you, Angie," Verna said.

"Why were you sleeping outside my window?"

"I'm a flower fairy, so I can only sleep in places where there are flowers blooming."

"Can't you just use magic to make flowers?" Angie asked.

"Not anymore. There's not enough magic." Verna tried not to remember how things were before. She didn't want to think about the beauty of pale pink roses pushing up through the snow around her feet. The memory was too wonderful and depressing.

"What happened to it?"

Verna shrugged. "I'm not sure. It just started to go away."

"When?" Angie asked.

"A long time ago."

"Oh," Angie said in a small sad voice. "I wish that it would come back."

"I do too."

"What happens if you can't find a flower to sleep next to?"

"I start to fade away, and I'll eventually disappear," Verna said.

"That's terrible! It's not fair!"

Verna shrugged. She didn't want to tell Angie that life was never fair.

"Well, you can sleep next to my flower anytime. And I'll see if I can get my mom to let me have more flowers for you."

Verna smiled and nodded her thanks, but she knew that Angie would probably forget about her within a few hours. That's the way things worked, now.

A voice called from within the house. "Angie, time for breakfast!"

Angie reached out and touched one of Verna's wings. "Will you be here when I come home from school?"

"I can be, if you wish," Verna said, enjoying the way the warmth from Angie's finger spread through her body.

"Okay. I'll try to get you another flower, too." Angie closed her window and vanished into the house for her breakfast.

•

Verna spent the day on Angie's roof, soaking in the weak winter sunshine. *She'll forget me*, she thought. *Angie will forget me, and forget her promise, and there won't be any new flowers.*

Angie's window sprang open, and the little girl's voice floated out. "Verna! Where are you?"

Joy filled Verna's chest as she fluttered down to the window.

"There you are! I was afraid that you'd gone. Look what I got!" Angie held up a tiny potted rosebush. Pink roses. Verna's favorite.

"You remembered." Verna stroked one of the tiny petals.

"Of course I remembered. No one at school believed me when I told them about you, but that's just because they're dumb." Angie sat the rose next to her violet. "Mom was happy to buy me another flower. She said that gardening is good for the soul."

"You'll forget about me eventually," Verna said as she climbed into the pot with the rosebush.

"Of course I won't!"

"Everyone does. It's because of the magic." Verna buried her nose in one of the pink blossoms.

"Well, I promise, even if I forget about you, I'll remember to keep flowers in my window. That way, you'll never have to worry about fading away."

"It would be nice to not have to worry," Verna said, feeling hope deep inside in spite of herself.

•

Verna spent the rest of the winter on Angie's windowsill. Even when spring came, and there were flowers everywhere, she still went to Angie's window every day. Verna's magic made Angie's flowers grow bigger and more beautiful than flowers in the most carefully tended gardens.

One day, Angie seemed distracted, and when Verna first fluttered up to her window her eyes skipped over her. She was losing her. Tears welled up in Verna's eyes, then Angie's eyes met hers. The little girl blinked.

"Verna! What's wrong?"

"You almost didn't see me. You're forgetting. You're going to grow up and forget me, and I'm going to miss you. I haven't had a friend in a long time."

"Verna, I won't forget you, I promise!" Angie held up a little leather book with golden embossed flowers on the cover. "I've written all about you in my journal, so I can't forget."

"You'll think you made me up."

"No! I wrote down that I didn't." She ruffled through pages. "See, right here. It says, *Verna is a flower fairy and she needs flowers to live, so I have to always have flowers. And I didn't make her up.*"

225

Verna nodded and blinked away her tears, but she knew that she was going to lose her friend. She'd enjoy talking to Angie for as long as she could, and try not to let her sorrow show.

•

Angie wasn't coming to the window. She was bent over something on her bed, laughing. Verna could just hear her through the glass. "Hello, kitty, my name is Angie." Angie took the kitten's paw and shook it. "What's your name? Violet? What a nice name."

Verna pressed her palms against the smooth glass as tears streamed down her cheeks. Angie had a new friend to replace her. Verna knew that she should be happy for her. Nothing good came of believing in fairies anymore.

But she was so lonely.

•

Spring turned to summer, then fall, then it was winter again. Verna found herself fluttering up to Angie's window. *She forgot about me*, she told herself. *Why should she remember that she promised to keep flowers for me?*

Verna reached the windowsill and froze, staring.

She could barely see through the mass of flowers in the little girl's window.

•

Angie grew up, and moved into a dorm room, then an apartment, then a house of her own. She stayed in Pittsburgh, and she always kept flowers on her windowsill. She could never explain why.

Angie's daughter was sitting on her bed one winter day, looking out the window, when Verna fluttered up to the flowers. The little girl cried out in joy and rushed to the window. She threw the window open. "Are you a fairy?" she asked.

"I am," Verna said.

"What's your name?" the little girl asked.

"Verna."

"That's my name, too!"

TOAST

Originally appeared in *The Drabblecast*

Elayne won't eat toast anymore. A week ago, she never would have dreamed of giving up toast. It was her favorite breakfast food, and breakfast is the most important meal of the day.

Last Saturday, Elayne woke up before her alarm went off and wandered into the kitchen to start her coffee. That done, she grabbed the loaf of Wonder Whole Wheat off of her microwave and plopped two slices of bread into her trusty toaster. She went to brush her teeth while she waited for her toast to pop.

The coffee pot began to burble and the toaster popped just as Elayne spat her spent toothpaste into the sink. She danced to the kitchen, humming to herself. It was going to be a great day.

She pulled the toast out with the toaster tongs her little brother had made her by gluing two tongue depressors to a clothespin.

"Oh, damn it." The bottom left corners of her toast were pale green with mold. With a sigh, she tossed them toward the trashcan, missing by inches. She glared at the toast for a moment, willing it to get up and deposit itself in the trash were it belonged, then she took two more slices of bread and carefully inspected them for mold before she inserted them into the toaster.

She was thinking about bending over to pick up the toast on the floor when her phone rang.

She dashed into the other room. The caller I.D. told her that it was Rick. Her gut told her that he was calling to cancel their trip up to the lake. They were supposed to go biking and camping and skinny-dip under the stars.

"Hey, sweetie," she chirped as she picked up the phone, hoping against hope that he was going to surprise her. Maybe he was calling to tell her how beautiful she was, or how much he loved her, or about the random pony that'd just run out into the road, missing him by inches.

"I'm not going to be able to go up to the lake today."

"Why not?" Elayne asked, half of her feeling disappointed. The other half felt smug and precognizant.

"Something came up at work, and I just can't get away."

Rick didn't even sound sorry. "What came up?"

"Just work stuff. It's complicated."

Why was she even dating this condescending asshole? "You know, if you didn't want to go, you could have just said so."

"Elayne, stop being unreasonable."

Unreasonable? "Rick, stop treating me like I'm a clingy slow-witted four-year-old."

"I'm not!"

"You are too! And you knew how much I was looking forward to this weekend, and you didn't even apologize for blowing it off."

"Is that what you want? An apology? Fine, I'm sorry!"

Elayne bit back her angry retort and tried to remember the last time she'd had fun with Rick. She couldn't. Anytime they did manage to find time to be together, all they did was fight or sit around trying to convince the other one to pick an activity. "No, Rick, that's not good enough. I'm tired of you standing me up and talking down to me." Elayne took a deep breath. "I don't think I want to see you again."

"Elayne, wait. You don't mean that."

"Goodbye, Rick." Elayne gently placed the phone back in its cradle. She waited for the tears to start, but to her surprise, they didn't. She felt fine. Hungry, but fine. And her toast would be cold by now. Stupid Rick, ruining everything.

Screw him. She'd go camping by herself and have a great time in spite of him. Or maybe one of her friends had the weekend off. She hadn't spent nearly enough time with her friends lately.

She walked back into the kitchen and saw her toast climbing out of the toaster. The moldy toast from the floor was helping it get over the plastic edge. They had tiny little arms that split into two fingered hands and stubby little legs. The two pieces of moldy toast had taken aluminum foil and made themselves silver eyes and little antennae that stuck up from either side of crease in the top of the loaf.

Elayne fainted.

She woke up surrounded by a small army of living toast. It looked like they'd toasted every piece of bread in the house. There were a couple of bagels, too, and an English muffin that she'd forgotten she had. They all had aluminum foil eyes and antennae and inch-long limbs. They were hopping up and down and making noises that sounded like the toaster popping. A few of them moved forward, holding up an aluminum foil headband with antennae attached. They held it out to her and hopped toward her, popping.

"You want me to put that on my head?"

The popping got faster, and they hopped higher.

Elayne's curiosity overcame her fear of the strange little creatures. "What the hell." Elayne took the headpiece and slipped it on. Suddenly, she felt a wave of happiness that she knew hadn't come from inside her brain. "You're communicating empathetically," she said. The happiness intensified. She felt almost giddy. "How is this happening?" Elayne knew that she should be more freaked out, but she just couldn't be with so much innocent joy pouring into her head.

The various toasted bread products had no idea. "Maybe it was some weird combination of the mold and the microwave and heat," Elayne guessed.

The toasts popped noncommittally.

"Well, what am I going to do with you?"

Again, the toasts had no suggestions.

"Swell. It's not like you were a present from some wise old man or anything. I didn't even get any warnings about when not to feed you. Will living toast need to eat?"

Elayne ended up spending the rest of the day teaching the toasts how to coordinate themselves to play *Dance Dance Revolution* using both dance pads. It took four or five of them hopping in unison to get the pad to pick up their movement. Watching them hopping up and down and shaking their tiny two-fingered fists in frustration when they missed a note was the most hilarious thing Elayne had seen in a while. She couldn't remember the last time she'd laughed so much.

Sometime after dinner, during which Elayne ate a chicken Caesar salad without any croutons and discovered that the toasts didn't seem interested in food, though they did like it when she read her romance novel out loud to them, the doorbell rang. The door opened before Elayne could get to it. "Elayne?"

She winced at Rick's voice as he slipped in through the door. "I told you I didn't want to see you again."

Rick held out a bouquet of pink roses. "I brought you these—what the hell is that on your head?"

"It's nothing." Elayne didn't think that Rick would react well to seeing her toasty friends. She didn't think they'd like him either—her agitation was upsetting them through their empathic link. She could hear them popping distressedly over the jazz she'd put on.

Rick pushed past her and strode into the other room. "Is there someone here with you?"

"No!" Elayne tried to block his view, but it was too late.

"What the fuck?" Rick stumbled back in shock, bumping into Elayne and sending her crashing onto the floor. Her head bounced off of the refrigerator handle on the way down. Pain and stars exploded in her skull.

Elayne felt a wave of rage through her empathic link with the toasts. They swarmed toward Rick as a mob, ignoring the fact that he was twice as big as all of them put together. He stomped on the English muffin, and it made a terrible *crunch*. The toasts continued to throw themselves fearlessly at Rick. Elayne's view of the carnage was fuzzy, but the crystal clear sound seemed to reverberate inside her skull as she listened to Rick methodically stomping on all of her little friends. She felt a wrenching empathic vacuum after each one.

"Stop it, Rick!" she shouted as she struggled to stand. Her body wouldn't quite cooperate. When she finally did manage to get up, she had to hold onto the fridge with a death grip to keep from falling over again. The floor seemed to be spinning. She was crying. She hadn't noticed when she'd started. She heard one last crunch over her sobs. She stumbled to the doorway and nearly retched at the sight of the massacre. Rick was surrounded by a field of crumbs that had been ground into Elayne's carpet. Tiny aluminum foil eyes and bent or broken antennae glinted from the dust.

"I hate you." Elayne fell to her knees, sinking her fingers into the crumbs that had moments ago been living toasts that had risen up to protect her. "Get out of my house."

"Elayne, you're bleeding." Rick knelt and touched the side of her head.

Elayne jerked away from his touch, ignoring the dizziness that her sudden movement caused. "I said get out." Tears and blood dripped onto the carpet, mixing with the corpses.

Rick left. A little while later, an ambulance came and took Elayne to the emergency room for her concussion. She came back from the hospital the next day with and found a fresh loaf of bread sitting on her doorstep. The note on it read *I'm sorry*. She walked over to the toaster, plopped two pieces into it, pushed down the button, crossed her fingers, and waited.

MEET CUTE

Originally appeared in *Unsung Stories*

Elayne dropped her keys in their spot and slipped her aluminum foil headband over her temples. A familiar wave of welcome enveloped her.

Her toasts clustered around the TV. Their aluminum antennae glinted in the dim blue light.

Elayne sighed. "Are you watching that Disney Singles Cruise infomercial again?"

The bagel (he was her favorite, but they all pretended not to know it) wobbled over to her on its tiny legs and bumped against her shins in greeting. "I keep telling you, we can't go. I can't afford it, and anyway, it's a boat. It's surrounded by water. What if one of you fell in? There's nothing worse than soggy toast."

The toasts beamed cheerful optimism at her. The bagel pointed to her computer.

Elayne obediently sat down. The toasts sent a telepathic image of her email icon, so she opened it.

There was an email from her mother at the very top. It had already been opened. "What are you up to?" she muttered.

Hi honey! I just got an email from one of your friends, a ToastyPal, which is a very strange name, by the way. This internet is such an odd place. Anyway, ToastyPal mentioned that you might like to do one of those "single's cruises," and even sent a link to a Disney version that looks super fun! Your father and I didn't want to say anything, but we're worried about you, sweetie. It's been over year since you stopped seeing your Rick. He was such a nice-looking young man!

We're getting you a ticket for this cruise for your birthday. Happy 30th, sweetie! I'm sure you'll have a great time!

Elayne rounded on the toasts. "You emailed my MOTHER?"

They burbled with excitement and filled her mind with images from the infomercial. Sexy young people, the on-deck pool, the waterslide, the buffet line—she held up her hands. "Stop, stop! We still can't go! You haven't solved the water problem!"

They suggested that she go without them. "No. This is your idea." She didn't know how far their telepathic link would stretch, and she couldn't imagine going a week without them. The thought made her queasy.

Bagel held up a box of Ziploc sandwich baggies, and the toasts hopped up and down in glee.

•

Elayne packed three boxes of Dramamine, her swimsuit, and some random clothes. The toasts insisted that she include a few nice dresses.

She sighed. "I don't want to meet someone. What if he's like Rick? What if he hurts you?" Painful memories of vacuuming crumbs out of her carpet bubbled up in her mind. "I—I can't do this."

The toasts beamed her a stream of scenes from romantic movies, then images of her eating dinner alone. They didn't like to see her lonely.

She sighed and threw the dresses in her suitcase. "You're worse than my mother. I never should have gotten you that Netflix subscription."

•

The people on the cruise were mostly older and all less attractive than the people in the infomercial. It was a bit of a relief. Her room was cute and tidy, and the soap was shaped like Mickey Mouse.

She opened her suitcase, and the toasts struggled out. They were never very fast-moving, and with their ziplock outfits, they were even slower.

"Well, we're here."

The toasts bobbled around the room, exploring every nook and cranny. Bagel and English Muffin peered at the event schedule. They pointed to a mixer that started in five minutes.

"I'd rather take a few minutes to settle in," Elayne said. The toasts beamed a stern glance at her. She rolled her eyes and adjusted the headband over her aluminum foil band. "Fine, I'll go. And I'll stay in constant contact, so you can all see the boat. Promise me that you won't get into trouble."

She opened the door and walked straight into a man. The toasts were delighted. They beamed at least twenty garbled meet cutes at her.

"Oh, I'm so sorry!" the stranger said, staring the floor. He twisted his hands together as if he wasn't sure what else to do with them. He was only slightly taller than Elayne, with short hair and a goatee.

"It's okay," Elayne said. "After all, we're supposed to be here to meet people." She plastered on what she hoped was a winning smile.

He giggled.

This is awkward, Elayne thought directly at the toasts. "I'm Elayne."

"Albert."

"I was going to the opening mixer. Want to walk with me?" Elayne asked.

Albert shook his head. "No, I—no. Thanks, though. It was nice meeting you." He held out his hand, and Elayne shook it.

"Is that aluminum foil in your hair?" he asked, leaning forward.

Elayne covered her head with both hands. "What? No, of course not."

"Right. Right. Sorry." Albert slipped into the room next to Elayne's. She went back into her own room, made herself a drink from the mini fridge, and ordered room service. The toasts beamed their disappointment at her till she took her headband off.

•

She slept late, then spent about an hour in bed wondering what she was doing with her life. Bagel waddled over and cuddled up under her chin.

She got up, put on one of the dresses, and went to the events that the toasts had circled on the schedule.

The waterslide was fun, especially with the toast's joy at experiencing it welling up in her mind. But she didn't really meet anyone. Other people coupled off all around her, and she eventually ended up alone at the dinner buffet. She imagined how miserable she'd be without the toasts cheerfulness in the back of her head. She stood at the end of the line with her tray and had flashbacks to the first day of middle school.

"I'm too old for this," Elayne muttered.

"Hi, Elayne."

"Oh, hello, Albert."

"Want to sit with me?"

Elayne's relief at the invitation was just as ridiculous as everything else about her life. She nodded. "Thanks." He led her to one of the many two-person tables. "How was your first day?" she asked.

Albert shrugged. "I didn't get a sunburn. That's good, I guess."

Elayne poked at her food. "This doesn't really seem like your thing," she said.

Albert shrugged. "My father got me the ticket, and I figured it could be good research. I'm writing a book."

The toasts were very enthused. "What kind of book?"

"A murder mystery. I'm only about halfway done, and I normally only have time to write on my lunch breaks at work, so I'm trying to get extra writing time in."

"I see."

"Can I ask you a personal question?" Albert asked.

The toasts flooded her with anticipation. "Sure."

"Why are you here? I can't imagine you having any trouble meeting people."

Elayne blushed. "I had a bad break up with my last boyfriend. And my parents got me my ticket, too."

"A bad breakup? Over what?"

A wave of dizzying terror washed over her. Images and sensations blurred together in her mind. She closed her eyes to try to sort it out. Vertigo and cold and fear and an image of the cruise ship from below. A trickle of water, leaking through a poorly sealed Ziploc baggie.

Bagel had fallen off the boat.

What were you doing on deck? She stood up, and her chair clattered on its side. "I have to go." She ran outside. Where had he fallen? Bagel tried to show her, but it was hard to tell from his perspective, and his mounting panic wasn't helping.

The cruise ship was moving fast. Bagel could see the stern, blocking out the stars above.

Elayne clamored up the railing.

Hands grabbed her shoulders and pulled her down. "What are you doing? No matter how bad it was, I'm sure it's not worth it!"

"Let me go!" She wondered how fast the ship was moving. "I'm not jumping off the boat because of Rick! I have to rescue Bagel!"

"What?"

"I—something important to me fell overboard!"

"So you're going to jump in after it?"

"Yes!"

"Without a life jacket?"

Bagel's panic curled in Elayne's chest. "Just let me go!"

Albert grabbed two life vests, shoved one into her chest and pulled the other one on. "I'm not letting you go alone."

He grabbed her hand, and the both clambered over the side.

The cold water hurt, and the bulky life jacket restricted her movement. She dropped Albert's hand and swam toward Bagel. She could see herself fumbling toward him through his tiny foil eyes. Her fingers touched slick plastic, and Bagel scrambled up onto her shoulder.

Albert splashed over. "Is that—is that a bagel?"

Elayne paddled back from him. "Yes."

"You jumped in here for a bagel?"

Bagel hopped on her shoulder.

"Holy shit, did it just move?"

"Yes."

"I—wha—how?"

Elayne shrugged, and Bagel bumped into her ear. The toasts trusted him. And he had jumped into the ocean with her. "Magic, I think. I'm not sure. I toasted a moldy piece of bread, and it came to life, and so did everything I toasted after that."

"Are they intelligent?"

"Yes."

"That is so cool."

They floated in the cold water. "Can I ask you something?" Elayne asked.

"Of course."

"Why did you ask me to sit with you?"

"Well, you were kind of a mystery. With the foil in your hair and everything. I like mysteries."

"The foil lets me communicate with the toasts."

"That—really doesn't make sense."

A searchlight swooped across the water and settled on them. Bagel slid into Elayne's shirt, and the next few minutes were a blur of shouting voices and bright lights. Hands pulled her from the water and wrapped a silvery blanket around her and Albert.

An official-looking woman knelt next to them. "I'm the safety officer. Are you two okay?"

The both nodded. Elayne was hyper aware of Bagel, squished against her chest.

"How did you end up in the water?" she asked, her voice stern.

Elayne stared at the deck. Excuses bounced around in her head. "I—"

"I was leaning too far out," Albert said. His eyes flicked to Elayne, then to the woman. "Showing off. I slipped and fell, and she grabbed us each a life vest and jumped after me."

The toasts were impressed by his story. The safety officer sighed. Elayne wondered how many men fell off the boat while trying to show off. "You should have called for help."

"I'm sorry," Elayne said. "I panicked."

"You're both going to want to get out of your wet clothes, and a hot shower. But you shouldn't be in any danger of hypothermia."

The safety officer ushered them back to their rooms. The toasts clustered around as Elayne pulled Bagel out of her bosom and peeled the damp plastic wrap away. He wiggled his tiny arms and legs, then hopped a few times. Elayne sagged onto the bed in relief.

Someone knocked on the door. "Elayne? It's Albert."

The toasts surged forward with a newly folded aluminum headband. "You really think this is a good idea?" Elayne asked.

The toasts' optimism buzzed in her head. They replayed him jumping into the ocean with her, his positive response to Bagel, then the way he'd covered for her. The montage did paint Albert in a pretty positive light. "Okay," Elayne said. "Okay."

She opened the door and handed Albert the headband. "Put this on, and come on in."

ABOUT THE AUTHOR

Jamie Lackey earned her BA in Creative Writing from the University of Pittsburgh at Bradford in 2006. Since then, she's had over 170 short stories published in places like *Beneath Ceaseless Skies, Apex Magazine,* and *Escape Pod.* Her fiction has also appeared on the Best Horror of the Year Honorable Mention List and Tangent Online Recommended Reading List.

Her debut novel, *Left-Hand Gods,* was published by Hadley Rille Books, and she's created four successful crowdfunding campaigns to self-publish two novellas, a novelette, and two flash fiction collections. She also has a novella and two short story collections available from Air and Nothingness Press.

She read slush for the award-winning Clarkesworld Magazine from 2008-2013, and she worked on the Triangulation Annual Anthology from 2008 to 2011. She edited *Triangulation: Lost Voices* in 2015 and *Triangulation: Beneath the Surface* in 2016.

She has volunteered with the Science Fiction and Fantasy Writers Association and organized the Steel City Speculative Series, a science fiction, fantasy, and horror reading series in Pittsburgh.

In addition to writing, she spends her time reading, playing tabletop RPGs, baking, mushroom hunting, and hiking. You can find her online at www. jamielackey.com.

ACKNOWLEDGMENTS

Laine Wilson
Nathan Griffith
Todd Sanders
Rose Dungeonwrecker
Julie Tennis
Betsy Bodamer
Bill Waugh
Mark
Jenn Scott
Linda McNair
Richard Novak
Nichelle Bauernfeind
Savannah Bozonier
Jeremy Zimmerman
JFBenedetto
Larry Ivkovich
Andrew Hatchell
casey
Chris Aumiller
Hamm
Cory Livingston
Frank Oreto
Isaac E. Payne
Bernadette Ulsamer
John McCurry
Patrick Ropp
John Frochio
Alan Stephen Bailey
Laura Pearlman
Elizabeth
Kimberly Coombs
Amy Treadwell
Stacy Seman
Christina Powers
Nancy Janda
Vicky Boardley

Tracey Levino
Cat Rambo
Jennifer Willis
Brooke Newdick
Sarah Doom
Crystal S
Pete Butler
Douglas Gwilym
Bees
Marc Plourde
Mike Ferdinando
Cassandra Sloan
Carissa Lackey
Jack Waddell
Tori
Kayla Carr
Seth Frost
Rebecca Young
Tom Flanagan
Aimee Picchi
Thomas Griffin
Matthew Lackey
Lynae Zebest
Clare Beams
Darren Radford
Phyllis Pigan
MikeBrendan
Nicholas
Ross Pollock
The Creative Fund by BackerKit
Julia Mulligan
Andrew Gunsch
Bill Moran
Debbie and Don Lackey
Lois Stefko

www.ingramcontent.com/pod-product-compliance
Lightning Source LLC
Chambersburg PA
CBHW072351020726
47506CB00004B/1094